SCANDALOUS

Desire, Oklahoma – The Founding Fathers 2

Lana Dare

MENAGE EVERLASTING

Siren Publishing, Inc.
www.SirenPublishing.com

A SIREN PUBLISHING BOOK
IMPRINT: Ménage Everlasting

SCANDALOUS DESIRE
Copyright © 2012 by Lana Dare

ISBN: 978-1-62241-360-7

First Printing: September 2012

Cover design by Les Byerley
All art and logo copyright © 2012 by Siren Publishing, Inc.

Printed in the U.S.A.

PUBLISHER
Siren Publishing, Inc.
www.SirenPublishing.com

SCANDALOUS DESIRE

Desire, Oklahoma – The Founding Fathers 2

LANA DARE
Copyright © 2012

Chapter One

Ignoring several curious stares, Savannah Perry strolled toward the general store, relieved that after weeks of waiting, she'd finally found her friend.

Maggie had gone inside just minutes ago, and she knew her best friend well enough to know that she would be in there for some time.

She smiled to herself, remembering all the times Maggie had insisted she come to the store with her when they were children.

It seemed like a lifetime ago.

She'd been a different person then, one who'd reached out to two men for comfort and had been swept away by a tenderness she'd never imagined.

On a cold, rainy night in Kansas City, Wyatt Matlock and Hayes Hawkins had made her a woman, and she'd never been the same since.

She doubted she ever would be.

Inwardly cursing that she'd allowed them to creep into her thoughts again, Savannah kept her gaze moving, her awareness of her surroundings having grown quite a bit in the last several months. A woman on her own had to be careful, but she'd already had an advantage. She'd learned how to watch her back from an early age.

She'd also learned that very few people could be trusted.

She'd trusted Wyatt and Hayes with her body—and her heart.

Thankful that her low-brimmed hat kept her red face shaded, she allowed a small smile. One of the few people in the world she trusted, Ebenezer Tyler, had just entered the store behind her best friend, who also happened to be his wife.

And his brother's wife.

The knowledge that Eb was near made Savannah feel safer than she had in months.

She hadn't felt this safe since the night she'd been in Wyatt and Hayes's arms.

Hellfire!

Folding her arms across her chest, she fought back memories of that night—the most magical night of her life. She'd never had such an amazing experience, but it was one she couldn't allow to be repeated. In order to get on with the life she'd chosen for herself, she'd had to leave and avoid both men at all costs.

They were a weakness she just couldn't afford.

Pushing thoughts of them out of her mind, she lifted her head and allowed herself to enjoy the scenery. It felt good to let her guard down, if only a little.

Rubbing at the back of her neck where the reoccurring tingling started again, she walked on.

She hadn't realized how much tension she'd been carrying until just now, when it felt as though a weight had been lifted from her shoulders.

Maggie was safe.

Reminding herself that she'd given up her own safety for independence, she went into the general store, a lump forming in her throat when she heard Maggie's voice coming from the rear of the store. Hearing the frustration in her friend's voice, Savannah smiled.

Some things never change.

"Eb, I swear, I'm gonna smack you if you and Jeremiah don't stop hovering over me. I'm not sick. I'm just fat."

Savannah paused behind one of the display shelves, taking advantage of the fact that neither one of them had spotted her yet. Listening to the tenderness in Eb's tone, a tone he'd only ever used with Maggie, Savannah closed her eyes, shivering in remembered delight as the memories of Wyatt and Hayes's soft words came back to her.

"You're not fat, honey. You're more beautiful than ever. You're also a little grouchy today, aren't you? I knew this trip would be too much for you. I should have made you stay at the ranch. Here, let me carry that."

Snapping her eyes open, Savannah came back to the present and let out a breath she hadn't realized she'd been holding.

She'd known Eb and Jeremiah would take good care of her friend, but also knew that Maggie had reservations about going away with them. The love and worry she heard in Eb's tone convinced her that Maggie was not only cared for, but well loved.

Savannah sighed, blinking back tears. After enduring years of loneliness, her friend deserved to be happy.

Enjoying their banter, she continued to eavesdrop, ignoring the dirty look the storekeeper sent her way.

"Eb, it's only a basket. I can carry it. And if you left me at the ranch, I'd never speak to you again. I wanted to come to town. I still need some things before the baby comes."

"I told you that I could get whatever you need. I should never have let you talk me into bringing you. As soon as we finish here, we're going to get something to eat, and then you're going to go up to the room and lie down."

"No. I'm. Not."

Savannah smothered a laugh at Maggie's belligerent tone and moved closer in time to hear Eb's reply.

"Yes, Margaret Tyler. You are."

Recognizing the tone that made grown men shake in their boots, Savannah started forward. Before her friend could get worked up, something she didn't think would be good for a woman in Maggie's condition, Savannah stepped into their line of vision.

"I see you're still giving Eb a hard time."

With a cry, Maggie spun in her direction, and with a low curse, Eb caught her in his arms to steady her. As recognition came into her eyes, her face lit up.

"Savannah!"

Fighting her way out of Eb's hold, Maggie launched herself at Savannah, earning another curse from her husband as he gripped her shoulders to support her.

With a laugh, Savannah caught Maggie. Although she stood several inches taller, she had to brace herself against her friend's weight and momentum.

"Easy, Maggie. Don't hurt yourself."

Maggie laughed and cried simultaneously.

"Savannah! I can't believe it. What are you doing here? Are you here with your uncle? When did you get here? How long are you staying? Are you staying at the hotel? You have to come to the ranch. Eb, make her come to the ranch."

Eb's eyes narrowed.

"Oh, she's coming to the ranch all right."

Ignoring that, Savannah laughed and hugged her friend, getting as close as Maggie's swollen belly allowed.

"Look at you! You look wonderful, Maggie." She meant it. Her friend glowed with happiness and good health.

Releasing her hold on her friend, Savannah braced herself and smiled at Eb.

"Hello, Eb. It's great to see you again."

Crossing his arms over his chest, he smiled faintly, but Savannah didn't miss the hard glint of anger in his eyes.

"Well, if it isn't Savannah Perry. Don't you know that a woman travelling alone is just asking for trouble?"

Maggie gasped. "Eb, don't you dare talk to Savannah that way. Savannah, where have you been? Did you really leave Kansas City alone?"

Not wanting to get her friend riled, especially in her condition, Savannah laid a hand on Maggie's shoulder.

"Now don't you go getting yourself all worked up. You know I'm more than able to take care of myself. I'm older than you, but you always want to take care of me. I'm a big girl, Maggie."

She hid a smile at the displeasure on Eb's face when he took in the men's clothing she wore. She had to bite her lip to keep from laughing out loud when he eyed her holster and raised a brow, his lips thinning.

Crossing her arms over her chest, she leaned against a wooden post.

"Eb knows I'm perfectly capable of taking care of myself, too. Don't you, Eb?"

He shot a quick glance at Maggie before turning back to her, his eyes glittering dangerously.

"You're a woman, and this isn't Kansas City. You're too vulnerable to be on your own. Leaving alone was dangerous—and stupid."

Savannah saw it in his eyes—the memory of a night long ago—a night when she'd been little more than a child.

A night he'd almost killed her uncle.

She turned away, a cold chill creeping up her spine.

Glancing pointedly at Maggie, she forced a smile, hoping that Eb hadn't told her friend about that night.

"I'm a lot stronger than I used to be." ·

When Maggie turned to her, frowning in confusion, Eb shook his head, wordlessly telling Savannah that he'd kept her secret.

Relieved, she smiled in gratitude, her smile falling when Eb's eyes hardened.

"You're still a woman and need the protection of a man. Or men. You shouldn't be alone."

Her face burned at the memory of her hurried escape from Kansas City.

Eb seemed pleased by that and smiled coldly.

"You should be ashamed of yourself. What do you think Wyatt and Hayes are going to say when they see you?"

Not wanting to disrespect a man who'd always been such a friend to her and who loved her best friend, she forced herself to answer calmly.

"I don't plan to see either one of them, so that won't be an issue."

Maggie gripped her arm.

"Savannah, did you leave without telling Wyatt and Hayes? Did you finally leave your uncle? Does he even know where you are? What's going on?"

Ignoring Eb's glower, Savannah patted her friend's arm.

"Yes, I left my uncle's house and, no, Wyatt and Hayes have no idea where I am. I left without saying anything to anyone, except my uncle." Her face burned even hotter at the shame of sneaking away into the night without even telling Wyatt or Hayes about her plans.

Clenching her jaw, she met Eb's glare.

"I want to be left alone."

Ignoring Eb's raised brow, she looked away, fingering one of the fabrics Maggie had been looking at.

"I told my uncle, the darling reverend, that I was leaving and what I would do if he tried to stop me."

Maggie hugged her, surrounding Savannah with the scent of freshly baked bread and wildflowers.

"Oh, Savannah! I can't believe you're actually here. I'm so glad to see you. It's all men at the ranch. It'll be wonderful to have you close by again."

Eb's face hardened even more, something Savannah hadn't thought possible, but the hand he ran down Maggie's back moved with slow gentleness.

"I want the two of you to stay here until I get back."

"But Eb, where are you—"

He dropped a hard kiss on Maggie's lips, effectively cutting off her question.

"I just have an errand to run. I'll be right back. I'll send one of the men to watch over you until I get back. He'll be right outside. Don't leave the store—either of you. Maggie, if I find out you lifted anything heavier than that basket before I get back, we're gonna have a nice discussion about it later on."

The emphasis on *discussion* wasn't lost on Savannah.

Stiffening, she glanced at Maggie, who didn't appear at all concerned and merely poked Eb in his flat stomach.

Maggie's eyes filled with love as they followed Eb to the door, a look more intense than Savannah remembered.

Her best friend had loved Eb and Jeremiah Tyler for as long as Savannah could remember, but it had been nothing compared to what she saw in Maggie's eyes now.

She remembered how heartbroken Maggie had been when they'd left one day with no warning, and how nervous she'd been when they reappeared after her father's death. Their decision to marry her and bring her to the land they'd won playing poker, and to adapt to a new way of life, had scared the hell out of Maggie.

They'd built a place where they could live with Maggie—a way that wouldn't be accepted in Kansas City.

Savannah had been in the church while her uncle, the reverend, looked down his nose as Eb and Jeremiah had *both* married Maggie. Smiling at the memory of her uncle's disapproval and his fear of defying Eb and Jeremiah, Savannah touched Maggie's shoulder.

"You look happy, Maggie. I'm so glad."

Maggie watched her husband walk away, not turning back until he'd disappeared through the door. She smiled and turned back, her face flushed a becoming pink.

"I am, Savannah. I'm happier than I ever thought I could be."

Wiping away a tear, she put her arm through Savannah's.

"Don't pay any attention to me. The baby makes weepy. Just don't tell Eb or Jeremiah that you saw me cry. They worry, and there's nothing to worry about. Sometimes, I cry for no reason at all."

Maggie sniffed and glanced toward the door.

"They worry because they love me. They always have. Can you believe that?"

Patting Savannah's arm, she beamed up at her.

"Those two act like I'm the first woman in the world to have a baby." Sobering, she shrugged. "I have to admit I'm scared. I wish Esmeralda was here."

Savannah nodded, forcing a smile, saddened that she would probably never see the sweet older woman again.

Esmeralda had always been more than just the housekeeper on the Tyler ranch where Maggie had grown up. She'd been a mother to Maggie, whose own had died in childbirth, and had tried to mother Savannah every time she got the chance.

Happy, but worried for her only friend, Savannah wandered with her around the store. Keeping Maggie's arm in hers, she surreptitiously shot a warning look at the shopkeeper, who eyed her as though she might steal something.

"Eb and Jeremiah obviously love you and are taking good care of you. You've settled here and are happy. That's all I needed to know."

Maggie paused and turned to her, a frown marring her features.

"That sounded awfully final, Savannah, like we're never going to see each other again. Aren't you staying here? I thought—"

Taking her friend's arm again, Savannah steered her away from the annoying shopkeeper and his apparent attempt to eavesdrop on their conversation.

"I just wanted to make sure that you were happy and settled in your new home before I moved on." She didn't want to mention that if Maggie had been unhappy, or mistreated, Savannah would have taken Maggie with her when she left.

Maggie stopped abruptly and yanked her arm out of Savannah's hold, almost knocking over a display of tins.

"What are you talking about? You're not staying? Where are you going? What happened to those two handsome U.S. Marshals who couldn't stay away from you?"

The fear in Maggie's eyes tugged at Savannah's heart. Wondering if there was something wrong that Maggie hadn't told her, she ignored the reference to Wyatt and Hayes. She couldn't talk about them, too sensitive about the subject to even try.

"Are you sure everything's all right with you? Are you really happy?"

Maggie slapped her arm, her eyes narrowing in impatience. "Of course, I'm happy. I've always loved Eb and Jeremiah. You know that. Now, stop trying to change the subject. Where are you going?"

Savannah sighed and turned to level a cold stare at the shopkeeper, who'd crept closer again. Inwardly pleased when he reddened, Savannah lifted a brow, not turning away until he harrumphed and went back to the counter.

Turning back to Maggie, she smiled and tried to inject some enthusiasm into her tone.

"I'm going to Texas. I hear it's wide-open country and a great place to disappear. If things don't work out for me there, I may head for California."

Maggie's eyes went wide.

"Disappear? You can't! Stay here. No one would ever be able to get to you here."

Maggie didn't even make an attempt to keep her voice down, the distress in her tone once again drawing the attention of the shopkeeper.

He rushed over, obviously pleased to have a reason to confront Savannah.

"Mrs. Tyler, is this woman bothering you? If so, I'll get rid of her right quick. I don't want no trouble in my shop, and I know the Tyler brothers wouldn't want you gettin' upset."

Savannah had always considered herself to be too tall for a woman, but took great satisfaction in it now. Straightening to her full height, several inches taller than both Maggie and the shopkeeper, she faced him straight on and planted her feet. Raising a brow, she kept her tone cool.

"Mrs. Tyler happens to be a good friend of mine, and I don't appreciate your interference or your eavesdropping one bit."

"Now, look here, you troublemaker—"

"That's enough, Tillman!"

Eb's voice cracked like a whip over the small store, making the red-faced shopkeeper flinch and back away.

With eyes glittering like ice, Eb rushed to Maggie's side, his concern evident as he pulled her close. He gestured toward Savannah, arrogance in every line of his body.

"This is Miss Savannah Perry. She's my wife's best friend and under my protection. I'll take any slight to her personally."

When the shopkeeper's face reddened even more, Eb nodded once, obviously satisfied that he'd gotten his message across.

"Anything Miss Perry wants, just add it to my bill."

Wishing she could take the time to enjoy the shopkeeper's discomfort, Savannah kept her voice low, gritting her teeth in frustration. "You're not paying for my things!"

Eb lifted a brow in that arrogant way she remembered, one that had the shopkeeper taking refuge behind the counter.

"Is that a fact?"

Savannah had a slight advantage over the terrified shopkeeper. She'd grown up around Eb and knew he had a soft spot for her. She knew, also, that he'd never yell at her in front of Maggie, especially in her condition.

Crossing her arms over her chest, she smiled.

"That's a fact."

Pleased with herself, she stood her ground, but only seconds later found herself shifting under Eb's steely glare.

His slow, knowing smile sent a chill through her, while his eyes promised retribution if she defied him further.

"I'm afraid you're going to find out things are a lot different in *my* town than they are in Kansas City. Until you accept a claim, you'll be our responsibility. Once we get to the ranch, everyone there will look after you and make sure you're safe."

Forcing a smile, Savannah raised a brow, amused that he'd become even more arrogant than she remembered.

"I know you think of me as the little girl you bought peppermint sticks for, but I've been on my own for months now. I appreciate all you've done for me, but I'm not, and never have been, your responsibility. Thank you for the offer, but I'm just going to have to pass."

Eb's rare grin made her even more nervous.

"Wyatt and Hayes are going to have their hands full with you. Good. We need some entertainment in Desire."

Savannah gasped at the mention of the two men she'd run from and had been trying to forget, wondering just how much he and Jeremiah knew. "Oh, dear God almighty. Please tell me they're not here."

Maggie, though, chose that moment to lift her head from Eb's chest. With her hands over her swollen abdomen, she stuck her bottom lip out in a pout that Savannah knew had always worked with Eb and Jeremiah.

"You're not coming to the ranch? You're going to ride off into the sunset—"

Savannah smiled. "I'm leaving at dawn, Maggie."

Maggie glared at that and stuck her lip out even farther. "You're going to leave me here to worry about you in my delicate condition?"

Savannah knew her best friend well enough and had watched her get around Eb and Jeremiah often enough in the past to understand exactly what she was up to.

With her hands on her hips, she grinned.

"You didn't look so delicate a few minutes ago when you were yelling at Eb."

After a shocked silence, Maggie sighed and smiled.

"Savannah, please stay. The ranch is wonderful." She smiled up at Eb. "Eb and Jeremiah are wonderful, but I'm lonely for a woman's company, especially with the baby coming. I miss you so much and I'm a little scared."

She ran a protective hand over her stomach as Eb wrapped his arms around her from behind. Hiding a smile from her husband, she stared at Savannah thoughtfully before nodding as though she'd come to some kind of a decision.

Recognizing the calculated gleam in Maggie's eyes, Savannah sighed.

Maggie looked up at her husband adoringly. "Eb, Savannah's delivered quite a few babies. I would feel much better if she would stay. Savannah, please stay, at least until the baby comes. It's only a few more months."

Eb nodded. "It's settled then. Savannah'll stay at the ranch until the baby comes. I have a feeling, though, that it's going to be much longer."

His eyes dared Savannah to defy him.

"Maggie wants you there, and I want you protected. No one would dare hurt you in my town."

Savannah smiled at his arrogance, having already made the decision to stay with her friend until she delivered. After all Maggie had done for her, she couldn't refuse her.

"Same old Eb. Always bossing everyone around. You know, the ranch got much quieter after you left again."

Lifting a brow, he smiled coolly. "How would you know? You left right after we did."

Savannah got a cold feeling in the pit of her stomach.

"How did you know that?"

"We told him."

Too shocked to hide her gasp at the deep masculine voice that came from somewhere behind her, Savannah swallowed heavily, staring at a wide-eyed Maggie. Taking a deep breath, she forced herself to turn around and face the men she dreamed about every night.

The sight of Wyatt Matlock and Hayes Hawkins, as always, stole her breath and made her insides flutter and grow warm.

Wyatt towered over her, his brown eyes appearing even darker and more watchful than usual. Steady on hers, they held a knowledge and intimacy that made her nipples tighten and her stomach clench.

The lines around his eyes, lines formed by years of squinting into the sun, seemed even more pronounced now than they did the last time she saw him, but it did nothing to detract from his good looks.

His features, always hard and masculine, seemed even harder now, the anger in his face and in his stance more intimidating than she remembered.

Sliding her gaze to Hayes, she swallowed again, fighting not to take several steps back.

Hard. Cold. Deadly.

Looking at him now, she had trouble believing he was the same man who crooned to her, holding her close and caressing her after taking her.

Standing an inch or two taller than Wyatt, Hayes eyed her coldly, his green eyes glittering like chips of ice. His hair appeared dark inside the store, but she knew that in the sun, it shone with a reddish tint, one that hinted at the temper that had been known to make even the most hardened criminals cautious.

For a split second, tenderness shone in his eyes, before it was quickly shuddered, and she saw a glimpse of the man he'd been that night. No matter how hard he appeared, he wanted her.

She knew it with a certainty she seldom felt about anything.

The knowledge scared her to death.

His hands clenched at his sides as though he had to restrain himself from reaching for her, but she knew that if they'd been alone, she would have already been pulled into his arms and nestled against his massive chest.

U.S. Marshals from head to toe, Wyatt and Hayes looked every inch the hard-nosed lawmen, men with reputations for being the best.

The coldest, the meanest of lawmen.

Men who went up against the worst outlaws and always came out on top.

Men who could track anyone, anywhere, at any time.

Men who made even the most seasoned gunslingers shake in their boots.

Men she hadn't seen since the night she left Kansas City.

The night they'd taken her virginity.

It took every ounce of self-control she possessed to smile coolly and nod in their direction, while her insides twisted with nerves.

"Wyatt. Hayes."

Unsettled by their anger, she ignored Eb's low chuckle coming from somewhere behind her. Her breath caught when Wyatt stepped closer.

Standing directly in front of her, he effectively blocked the shopkeeper's view and reached out to touch her cheek, leaving a trail of fire behind.

"Don't take that cool tone with me. I know better. You're trembling."

Savannah's face burned, and she tried to step back, but he caught her arm, preventing it.

His gaze moved over her face for several long seconds before he nodded once in satisfaction. "You should be embarrassed for running away like that. You were almost attacked twice, and it's only because Hayes and I took care of those men before they could get to you that you arrived here unscathed. Don't make the mistake of thinking you'll be allowed to be alone again."

Glancing at Hayes, Savannah swallowed again, his intense scrutiny leaving her shaken.

"What are you talking about? You had no idea where I was. You couldn't have tracked me."

Lifting a brow, Wyatt grinned coldly.

"We've been following you ever since you left Kansas City."

Savannah blinked, not even attempting to hide her surprise. "Why?"

Shaking his head, Wyatt smiled faintly. "You know the answer to that, Savannah."

She couldn't stop glancing at Hayes, unnerved by his cold silence. "What you want from me isn't possible."

Wyatt's smile widened. "Of course it is. We want you with us. We'll make it possible."

Suddenly aware of Eb's and Maggie's attention, she forced a sarcastic smile. "If you wanted my company so badly, why didn't you ride with me instead of trailing behind?" The thought of being watched made her uneasy.

Wyatt stepped closer and bent, keeping his voice low. "We wanted to know where you were headed." Cupping her jaw, he slid his thumb over her bottom lip.

"We figured you were shaken by leaving—and other things—and that you needed some time alone."

Hayes, with his hands on his hips, dangerously close to the guns he wore there, turned his head to glare at the shopkeeper, who'd moved closer in an obvious attempt to eavesdrop on their conversation.

"What do you want?"

The shopkeeper paled. "I couldn't, uh, help but overhear. Uh, she called you Wyatt and Hayes. You, uh, wouldn't happen to be the U.S. Marshals, Wyatt Matlock and Hayes Hawkins, would you?"

Every hard line of Hayes's body tightened with threatening menace.

"Yeah. So?"

Shooting a smug look at Savannah, the shopkeeper came forward, pointing at her.

"I knew she was trouble. She's a thief, isn't she? And look how she dresses! What kind of woman, other than an outlaw, wears pants and a holster? I knew she was no good. I knew it. I told Emma that she looks like trouble. I been watchin' her every time she comes in here, just to make sure she don't steal nothin'. She must have really done something bad for *you* to be after her. Did she kill somebody?"

He eyed Eb nervously, but straightened to his full height as though proud that he'd done something that Eb would be thankful for.

Amused, Savannah lifted a brow, sharing a look with Maggie.

Wyatt, on the other hand, looked far from amused. His face turned to stone, devoid of all expression as he turned and faced the other man squarely, placing his body between the shopkeeper and Savannah.

A muscle worked in Hayes's jaw, his eyes turning even colder.

"Miss Perry is no outlaw. She's the daughter of a preacher and happens to be our woman."

He took a step toward the shopkeeper, beating Wyatt by a split second.

"If I hear any talk about her, or if I hear about you treating her with anything but the utmost respect, I won't be happy at all."

Reaching out a fist, he grabbed the shopkeeper by the collar and lifted him several inches off the floor.

"You might want to pass that along."

Even Savannah shivered at his icy tone.

She imagined the looks on their faces as the ones they wore when facing outlaws and, seeing them this way, understood just how they'd earned their reputations.

The shopkeeper looked as though he might pass out.

"Y–Yes, s–sir."

Hayes spent no more time on him, releasing the stuttering shopkeeper to scramble away before turning back to Savannah.

"We've been staying in the room across from yours in the hotel." At her look of surprise, he raised a brow, as though daring her to protest.

"You really didn't think we were going to let you out of our sight, did you?"

Her face burned at the intimacy and possession in his hooded gaze, a look she saw in her dreams, night after night. Shifting restlessly at the moisture that dampened her thighs, she looked away, promising herself she wouldn't be taken in by that look ever again.

Aware of Maggie's rapt attention and the amusement and suspicion gleaming in Eb's eyes, Savannah cleared her throat, careful to keep her voice at an angry whisper.

"Perhaps you didn't understand when I told you that there could never be anything between us, especially...you know."

Wyatt stepped closer, touching her arm.

"With both of us?"

With her face even hotter, Savannah nodded. "Yes, and I don't appreciate you telling the shopkeeper otherwise."

She eyed both of them and straightened to her full height in an instinctive effort to intimidate them, clenching her jaw at the amusement in their eyes at her ineffective ploy as they towered over her.

"You expect something from me that I just can't give you."

Wyatt's slow, devious smile made her belly tighten with arousal and more than just a small amount of trepidation.

"We're the sheriffs in Desire. Living there, you can give us exactly what we want."

With his hands on his hips and the hard glint of challenge in his eyes, he looked every inch the dangerous lawman, the amusement curving his lips making him even more dangerous to her senses.

"Appreciate you getting here on your own and saving us the trouble of dragging you here."

The knot in her stomach turned cold.

"I'm not staying."

Hayes gave her one of his rare smiles.

"Oh, yes. You are. And you're going to marry us. Both of us."

Chapter Two

After the meal at the hotel the men had insisted on, Savannah had a full belly for the first time in weeks. Not long after that, she found herself and Maggie surrounded by not only Eb, Wyatt, and Hayes, but several of the Circle T ranch hands as they rode out of town.

She couldn't blame the people who stopped to stare as the large group of them rode by. From what she'd seen so far, the men who worked at the Circle T were an intimidating bunch.

All tall, broad shouldered, and hard eyed they drew the attention of every person they came across. Even in a town filled with men, they stood apart.

Men eyed them with respect, while women eyed them with fear and scurried to get out of their way.

The first they appeared to take as their due, while the second seemed to irritate them more each time it happened.

Once they left the outskirts of town, the men seemed to become even more alert, scanning the area constantly with their razor-sharp eyes, but within minutes, broke their cold silence and began to talk.

Distant from the others in town, the men seemed very comfortable with each other, allowing her to see a side of them she wouldn't have expected.

Because of Maggie's condition, Eb had settled her as comfortably as possible on the buckboard he drove, and kept travel slow.

Staring straight ahead, Savannah let the men's low conversation flow around her, a little surprised at their camaraderie with Wyatt and Hayes. Soothed by their low, sometimes teasing, conversation, she shot several glances at Maggie, curious about how she got along with such a group of men, but her friend leaned heavily against Eb and drowsed.

It gave Savannah time to think.

All hard masculinity and obvious caring and respect for each other, the other men fascinated her, but nothing could distract her from Wyatt and Hayes.

They sat tall in their saddles, their gazes always shifting, mostly in her direction. The self-confidence and intelligence in their eyes spoke volumes, letting the world know that they would have no trouble handling whatever trouble came their way.

Their arrogance, a source of both pride and annoyance with her, couldn't be contained, evident in every hard line of their bodies and steely glint of their eyes.

They flanked her, staying close enough to make it clear that she was with them, their eyes daring her to run.

The knowledge that she wanted to gleamed in Wyatt's dark gaze and Hayes's brilliant green one.

The anticipation of catching her glittered bright, a look they probably used on their prisoners, a look that would have stopped her from running if she'd considered it.

So, she rode along in silence, too aware of their intimate knowledge of her to attempt conversation.

Swallowing her impatience, she kept her mount at a steady, even pace. She could feel the others' curious gazes and didn't want to draw any more attention to herself than necessary.

She'd promised to stay until Maggie had her baby, and Savannah never broke a promise. She'd had too many promises made to her broken and had vowed that she would never do that to another.

She would, however, do this on *her* terms.

She'd keep her head down, spend as much time as she could with Maggie, and leave just as soon as possible.

Even after several hours of riding, her awareness of Wyatt and Hayes and their sharp attention never lessened.

If anything, it grew stronger, the affection they'd shown to her in Kansas City shining in their eyes more frequently now, but remained tempered with frustration and anger.

Her skin prickled, a sensation that intensified every time they looked at her.

Their attention kept her on edge, making her stiff in the saddle, and renewed a closeness with them she'd thought long forgotten.

It brought back too many memories of the night they'd taken her.

No matter how hard she tried, she couldn't forget the way their warm strength felt against her body. Instead of being scared and vulnerable, she'd felt protected and safe in their arms, something she hadn't expected at all.

Hayes had taken her first that night, holding her and murmuring sweet words to her, raining kisses over her face as he apologized for hurting her.

It had been the most amazing night of her life. She'd felt closer to them than she'd ever felt to anyone in her entire life.

As he rode beside her, she couldn't help glancing at his gloved hands, remembering the scars on them and how they'd felt moving over her body.

Finding it difficult to believe that the hard man watching her with such anger in his eyes could be the same man who'd taken her with such tenderness, she looked away, rubbing her arm against the chill that went though her.

She knew they both had a right to be angry with her, but she hadn't thought she'd have to face it.

He moved closer, keeping his voice low and even as though trying not to spook her, but nothing could disguise the danger he exuded.

"Wyatt and I are the sheriffs in Desire now. Good group of men."

Experienced at hiding her emotions, she kept her expression bland.

"Why would you give up your job as Marshals to be sheriffs of a small town in the middle of nowhere?"

Hayes moved closer.

"To be with you. Everyone will recognize you as wife to both of us there. Eb and Jeremiah's men have already built the jailhouse. We ,just have to get a house built for you before winter sets in."

She trembled as Wyatt moved in on her other side, shrugging and staring straight ahead.

She wouldn't allow herself to want something that could never be with men she could never hold.

"I don't have any need for a house. I'll be staying with the Tylers just until Maggie delivers the babe. I'm hoping to be long gone before winter sets in."

All conversation around them stopped, the rapt attention of the other men a tangible thing.

After several heart-pounding seconds, Hayes spoke, the muscle working in his jaw making his scar appear more prominent.

"No. You won't."

Savannah couldn't help but smile at the arrogance in his tone. His arrogance didn't stand a chance against her determination.

"I hear Texas is wide open and full of opportunity."

"What kind of opportunity?"

Wyatt's icy question had her turning to glare at him, struck again by his blatant masculinity.

Her mind went blank as a surge of longing hit her.

She didn't know how a man so hard looking could be considered handsome, but somehow Wyatt managed to be both.

All hard lines and angles, and with the scar on his cheek, Hayes could be downright scary, intimidating all but the bravest men. Wyatt, on the other hand, had women chasing him all over Kansas City— women determined to tame the gorgeous and dangerous Marshal.

Wyatt's charm drew people while Hayes's icy demeanor and scarred face kept them at a distance.

Even wearing the cold expression Wyatt wore now, his masculine good looks made her tongue-tied.

Savannah turned away, her face burning and her heart beating nearly out of her chest.

"What I do is really none of your concern."

Wyatt's eyes narrowed dangerously. "You know better. Everything about you is my concern, Savannah."

From the other side, Hayes touched her shoulder, leaning close enough for her to clearly make out the possessive gleam in his eyes.

"And mine."

Savannah gulped, finding it difficult to breathe. When Wyatt's easy charm turned to ice, it chilled her from within, while the warmth Hayes displayed now left her frazzled and confused. It was as if both allowed her to see a side of them they hadn't before.

"If she accepts your claim. Until then she's under our protection." The underlying iron in Eb's tone left no room for argument.

Wyatt kept his gaze steady on Savannah.

"Hayes and I have already declared our intentions. We'll keep Savannah safe and care for her."

Several whoops from the other men made Savannah's stomach tighten. If not for the fact that she'd promised Maggie she'd stay, she might have ridden away right then and there.

"I don't need your protection, and I have no desire to be *claimed*."

Hayes moved in closer, keeping his voice low enough not to be overheard.

"You've already given yourself to us. You're ours now. There's no turning back." Straightening, he nodded once. "We'll talk somewhere private."

Eb eyed her for several seconds before inclining his head. "I'll allow that."

Bristling at the arrogance in Eb's tone, Savannah whirled in the saddle.

"I don't need your permission to talk to them or anyone else."

Eb bent low to say something to Maggie, who appeared agitated. Once he settled her, he turned back to Savannah, still caressing Maggie's shoulder.

"So you feel as though you could handle talking to Wyatt and Hayes alone? I don't want you putting yourself in a situation where you might be in over your head. I trust them with you, though."

His smug smile set her teeth on edge. He shrugged and adjusted the blanket on Maggie's shoulders.

"Until I hear from your lips that you're going to marry them, you're my responsibility."

Savannah's strict upbringing kept her from cursing out loud, but her anger had them running through her head.

"In case you haven't noticed, I'm a grown woman now, not the child you knew in Kansas City."

To her surprise, instead of snapping back, Eb chuckled.

"Always did have a temper underneath all that politeness." He shared a look with Wyatt and Hayes. "She's always been polite, sometimes *too* polite—just apparently not with the two of you."

Wyatt's lips twitched, his twinkling eyes making him even more breathtaking. "We noticed. Fascinating, isn't it?"

Eb sobered, his gaze holding hers and filled with determination and tenderness, bringing back memories of a night long ago, a night in which he'd rescued her from the most frightening experience of her life.

"Savannah, you're under our protection, and you'll obey the rules we laid out for you. You'll do nothing to endanger yourself. My men have all sworn to keep every woman on the place safe. If they tell you to do something for your own safety, then you'd better do it."

He smiled, taking some of the sting from his words. "Besides, I don't want to have to be the one to answer to Maggie if something happens to you."

Savannah blinked, slowing her horse and looking at each of the men in turn. Amazed that they all wore the same sober expressions, she turned back to Eb, carefully avoiding the searching looks both Wyatt and Hayes gave her.

Knowing she owed Eb Tyler a debt she could never repay, she bit back her anger.

"I have no intention of putting myself in danger and—"

Eb had already started shaking his head.

"No, I don't believe you would, but you'll abide by the rules we've established here, rules designed to—"

"Bully women around?"

The words slipped out before she could stop them, her anger bubbling at the amusement in Wyatt's eyes.

"It's not enough that men are physically stronger. They don't want women to read, unless they get to pick the reading material. They don't want them to have minds of their own. They'd rather tell them what to do every waking moment of their day. They want slaves and make whatever laws they have to make in order to keep women under their control."

Thinking of her mother and some of the women she'd helped in Kansas City only made her angrier. Turning to face Wyatt fully, she clenched her fists on the reins.

"They suck the life out of a woman, making her old before her time and desperate enough to believe whatever a man says. Meanwhile, men go out and do whatever they want to do, sometimes staying out all night with one of their painted ladies, while the woman stays home and works like a dog."

By the time she finished, she was breathing heavily, her heart pounding in her chest.

Shifting in embarrassment at the ensuing silence, Savannah turned away from Wyatt's speculative look and Eb's knowing one.

She didn't have the courage to look at Hayes.

Gritting her teeth in frustration, she turned her horse and continued on at a much faster pace.

She knew better than to let anyone know what she was thinking or feeling.

Keeping her thoughts and feelings to herself had always been one of *her* rules, one self-imposed, and that had always worked well for her.

Letting her anger loosen her tongue only made her angrier.

Eb looked furious. "Those rules are for the sole intention of keeping our women safe!"

Savannah snorted inelegantly, saying nothing.

Hayes closed in on her other side, his tender smile surprising her.

"Savannah, Wyatt and I swore to uphold those laws. If we didn't think they would keep you and all the other women safe, we wouldn't have agreed to become the sheriffs."

Remembering all the times Eb and Jeremiah had confronted her uncle on her behalf, and their patience in letting her tag along with Maggie, she sighed, her temper cooling.

Well known for his patience, Eb waited until she met his gaze again, nodding in satisfaction when she did.

"You know I would do anything to protect the women I care about. When have I ever stood by and let anyone hurt a woman?"

She glanced at Wyatt, breathing a sigh of relief when his speculative gaze slid from her to Eb and back again.

He didn't know.

She hoped he never would.

Meeting Eb's sharp eyes, she nodded and focused her attention straight ahead.

"Never. I trust *you*."

Gesturing toward the men approaching from a distance, she put a hand over the butt of her gun, a little surprised that the men didn't.

"That doesn't mean I trust anyone else. Trust has to be earned."

Hayes laid a hand over her forearm, the tingling awareness from his touch shooting straight to her nipples.

"You can ease up on that pistol. That's Jeremiah, Phoenix, and Hart up ahead. I'm sure Jeremiah can't wait to see Maggie, and Phoenix and Hart are probably checking to see if they brought any women back with them. They all know that you're already spoken for."

Something had already told her that the approaching riders posed no threat. The men had obviously seen and identified them, probably long before she'd even noticed them.

Uneasy at her own lack of vigilance, she took her hand from her gun.

Wyatt glanced at Eb, but Savannah could feel his attention on her.

"We're on Tyler land now, Savannah. Eb, Hayes and I are going on to the pond with your charge. We've got a few things to discuss before we get to the ranch. She's safe with us."

Eb nodded without hesitation.

"Didn't doubt that at all."

Savannah thought about objecting, but one look at the worry in Maggie's eyes changed her mind. She didn't want to upset her friend by arguing with Wyatt and Hayes in front of her, and figured this would be as good a time as any to set them straight about a few things.

"I won't be long, Maggie. I know you're tired. Why don't you go on up to the ranch and get a little sleep? We can talk later."

Not bothering to wait for Maggie's reply, she turned away, a little surprised at the looks of respect and indulgence from Eb's ranch hands.

She hadn't expected that, assuming that they would think less of her after hearing that both Wyatt and Hayes had an interest in sharing her.

She thought about it as she rode in silence between Wyatt and Hayes, staring straight ahead as they made their way through a small grove of trees.

Perhaps the other men had been forced to accept what Eb and Jeremiah had with Maggie. After all, their pay depended on respecting their bosses' wishes.

When the trail narrowed, Hayes urged his horse forward to lead the way, while Wyatt fell back to ride behind her.

Her position between them filled her with an inner warmth she didn't want to examine too closely.

It struck her suddenly that ever since they'd approached her in the store, she'd let her guard down, relying on them to keep her safe in a place where danger lurked around every corner.

No matter what she'd said to Eb, she trusted Wyatt and Hayes with her safety every bit as much as she trusted them with her body.

Somehow she felt connected to them, and in ways she hadn't even considered. Even now she couldn't keep her eyes from the compelling sight of Hayes riding in front of her. Staring at his broad back, she couldn't help but admire his wide shoulders as he sat straight and tall in the saddle.

The coat he wore against the early autumn evening only emphasized his rugged build, a build she knew intimately.

It hit her suddenly that the night they'd spent together in Kansas City would always be between them—an intimacy they'd shared that nothing could ever change, and one that no one, not even her uncle, could ever take away from her.

Her stomach tightened at the memory of just how firm and sleek those shoulders she couldn't stop staring at felt under her hands. How safe and solid his body felt as he cradled her against him.

How hot. How strong.

How those wide shoulders could block out the rest of the world and make a cocoon of warmth and safety just for them.

How they'd blocked her view of the fire he'd built as he held her, whispering words of affection and encouragement as he took her virginity.

"I think you were right in suggesting some sleep. Mrs. Tyler was looking a little under the weather."

Wyatt's low tone coming from right behind her snapped her back to the present. Raising her collar around her burning face, she nodded and looked around, taking in the small clearing they'd entered and the cluster of large rocks by the pond.

"Yes. I'm sure she needs more rest now. I just hope Eb and Jeremiah are taking care of her."

Glancing in her direction, Hayes brought his mount to a stop beside the pond. He slid from his horse in a graceful move and headed straight toward her, frowning when she dismounted without waiting for him.

"Of course Eb and Jeremiah take care of her. They worry about her all the time and check on her constantly. Sometimes I wonder if she's strong enough for life out here."

From behind, Wyatt touched her shoulder, making her jump because she hadn't even heard him approach.

"It's a hard life, but I have to give them credit for making sure she's as protected as possible. I just don't know if she's got the sand to make it here."

Insulted, Savannah rushed to defend her only friend.

"You know nothing about Maggie, you sidewinders!"

Ignoring their looks of surprise, she rushed on, not giving either one of them a chance to speak.

"You don't know her at all! She might have been surrounded by people who loved and protected her, but she's never been spoiled."

Wyatt straightened to his full height, several inches over six feet, and crossed his arms over his chest.

"I know she's nothing like you. I know she didn't have the kind of life you had to endure. Your friend's been protected and spoiled her entire life—"

"No!" She shoved at him, infuriated when she encountered rock-hard muscle on an apparently immovable frame.

"Maggie was my friend when no one else wanted to be seen with the daughter of a loose woman and the niece of the crazy Reverend Perry. She included me in everything and shared everything with me—even her family. The Tylers looked after me because I was Maggie's friend. Every time Esmeralda made a dress for Maggie, Maggie had her make one for me. Even Eb and Jeremiah looked out for me because of Maggie. She made them stop for me every time they went to town. She always made sure I had as many of the treats they bought as she had."

Turning away from their probing gazes, she stared at the pond behind them, furious at herself for letting her mouth get away from her. Apparently, she'd dropped her guard too much and scrambled to create some sort of distance between them again, and at the same time defend her friend.

Memories crept in again, memories of a night long ago, the night Eb rescued her from the man who was supposed to be taking care of her. If not for her friendship with Maggie, he wouldn't have been there to collect her, and her life would have been changed forever.

Lifting her head, she met their gazes.

"Maggie's friendship has always been the best thing in my life. I don't know what would have become of me if not for that."

Some unspoken message passed between Wyatt and Hayes, one filled with pity that made her uncomfortable enough to look away.

Staring back at the pond, she took a deep breath and let it out slowly, determined to get her emotions back under control.

It was important to her to make them understand Maggie.

"Maggie taught me how to shoot and ride, even though my uncle forbade both of them. She went toe-to-toe with both Eb and Jeremiah when they found out and somehow managed to get them to not only keep it a secret, but to help teach me. When she's determined to get her way, Eb and Jeremiah don't stand a chance."

Her smile widened at their looks of surprise.

"Maggie's always been hard working, courageous, and full of life. She has the kindest heart of anyone I've ever known, but don't ever make the mistake of confusing that with weakness."

Hayes smiled, a sad smile that Savannah had seen more than she cared for. On Hayes, however, it made her want to cry.

"But she didn't have it as hard as you did, did she, Savannah? You were a slave to whatever chore your uncle wanted you to do. He had you running all over town to tend to the sick members of his church, making excuses about being busy because he didn't want to be around them. Cleaning the church and his house. Cooking for him and for folks he wanted to impress so that they would give him donations."

Wyatt's jaw clenched.

"He ran you ragged and then expected you to sit and read scripture to him every night because he wanted to instill it into you and was too damned lazy to read it himself."

Savannah blinked, too surprised to hide her reaction.

"How did you know that?"

Hayes smiled and took a step closer, his eyes narrowing when she stiffened. "Don't. Don't be afraid of me."

Lifting her chin, she met his gaze squarely, surprised at the vulnerability darkening his eyes.

Wyatt closed in on her from the other side, running a hand over her trembling arm.

"We watched you like hawks, and have no intention of changing that. You really didn't think we were going to give your uncle a chance to put any more of those bruises on you, did you?"

The fire in Hayes's green eyes reminded Savannah far too much of the night they'd both taken her, a fierce possessiveness combined with tenderness that made her weak in the knees.

"We'd wondered if we'd made a baby with you that night."

The hand he slid a hand inside her coat moved over her abdomen with the same tender possessiveness, the shock of sizzling heat making her gasp aloud. Her stomach tightened in response, the sharp stab of intense heat making her pussy clench and dampening the place between her thighs.

His eyes narrowed.

"We didn't, but we will."

She tried to pull away, but Wyatt caught her from behind, wrapping an arm around her waist while nuzzling her neck.

"Why did you run away, honey? You know how much Hayes and I want you. We told you that we both wanted to marry you. We would have handled your uncle for you."

With a surge of inner strength she didn't realize she possessed, she pushed out of their arms, her heart pounding.

Keeping her back to them, she took a few precious seconds to get herself under control before adopting the cool dismissive look she'd long ago become accustomed to wearing.

"I don't want you handling things for me. I can take care of myself. I've been doing it for years. I have no intention of being under the control of any man ever again. I left one. What makes you think I'd let myself belong to two?"

Hayes's eyes darkened and narrowed into that terrifying look he must have perfected during years of facing down outlaws.

"Take that tone with me again, Savannah, and I'm going to turn you over my knee and paddle that perfect little bottom of yours."

Savannah's jaw dropped, hardly believing the always stoic man standing before her would even say such a thing.

Gathering her wits, she chuckled, reminding herself that she no longer had to answer to anyone.

"What would make you think that I would be interested in tying myself to a man who wants to hurt me? If your arrogant attitude is supposed to make me swoon and fall into your arms, you're in for a big disappointment."

Gripping her forearms, Hayes yanked her against him, his eyes narrowing to slits.

"My *arrogant attitude* is what kept you alive and unharmed during your trip here. We sat up nights watching you—taking turns sleeping. We moved closer and closer every day, but you're so green, you didn't even realize it. You were almost attacked twice, but we got to them first and you slept right through it. My *arrogant attitude* will deter other men from thinking they can even get close to you. This isn't Kansas City. This is wide-open country and is only as safe as those who uphold the law make it."

Wyatt slipped his arms around her from behind.

"We want you, Savannah. We quit our jobs with the Marshals in order to become sheriffs in a town where we can marry you."

Staring into Hayes's hypnotic gaze, she moaned as her hands moved of their own volition, flattening on his muscular chest.

"You shouldn't have done that."

Surrounded by the heat of their bodies, she trembled with a need so strong it scared her, her stomach muscles tightening as Wyatt moved her braid aside and touched his lips to her neck.

Somehow her head fell back and tilted to the side at her involuntary need to give him access to the vulnerable place on her neck.

Closing her eyes, she moaned again at the delicious heat that sizzled through her, from her neck to her breasts and back again, the pinpricks of pleasure making her ache everywhere.

Wyatt ran his lips over her neck, his voice low and intimate.

"We couldn't have done anything else. Don't you realize by now that we would do anything for you? We couldn't just ride away and leave you there."

His hands closed around her waist, the tension in his big body unmistakable.

"We couldn't take you with us and subject you to the kind of danger we dealt with every day. We all want to build something here, Savannah. A place where folks can live any way they desire as long as they're not hurting anyone else. A place where the women's safety is the main priority. Stay here with us, Savannah. Help us build this place. Help us be a family."

Hayes slid his hands from her shoulders and into her hair, tilting her head back, his eyes hooded.

"No more running. You'll be safe here. Stay."

Savannah gasped at the feel of his warm breath on her lips, the anticipation of his kiss making her heart race. Remembering the slow way he kissed her, a way that made her feel as though she was drowning, she fisted her hands on his jacket and waited.

As he'd done before, he teased her lips with his, enticing her to open to him before he ventured inside.

Her lips parted in another gasp when Wyatt closed his hands over her breasts, his touch so light she wondered if she imagined it.

But the heat, oh God, the heat from his hands burned through her shirt, making her breasts feel even more swollen. The tingling sensation in her nipples made her squirm against Hayes as he covered her mouth completely with his.

He swallowed her cry, lifting her against him and urging her to wrap her legs around his waist. With one hand tangled in her hair and the other firm beneath her bottom, he held her, sliding his tongue over hers in an erotic dance that made her head swim.

From behind, Wyatt nuzzled her neck and shoulder, his chest hot against her back as he teased her nipples through her shirt.

An inner passion she didn't know she possessed broke free, and before she could stop herself, she began sucking on Hayes's tongue, drawing it into her mouth and caressing it with her own.

His reaction both stunned and delighted her.

At first, he stiffened as if surprised, but he recovered quickly.

Tightening his hand on her bottom and in her hair, he pulled her impossibly closer and moved her body against his, pressing the hard bulge at the front of his pants against her center.

Lifting his head, he held hers steady, forcing her to meet his gaze.

"Do you know what it did to me when you left?"

His beautiful eyes glittered, the distress in them melting something inside her that had been frozen for years. The rare glimpses of tenderness this wonderful man seemed to have trouble showing made each one even more special.

The sudden warmth hurt, making her feel things that she'd only gotten a glimmer of the night they'd taken her.

It made her feel vulnerable and soft, two things she couldn't allow.

Frightened, she tried to pull away, but Hayes held strong.

"Let go of me."

With a hand wrapped around her braid, he set her on her feet and reached between them, caressing her mound.

"I'll never let go of you, Savannah. I ache every night with wanting you. Why did you leave Kansas City without telling us? We would have taken you out of there and away from your uncle any time you wanted."

From behind her, Wyatt massaged her breasts, his fingers pulling away the ends of her shirt as Hayes unbuttoned it.

Wyatt groaned against her neck. "You should have come to us."

Savannah couldn't catch her breath as they bared her breasts to the cool evening air. Her knees weakened, threatening to give out on her when each man began to toy with her nipples, teasing them into throbbing points.

"I, oh, God. I didn't want your help. Oh!" Defenseless again the intoxicating pleasure, she let her head fall back against Wyatt's chest and closed her eyes.

They'd paid quite a bit of attention to her nipples that night in Kansas City. She'd been too nervous and overwhelmed by their hands everywhere else, though, to notice how incredible the lightest touch there could feel.

Each brush of their rough fingers sent a surge of pleasure through her, making her pussy clench with need and her clit feel swollen and tingly. Tightening her fists on Hayes's coat, she struggled to concentrate.

"I didn't *need* your help."

She gasped at the pinch to her nipple, crying out at the sharp pleasure of Hayes's touch.

Wyatt caught her with an arm around her waist, steadying her.

"Yes, you did." His hand closed over her breast, a sharp contrast to the cold air on her other.

"You put yourself in a dangerous position. Your impulsiveness could have gotten you hurt, or even killed. Those men who tracked you weren't looking for a cup of coffee at your fire, and the outlaws you almost ran into would have done a hell of a lot worse to you."

Hayes rolled her nipple between his thumb and forefinger.

"When I think of what could have happened to you—"

With a curse, he gave her nipple a sharp tug. "I'm not used to caring about anyone, Savannah. Hell, it took me years to warm up to riding with Wyatt. This doesn't come easy for me at all, and your blatant disregard for your own safety infuriates me. I won't be able to take it if something happens to you."

Wyatt buried his face against her neck.

"You should have come to us."

The need inside her frightened her, becoming far stronger than it had been the night they'd taken her. That night, they'd spent most of the time easing her fears and comforting her. This time, however, they seemed different—more intense.

Before they'd been calm and their caresses tender and smooth. Now, their hands shook slightly, their touch more desperate, and they clenched their jaws as though struggling for control.

Having no idea what two such men would be like if that control snapped, Savannah shook helplessly with nerves, and a need so enticing, it scared her.

Their fingers tugging at her nipples and caressing her breasts felt hot against skin cooled by the late-afternoon breeze. Her stomach muscles contracted with each panting breath she released, and her skin felt too tight for her body.

The unfamiliar sensations made it nearly impossible to think clearly, but her mind screamed at her to stand her ground and maintain her newfound independence.

"No. I couldn't. I don't want to, oh, God, be beholden to…to you or any other m–man."

Both men stilled, making her squirm with the need to get their hands moving again.

To her extreme disappointment, Hayes lifted his hand from her breast to cup her chin, his hand so large that his thumb brushed against one ear and his fingers the other.

His eyes went flat, the danger surrounding him more exciting than scary now.

"Beholden? You think that's what we want from you? To be *beholden* to us?"

Unsettled at the wave of longing his rumbling tone sent through her, she tried to pull out of his grip. Used to dealing with her uncle, she was shocked at Hayes's strength and realized just how gentle they'd both been with her that night.

Shivering in delight at the rough texture of Wyatt's hands cupping her breasts, Savannah lifted her gaze to his.

"Please understand. I don't want to be helpless ever again."

Brushing his lips with hers, Hayes groaned.

"As long as there's breath in my body, you'll never be helpless."

He swallowed the cry she made, taking her mouth in one of those slow, thorough kisses that made her head spin.

Finding it hard to believe that a man like Hayes could be so feeling, she fisted her hands in his shirt, her heart beating out of control.

In the meantime, Wyatt made quick work of unfastening her pants and yanking them down to her knees. Running his hands over her bare bottom, he touched his lips to her ear.

"We want you to look to us for protection and to provide for you. We want you to come to us when you need or want anything. We want you to reach for us when your body's on fire the way it is now."

Hayes lifted his head, running his tongue over his bottom lip as though savoring the taste of her.

She'd never realized the level of intimacy that men and women could share. What they did to her now couldn't compare to being held in the dark with her face hidden, but she'd been so scared and overwhelmed that night, she hadn't been able to relax enough to enjoy it.

Their tenderness and affection had made it a wonderful experience for her, but the need she felt now made it so much different. Combined with their obvious affection for her, their lovemaking affected her even more strongly than before.

With a hot hand on each hip, Wyatt turned her to the side and watched her as his firm hands slid over her abdomen and between her thighs, separated her folds to the cool air.

The effect knocked her legs out from under her and she grabbed at Hayes to stay upright, thankful that he already held her securely.

Stunned at the feel of the cold air blowing over her swollen clit, Savannah stood frozen in place.

Naked from her neck to her knees, she should have felt cold, but the heat of their bodies surrounding her and the warmth of their hands kept her toasty warm. It made the contrast of the cold air blowing over her clit even more intense.

She whimpered at the too extreme sensation, reaching to cover herself, but Wyatt caught her hands in his, lifting it to his shoulder.

Holding her upright with an arm around her waist, he caressed her breast, his slow, tender touch sending jagged shards of white-hot pleasure through her.

"When you need to be loved, to be pleasured, when you ache, you come to us. We'll always take care of you, Savannah. In every way."

Looming over her, Hayes clenched his jaw, making the scar on his cheek even more pronounced.

"I've got to have my mouth on you. I didn't get a chance the last time, and I've been regretting it for months."

Savannah eagerly parted her lips and leaned forward, anxious for one of his slow kisses, one that made her feel all woman.

Touching his lips to hers, he smiled faintly, his eyes dancing with amusement.

"I'm glad to see you open so readily for my kiss, but that's not where I was talking about putting my mouth."

Savannah blinked, wondering if he could mean what she thought he meant. Her clit throbbed, the cold air so foreign on that part of her that she could hardly stand it. Between that and being exposed so completely, she shook with apprehension and a need so strong it threatened to consume her.

It thrilled her that she could put that look on his face, but the look itself filled her with apprehension.

"Something's wrong." Unsure and scared, she held on to Wyatt's forearm with one shaky hand and twisted her other free of Hayes's grip to reach for her pants.

Hayes ran a finger through her folds, smiling when she gasped and her knees buckled again.

"I'll fix it for you, darlin'. Don't fight it. There's nothing to be afraid of."

Wyatt tilted her head back, keeping her gaze on him as he covered her breast and squeezed her nipples between two strong fingers.

"There isn't a thing wrong with you. This is how it's supposed to be between a man and a woman."

She felt more than saw Hayes crouch down in front of her, shaking even harder when his hands came around her to grip her buttocks. Sucking in a breath when his warm breath heated her damp center, she fought to close her thighs, but his knees between hers kept them spread wide.

A second later, the warmth became fire as his tongue made a slow trail over her slick flesh, the sensation so astounding she grabbed at Wyatt again for support.

"Oh, God. You can't. It's so..."

Wyatt smiled, his eyes glittering with indulgence, affection, and something hot and wicked.

"Naughty. Delicious. Sweet."

Hayes lifted his head. "All of the above. I think we should make her wear skirts all the time just so we can throw them up whenever one of us gets a hunger for her."

Groaning, he buried his face between her thighs again, lapping at her, each stroke making her jolt, her entire body shaking with need.

She couldn't hold back her cries, so alarmed at the strength of the amazing pleasure, the feel of his tongue sliding over her clit so naughty and sinful she knew she should have objected.

But, God, she wanted it.

Hayes growled, the sound of it vibrating over her clit. "Damn, honey. You taste so good. I could make a meal of you. Come for me. Give me more of those juices."

Having no idea what he was talking about, Savannah struggled to be free, frightened at his complete dominance over her senses, one that she couldn't fight, no matter how hard she tried.

The pressure inside her built with each stroke, becoming too intense to bear.

It scared her even more that Wyatt and Hayes didn't even seem to notice.

It felt incredible, and the fact that a man as hard as Hayes would get such enjoyment from doing such a thing to her made it even more exciting.

Fisting her hands on Wyatt's chest, she looked up at him, licking her dry lips.

"Wyatt! Please. Help me."

A remarkable change came over his features, the wickedness in his eyes softening with tenderness and emotion.

"Don't be frightened, Savannah. Yes, that's it. Let go. Take your pleasure."

The heat between her thighs grew even hotter. The tingling awareness in her pussy and clit sharpened, becoming almost unbearable.

And still the pressure built.

Gulping in air, Savannah shook her head helplessly. "No. Something's happening to me. Make it stop."

The tingling grew, as did her trembling. It felt so good, better than anything had ever felt, but she couldn't take much more of it. The intensity of it scared her out of her wits, but she just couldn't stop reaching for more.

Without even meaning to, she pushed against Hayes's mouth even as she struggled to push out of their arms.

Hayes moaned against her folds before lifting his head, holding her gaze as he slid his finger into her pussy and began to press at her inner walls.

"I'm not going to let you fight this. There's nothing to fear, Savannah. Trust us."

He pushed his finger deeper, at the same time sucking her clit into his mouth. His movements became more forceful when she cried out as the pressure inside her seemed to explode. He kept sucking and stroking as the rippling waves of the most supreme pleasure went through her—wave after wave of it until she couldn't think about anything else at all.

It was like nothing she'd ever experienced, the pleasure making her body tighten and jerk out of her control. She couldn't stop it, each flick of Hayes's tongue and slide of his finger into her moist opening making the sensations even stronger.

Her entire body stiffened as his attention to her throbbing clit went on and on. Her pussy clenched repeatedly on the slow-moving finger inside her, intensifying the sensation of being filled.

Everything became focused on her clit and pussy. Nothing else mattered. Not her nakedness, not her need for independence, not her uncle.

Nothing.

Just this incredible feeling that made her entire body tingle and shake until she went limp, her muscles so weak she couldn't even support her own weight.

Closing her eyes, she let her head fall back, trusting Hayes and Wyatt to keep her from falling.

As if from a distance, she heard Wyatt croon to her, words that jumbled in her mind and made no sense at all, but the gentleness in his tone came through. It filled her with a warmth that reached deep inside her, the strength of his hold making her feel safe and secure while the world spun all around her.

She collapsed against him, thankful that he caught her in his arms.

Barely aware of Hayes coming to his feet and wrapping his arms around her from the other side, Savannah slumped, positive she couldn't have stood on her own even if she'd wanted to.

Wyatt held her close, running a hand up and down her back to her bare bottom, which suddenly felt cold.

"That's the kind of pleasure we'll give you. You were too nervous when we took your virginity, but now you see what it feels like and won't be afraid anymore."

It took every ounce of effort she possessed to push out of their arms, her hands and knees shaking as she struggled to right her clothing, brushing aside their attempts to help her.

Dizzy, she had trouble balancing, but each time they reached for her, she slapped their hands away, too shaken by what had just happened to want to be touched again.

It took several minutes of struggling to catch her breath before she could even speak.

"Do you mean that it's supposed to feel like that when you...you know?"

Wyatt chuckled. "If we do it right. Don't you worry about it. That's up to us. All you have to do is enjoy it."

It seemed stupid to turn away from them to finish dressing, especially since they'd already seen and touched everything, but Savannah couldn't help it.

Looking over her shoulder, she finished fastening her pants and started buttoning her shirt, her shaking hands making the simple task difficult.

"That can't happen again. I told you. I'm not staying."

Hayes's eyes narrowed as he turned her to face him. "If you go, we go with you."

His flat tone told her he would do it.

She couldn't let them follow her. They could never live the way they wanted to live anywhere but here, and if she stayed, her uncle would ruin things for everyone. She had to be far from here before he found her.

She couldn't let them want her.

"No! I want you to stay away from me."

Hayes stepped forward and yanked her against him, licking his lips, still shiny with her juices.

"There's nothing on God's green earth that'll keep me away from you. Belonging to us is going to be nothing like belonging to your uncle. With us, you'll be loved and cared for."

"Loved?" Savannah snorted inelegantly, pulled from his grip, and started for her horse. "My uncle told me he loved me all the time. If that's love, I want no part of it. Besides, you can't love me. You don't even know me. Just leave me alone." She mounted her horse, but Wyatt and Hayes were already there, Hayes taking the reins out of her hands before she could stop him.

His eyes turned icy, the hard lawman returning.

"I know what I feel, Savannah. I'm not a schoolboy. I told you I loved you back in Kansas City, and I meant it. I've never said that to another woman, and I don't appreciate having it thrown back in my face."

"Neither do I." Hayes ran a hand up her thigh, sending another one of those jarring thrills through her.

"I never would have taken your virginity if I hadn't loved you. I've never taken a virgin before, and I didn't do it lightly." Lifting a brow, he smiled coldly. "I wouldn't have taken you for the kind of woman to give your virginity to two men you don't love."

Savannah turned away, hoping the darkening sky would keep them from seeing her burning cheeks.

She hadn't given her virginity lightly at all. She'd fallen in love with both of them almost from the first time she'd laid eyes on them, and she hadn't been able to resist their lovemaking for long.

She'd been lonely for so long, her only source of love and affection coming from the Tylers, Esmeralda, and Maggie at the Bar T.

She'd been starving for tenderness and hadn't even realized it until the night Wyatt and Hayes had shown her the kind of closeness she'd never even known existed.

Her plans to leave town had been made long before they'd gotten there, but once she gave herself to them, she knew she had to escape as soon as possible.

Each moment with them made her more aware of what she'd been missing in her life. The taste she'd had of it made her hungry for more—something she knew she couldn't have had in Kansas City. Her uncle would never let her go, and even if he had, she wouldn't have been able to live with both Wyatt and Hayes there.

So, she'd run away, intent on finding happiness, and she had no intention of stopping now.

"I didn't give myself lightly, but that doesn't mean I want two men telling me what to do. Believe whatever you want. But, just as soon as Maggie has her baby, I'm leaving Desire. Alone."

Wyatt reached up to caress her breast through her shirt, drawing a gasp from her as he stroked a too-sensitive nipple.

"You're wrong on all counts. You already belong to us, and you won't be leaving Desire at all. You're ours, Savannah. Make no mistake about that."

"Never." Savannah yanked the reins out of his hands and started back the way they'd come, having no idea how to get to the Circle T.

She needn't have worried.

They caught up with her almost immediately, flanking her as they rode back to the ranch.

Riding in silence for several minutes, Savannah's mind wandered with thoughts of how it might have been if she could have stayed there. When Hayes moved closer, she jerked back to the present, stiffening.

Leaning toward her, he touched her arm, wrapping his strong fingers around it until she met his gaze.

"The only reason we didn't take you tonight is because we didn't want to betray Eb's trust. Or yours. That doesn't mean we're going to leave you alone. Ever."

Wyatt laughed beside her, a cold sound that chilled her.

"Be on your guard, honey. Every time we get the chance, we're going to give you so much pleasure, you'll never want to leave us. We'll get through that stubbornness of yours no matter what it takes."

Savannah rode on in silence toward the lights burning in the distance, very much afraid that they spoke the truth.

Chapter Three

After putting away the horses, they made their way toward the large chow building, her stomach rumbling at the delicious smells coming from inside.

Hayes took her arm and guided her through the heavy door.

"Damn, it smells like Duke outdid himself again."

Feeling all eyes on her, Savannah paused just inside the doorway, automatically seeking out Maggie.

Seated at what appeared to be her usual place, her friend waved and started to get up, but Jeremiah stopped her with a hand on her arm, bending to say something that had Maggie nodding, her fatigue apparent even from several feet away.

Eb came to his feet and approached, his eyes narrowing as they moved over her face.

Uncomfortable and feeling a little insecure, she instinctively moved closer to Hayes, a gesture that made Eb's gaze sharpen and seemed to amuse several of the other men sitting nearby.

Recognizing her mistake, she tried to move away, but Hayes caught her with an arm around her waist, keeping her at his side.

Wyatt closed in on her other, raising his voice loud enough for everyone to hear him. "Eb, your charge is here safe and sound. Hayes and I have already declared our intentions and made a claim on Savannah."

Eb inclined his head.

"It appears she's accepted your claim. She went off alone with you of her own free will and goes to you for safety. Congratulations. We'll see the preacher the next time we go into town."

The men started cheering, drowning out her gasp.

Shaking off Hayes's restraining hand, Savannah ran after Eb, grabbing his forearm until he turned back around.

"Eb Tyler, I said no such thing! I thought you said I could choose."

A dark brow went up, his lips thinning.

"You're going to have to make up your mind, Savannah. I won't have fights breaking out between my men and the new sheriffs because the men can't figure out if you're taken or not. If you're not taken, they're going to make a play for you."

Gesturing toward Wyatt and Hayes, who accepted congratulations and teasing comments from the other men, Eb sighed.

"Wyatt and Hayes would kill any man who touched you. You know that as well as I do. I don't want trouble, Savannah. The men want wives. They want women to warm their beds and make homes for them."

He gestured toward Maggie, his expression softening.

"We all want children. We want to build something here, Savannah. A home. A life. It's damned lonely without a woman to share it with."

Turning back to her, he nodded in Wyatt and Hayes's direction.

"That's what they want. They're smitten with you, and gave up their positions with the Marshals just to be able to make a home with you here. They won't take kindly to being toyed with."

A delicious warmth seemed to swell up inside her as she thought about their hands on her body and the way they *toyed* with her only minutes earlier.

Embarrassed that she'd messed everything up, she gritted her teeth and rubbed her eyes in frustration. She turned to find both Wyatt and Hayes watching her, the possessiveness and concern in their eyes unmistakable even at this distance.

Looking away, she scanned the room, noticing that the men who'd eyed her with curiosity and male interest when she'd walked through the door smiled politely or nodded with respect before looking away.

"Hellfire and damnation."

Eb chuckled. "And then some. Your men will get you some supper. According to everyone here, you're already spoken for. I'm beginning to think Wyatt and Hayes planned it that way. Smart men."

Savannah bristled. "Good. That'll keep everyone from bothering me until I can leave. Hopefully by then I'll be able to get Hayes and Wyatt to understand."

She turned again to find both men starting toward her, each with two plates piled high with food.

Eb took her arm and turned her toward the table where Maggie waited.

"Good luck with that, honey. They seem real determined."

Taking the seat across from Maggie, she nodded at Jeremiah, who sat on the other side of her friend, before looking up at Eb over her shoulder. "So am I."

Eb grinned and took his seat on the other side of his wife. "My money's on them."

* * * *

Of course Wyatt and Hayes sat on either side of her, making it impossible to move without brushing against one of them.

She ate, but tasted nothing.

When they finished eating, the four men walked Maggie and Savannah back to the house, each seemingly preoccupied with his own thoughts.

Maggie tried several times to make conversation, but Savannah just nodded, finding it difficult to concentrate. Eventually, Maggie smiled in understanding and gave up.

Once inside, Savannah walked ahead of Maggie and Jeremiah, making her way up the stairs on shaky legs. She made her way to her room and listened to the men, who stayed outside talking for what seemed like hours.

She knew the looks Wyatt and Hayes had given her as they bid her good night would keep her awake for hours.

Filled with desire, their eyes flashed with impatience that they couldn't give her a more intimate good-night.

She couldn't hear what they said, but she could easily distinguish the rumble of Hayes and Wyatt's voices. After hours of tossing and turning, she finally fell asleep and dreamed about being held between them.

Restless, she curled into a ball and wondered what it would be like to be on the receiving end of the pleasure their eyes had promised.

* * * *

Her lack of sleep made her grouchy the next morning, and she blamed them. Angry and ashamed of herself for responding so readily to them, she stomped down the stairs and got even madder.

Shocked at her own delight at finding them waiting for her, she swallowed heavily, hoping they would assume her red face was due to anger.

"Where is everyone? Maggie and I were supposed to go out together."

Hayes took a step toward her, his eyes sharpening when she took a step back.

"Jeremiah took her out. She needs to eat, and it's still dark outside. He didn't want her to trip on anything. Besides, we wanted to say good morning to you in private, especially since we didn't get to give you a proper good-night last night. Eb's not as comfortable leaving us alone with you now that you told him you don't want to marry us."

Already trembling, Savannah took another step backward, sucking in a panicked breath when she backed into the wall. Her gaze slid to where Wyatt stood watching her, the anticipation and impatience glittering in his eyes making her stomach tighten and her pussy clench with an awareness that never failed to unsettle her.

"I don't want to marry anyone."

With her attention diverted, Hayes took advantage, closing her in with a hand on the wall on either side of her head. He bent over her, his wide shoulders completely blocking her view of Wyatt.

"Good morning, darlin'. Did you dream about me last night?"

Each time he spoke to her in that low, intimate tone, it sent ripples of delight over her skin.

He'd never shown even the smallest amount of playfulness toward her or anyone else in Kansas City, but here he seemed more relaxed.

She stared at his lips, her nipples beading at the memory of how it felt to have his hot mouth on them.

Biting her lip at the memory, she straightened, inadvertently brushing her nipples against Hayes's chest.

Unnerved by the glint of amusement and determination in his green eyes, she swallowed heavily, finding it hard to keep from staring at his lips.

"N–Not at all. When I dream, it's about being on my own, where no one can tell me what to do and I answer only to myself. I like it."

His lips moved, capturing her attention again, remembering how firm they'd felt when taking hers. She couldn't forget how soft they'd been brushing over her temple and cheeks when he took her. She knew the heat of them and dreamt of feeling them moving over every part of her.

The kind of pleasure he could give just using his mouth should have been illegal—but she was glad that it wasn't.

She couldn't help wanting more.

With her mind swirling with sinful thoughts, she tore her gaze away from his lips to look into his eyes, startled by the indulgent laughter and expectation in them.

He seemed so different from the man he'd been in Kansas City that she sometimes wondered if she'd imagined the man he'd been before.

Belatedly realizing that he'd spoken, she swallowed heavily, her face burning.

"What did you say?"

With a gleam in his eyes she didn't trust, Hayes ran a finger down the front of her shirt, pausing to tease a nipple.

"You seem distracted. I said that Wyatt and I are going to have to do something about that. You should be dreaming of being snuggled into a warm bed between us, where you'll sleep every night for the rest of your life."

He tapped her nipple, grinning when she cried out, a rare grin that made her heart skip a beat.

His smile fell, his eyes narrowing as he switched his attention to her other breast, this time ignoring her nipple entirely. Using one finger, he caressed the underside, making her nipple bead even tighter.

Fisting her hands at her sides to keep from reaching for him, she let out a shaky breath.

"I–I'm n–not interested. I w–want to b–be on m–my own."

Bending low, he brushed her lips with his, sliding his hands up to cup both of her breasts, his thumbs stroking her nipples over her shirt.

"What do you want to do on your own that you can't do living here and married to us?"

Dying for his kiss, to feel his incredible mouth against hers, she parted her lips in an automatic invitation she didn't even intend to extend.

To her delight, he accepted immediately, using his lips to part hers even wider and sweeping his tongue inside.

Tasting coffee and sin she grabbed onto him, rising to her toes to get even closer.

Her head spun at the slide of his tongue over her teeth, her breath catching when he curled his tongue around hers, encouraging her to follow his into his mouth.

Surprised at her own daring, she pushed to get even closer.

She couldn't get enough of him, wanting more, closer, harder.

Wicked. Sensual. Hot.

She didn't know how something so sinful could feel so natural and right, almost as though she'd spent her life just waiting for this.

She hadn't even known she could experience this kind of closeness with a man, a connection that included not only sex, but trust and respect.

At that moment, she wished with everything inside her that she didn't have to leave.

When he wrapped his arms around her and drew her even closer, she could all but feel herself melting against him. When he started to lift his head, she moaned her distress, nearly climbing his body in an effort to keep his lips against hers.

Hayes took a shuddering breath and groaned, letting her know without words that he suffered the same way she did. He dipped his head again, taking her lips in a lingering kiss, one with a hint of desperation.

Lifting his head, he brushed his lips over her cheek, his breath warm against her ear.

"You belong here. With us. There's nothing out there for you that you can't find here with us."

Savannah pushed against his flat stomach to put some distance between them, both surprised and disappointed that he allowed it.

"How about freedom?"

Wyatt closed in on her other side, taking her arm to pull her to him. Running his hands over her hair, he tilted her head back, searching her features.

"You'll have a hell of a lot more freedom with us than you had with your uncle—just not enough to get into any trouble. You'll be safe with us, Savannah, and we'll do everything in our power to make sure you're happy."

Picking her up with hands at her bottom, he slid them to her thighs, silently urging her to wrap her legs around his waist.

Savannah rubbed against him, unable to stop herself, her breath catching when Hayes moved in behind her and nuzzled her neck.

Focusing on Wyatt's eyes, she shook her head.

"What do you mean—just not enough freedom to get into trouble?"

Wyatt's eyes narrowed.

"You'll stay the hell away from other men, and you won't do anything, *anything*, that would put you in a dangerous situation."

Threading her fingers through his too-long hair, Savannah watched his mouth as he lowered it, holding her breath in anticipation of his kiss.

"I would never do either one of those things." Just the thought of allowing another man to touch her made her sick to her stomach.

Wyatt paused, sliding one hand to her bottom again and the other behind her neck to pull her closer.

"Then there's no reason not to marry us."

* * * *

With Wyatt's words still ringing in her ears, Savannah put aside the shirt she'd just finished mending and reached for another.

"You have a lot of mending to do on your own."

Maggie shrugged.

"A lot of the men do their own, but I offered to help. Duke and his men do all the cooking, and cleaning the house takes very little effort. I'm lucky enough to have husbands who can afford to buy candles and soaps in town so I don't have to make them. The real chore is the washing, but a few of the men help me with the water, especially now, so it isn't that bad."

Savannah smiled. "Do you remember when I begged to help you and Esmeralda, but I didn't know how to sew?" Smiling at the memory, she met Maggie's gaze. "Esmeralda was horrified and said that I would need to know how to mend when I marry. The three of us would sit by the fire and talk for hours."

Pausing, she frowned. "I didn't realize how much I missed that until now." She'd only remembered the long hours she'd spent sitting alone and mending her uncle's clothing.

Maggie's sad smile tugged at her heart.

"I miss Esmeralda so much, and I've missed you, too. I'm so glad you're going to be here when the baby's born. I hope you'll stay afterward. Eb and Jeremiah say that Wyatt and Hayes are good men. He thinks they'll convince you to stay. I'd hoped you would marry them."

Her eyes brimmed with tears.

"Oh, Savannah, it would be so wonderful to have you here with me. Other women will be coming along—mail-order brides—but you and I have been friends forever. Please stay. Marry Wyatt and Hayes. They care for you so much."

Savannah shook her head, trying to ignore the surge of delight at the reminder of how much Wyatt and Hayes professed to love her.

"Maggie, I don't want to get married." Looking away, she sighed. "I couldn't stay here even if I wanted to, and it's obvious Wyatt and Hayes belong here." The fact that both Wyatt and Hayes seemed more comfortable than they'd been in Kansas City supported that.

With the ease of long practice, Savannah picked up another shirt and began mending the torn sleeve, hurriedly changing the subject.

"You know the only reason my uncle even allowed us to be friends is because he was afraid of Mr. Tyler and couldn't figure out a way to put an end to it without offending him."

Smiling to hide the hurt she could never quite shake, Savannah glanced at Maggie.

"After you left, I had no freedom at all. I like having it now. I can do whatever I want to do."

Savannah kept her head down, afraid that the person in the world who knew her better than anyone would see too much.

"I'd been planning to leave for a long time. You know how much I hated him. After I took care of his chores and favors, I did everything I could to earn money. I took in sewing, cleaned stables, anything I could do to earn enough to leave."

Dropping her sewing, she stared down at her hands.

"He was evil, Maggie. You never knew some of the things he did to me. Beatings that would take me days to recover from—"

She stopped abruptly and picked up her mending again, afraid she'd already revealed too much. Her hands shook so hard, she set the sewing aside. She wouldn't be able to mend anything until she calmed down.

The memory of a terrible night, a memory never far from the surface, rose again, threatening to choke her. She didn't want to think about what would have happened if Eb hadn't come by and saved her.

Another vision rose, one of the night Wyatt and Hayes had taken her. They'd been so tender and loving, and she'd soaked it up like a sponge.

Since then, no matter how they touched her, she fell under their spell, making her wonder if her uncle had been right about her after all.

She'd spent her entire life fighting not to be like her mother. It unsettled her that if her mother were alive, she would be applauding the fact that Savannah had given herself to two men.

Her mother would be proud.

The thought sickened her.

Turning her head, she looked again at Maggie.

Glowing with health and happiness, Maggie stared at her in horror.

Savannah couldn't help but smile, unable to imagine a woman more unlike her mother.

Maggie's love for her husbands showed, and it was plain for anyone to see how much Eb and Jeremiah adored her.

Dropping the shirt she'd been working on, Maggie reached for her.

"Oh, Savannah! I didn't know it was that bad. I knew he was hitting you, and I told Mr. Tyler. I'd hoped he'd stopped."

Fighting back nausea, Savannah forced a smile. Not wanting Maggie to start crying again, Savannah came to her feet, stretching to ease the sore muscles in her shoulders.

"Don't cry for me. All of that's over now. I love being free, Maggie. I don't want to give that up. I can do whatever I want to do, and I don't have to answer to anyone."

Frowning, Maggie sat back, rubbing her swollen abdomen, something Savannah noticed she did quite a bit.

"Jeremiah told me that you were almost attacked twice on your way here. If not for Wyatt and Hayes intervening, you could have been hurt, or even killed, Savannah. It's not safe for you to be alone."

Maggie's eyes darkened in concern.

"I thought you were sweet on Wyatt and Hayes. Back in Kansas City, I heard them talking about kissing you. They're very protective of you, Savannah, and talked to Eb and Jeremiah about you several times. They told them they wanted to marry you and that they couldn't start their positions here as sheriffs until they got you here. They won't stay if you don't. They'll follow you wherever you go."

Savannah turned and moved away to hide her burning cheeks, not stopping until she got to the window. She stopped abruptly, her heart leaping to her throat at the sight of Wyatt crossing the yard.

She'd know his deceptively slow, long-legged stride anywhere.

To her shock, he stopped in his tracks and turned his head, lifting it in her direction as if somehow knowing she was there. His sharp eyes held hers, steady and warm, with an underlying possessiveness that felt more right than it should have.

She didn't know what Maggie would think if she knew that she'd done far more with Wyatt and Hayes than kissing.

She burned at the memory of what they'd done to her. Each time they touched her, it felt better than the time before, and she knew if she kept allowing it, there would come a time when she wouldn't be able to walk away.

The thought that she could have them for the rest of her life became harder and harder to resist each day.

Still, she had no choice. If she stayed, it would ruin everything they were all trying to build here. If her uncle found her here, he would see to that.

With a sigh, she ran her finger down the cool glass and over the place she stared at Wyatt, as though by touching the glass, she could touch him. When he smiled, she realized what she'd done and dropped her hand.

"I can't give them what they want from me."

Maggie touched her shoulder, startling her.

"Eb and Jeremiah want to love me, protect me, take care of me, and in return, they want me to love them back and to look to them for safety and security. They can be hard, but this land calls for it. When we go to bed—God, they make me feel so good."

Savannah turned away from the window.

"What did you mean about them making you feel good? Are you talking about…intimacy?"

She couldn't believe she'd even asked the question.

Maggie's giggle gave her all the answer she needed.

"Oh, Savannah. I haven't had anyone to talk to about this. It's incredible, and they seem to like it just as much as I do. We can't get enough of each other. Esmeralda told me some things, but I never dreamed..."

Swallowing heavily, Savannah blinked back tears of relief.

"So, it's not just loose women who enjoy being...intimate?"

Maggie laughed and hugged her.

"Not at all. Just wait until—"

Maggie must have felt Savannah stiffen because she stepped back, her eyes going wide.

"Oh, my God! You've already...are you expecting?"

Savannah's face burned even hotter. "Of course not. Maggie, I—"

Maggie moved away and put her hands over her ears.

"No. Don't tell me anything. If Eb and Jeremiah find out, they'll force you to marry Wyatt and Hayes before you're ready. If I know anything, Eb and Jeremiah will get it out of me. If they think I'm lying, they'll spank me. As much as I like it, I don't want to tell your secrets."

Memories of being punched and kicked raced through Savannah's mind, and she doubled over in remembered pain.

"Oh, God! They hit you? Pack. I'll get the horses and we'll get out of here as—"

Maggie caught her arm.

"Savannah! Stop it. I'm not going anywhere."

"You're damned right you're not."

Savannah whirled to see Jeremiah coming into the room, his eyes alight with anger.

"Jeremiah! Maggie, get back!"

Terrified, Savannah jumped in front of Maggie as instinct took over. Closing her eyes and putting her arms out on front of her, she braced for the blow that she knew would knock her off her feet.

After several long seconds of stunned silence, she opened her eyes to see Jeremiah staring at her in disbelief.

"Savannah? What is it, honey? You didn't really think I would hit you, did you?"

His incredulous tone made her feel even more stupid. Of course Jeremiah wouldn't hit her. They'd done their best to protect her when she'd needed it.

But—

Turning to meet Maggie's stunned look, Savannah drew a shaky breath.

"They *spank* you?"

The sound of footsteps racing up the stairs had Savannah turning back toward the door, mortified to see Wyatt coming through it.

He took in the room at a glance before rushing toward her, his gaze sliding to Jeremiah's.

"What the hell's going on? I heard Savannah scream."

Savannah grimaced and tried to avoid Wyatt, but as soon as he reached her side, he pulled her against him, somehow holding her while placing his big body between hers and Jeremiah's.

"Nothing's wrong with me." She hated to admit, even to herself, that she drew strength from Wyatt's presence.

"It's Maggie. Jeremiah and Eb hit her."

"What?"

All three shouted simultaneously, Jeremiah and Wyatt turning to stare at Maggie.

Maggie stared at Savannah, her face bright red.

"Savannah, I didn't say that. I said that they spanked me."

To Savannah's astonishment, Jeremiah burst out laughing and the tension drained from Wyatt, who seemed to be having a hard time keeping a straight face.

Furious and embarrassed, Savannah lifted her chin and glared at Wyatt. "I don't appreciate having all of you laugh at me, and I certainly don't think it's funny to hit a woman."

Wyatt curved an arm around her shoulder and led her from the room, his smile falling.

"You're right. It's not. Come with me, and maybe we can straighten this out."

"You'd better not hit me."

"I'll make you a deal. I'll show you what your friend was talking about, and then you and I can talk about how cruel it is."

Running a hand over her back, he leaned close, whispering in her ear.

"Brace yourself, darlin'. This isn't going to be like any spanking you've ever heard of."

Chapter Four

"If you think I'm going to let you get away with spanking me, you're crazy."

Wyatt only smiled and finished bundling her into her coat and plopping her hat on her head before leading her outside.

His silence filled her with foreboding, leaving her in no doubt that he had every intention of turning her over his lap.

For a split second, she figured he wouldn't dare do it, but almost as quickly remembered who she was dealing with.

She'd just have to figure out a way to stop him. Looking up at him, she hid a smile as an idea came to her. She'd threaten him with Eb. Fear of the big, fierce rancher and his brother had kept her uncle in check for years.

Sobering at the realization that even Eb and Jeremiah wouldn't intimidate Wyatt, she started to panic.

As they crossed the yard, Savannah tugged unobtrusively to get free, not wanting to cause a scene in front of the others. She could already feel several pairs of eyes on her from the men who paused in their chores to watch them.

Savannah realized that, other than Maggie, she was the only woman on a huge ranch, and knew that the others would be curious about her, but she hadn't counted on so much attention.

A very tall, very large, very *mean*-looking Indian, dressed in buckskins, straightened from the fence where he'd been watching another even meaner-looking Indian break a horse. Inclining his head in her direction, he slid a warning glance at the hand Wyatt had on her arm.

"Problem?"

Savannah tensed, scared that a fight would break out. Looking back and forth between the two of them, she had no idea who would come out the winner.

She only knew it would be ugly.

She hated violence in any form, but the thought of Wyatt and the fierce Indian fighting terrified her. She started to step between them, only to have Wyatt yank her back.

"Hello, Blade. This is Savannah, the woman who's going to marry Hayes and me on the next trip to town. We're off to have a little talk about the way things are done in Desire. She seems to think Jeremiah beats Maggie."

Blade's brows went up as he studied Savannah, his expression never changing.

"Neither one of them would ever hurt a hair on that woman's head. Don't ever step between two men when you think a fight might break out between them."

Savannah lifted her chin, bristling at his arrogance. Apparently, what she'd heard was true.

The men of Desire seemed to think they had the right to tell her what to do.

"I appreciate the advice, but I can take care of myself, thank you very much."

Blade smiled, a flash of white in his dark face, the transformation nearly taking her to her knees. Gorgeous and absolutely breathtaking, he took a step closer.

"Spirited, too. Yes, it sounds like you'd better have that talk. I don't think your woman realizes that every man on the place has sworn to watch out for her."

His eyes narrowed on Savannah's, making her nervous as hell.

"I wouldn't be happy if I lost my job and my home because something happened to her on my watch."

Savannah gritted her teeth and tried once again to pull from Wyatt's grasp.

"I'm not your responsibility."

Wyatt shared a look with Blade, one of male superiority.

"Hayes and I are responsible for your protection, but everyone else is committed to keeping you safe as well."

"I can take care of myself." She tried once again to pull away, but Wyatt's iron grip didn't allow it.

"Damnation! Will you let go of me? I'm not going anywhere with you."

Blade's smile widened, the pure sin in his eyes enhancing his startling good looks.

"You know, I never saw the draw of that spanking stuff, but now I do. Yours certainly needs one. After listening to her, I understand what Eb was talking about. Hardheadedness on a woman out here will only get her killed. Interesting concept and one worth exploring."

His eyes sparkled with mischief. "Phoenix will love it."

Enraged and more than a little concerned, Savannah gasped and tried to pull away again, but Wyatt merely chuckled.

With an ease that she found nothing short of amazing, Wyatt lifted her onto his horse, the muscles under her hands bunching and shifting as he settled her in place. With equal ease, he quickly mounted behind her.

Much to the obvious amusement of Blade and the other men watching, their grins and low chuckles making her stomach tighten, he settled her on his lap and rode off at a gallop, forcing her to hold on to his forearm for balance.

She tried not to think about the warmth of the muscular forearm brushing against the underside of her breasts, just as she tried to ignore the hard bulge pressing at her bottom.

Wyatt seemed tense behind her, his hand hard at her waist. The brief glance at his features reminded her very much of the night they'd taken her to the pond.

Savannah kept silent as they headed west, attempting to rein in her temper, a temper she'd been able to control, with very few lapses, until she'd met Wyatt and Hayes.

Once they'd ridden from view of the ranch, she turned her head, not quite ready to meet his eyes. "You'd better be teasing. You'd better not be thinking of really spanking me. I don't know why men feel the need to be such brutes, but you're not going to get away with it with me."

Being so close to him, close enough that his body brushed against hers with every movement, filled her with longing. The heat from his hard body warmed the entire back of hers, making the front of her feel even colder in contrast.

Her breath caught when Wyatt slid his hot hand higher to cup her breast, his fingers unerringly finding her nipple.

She wished she had the willpower to push him away, but his touch just felt too good, his caress both demanding and tender at the same time.

His warm lips moved over the outer curve of her ear, making her shiver and beading her nipples even more.

"I've never been anything but gentle with you, and you know it. If you deserved a spanking, you would sure as hell get one, but it wouldn't be anything like what your uncle did to you. I could kill him for the bruises he left on you."

Slowing his horse, he led them to a small clearing where a slight breeze blew. Other than her own heartbeat, only the sounds of rustling leaves broke the silence.

His gloved hands moved to her thighs, caressing lightly before sliding back up to cup her breasts again.

"We've both promised to love and protect you. If you get bruises from us, darlin', it'll be from sex."

Swallowing heavily, Savannah fought not to lean into his caress, not about to let him see how strongly he affected her. Her shirt came undone under his quick hands, allowing the cool air to blow over her nipples, pebbling them even tighter.

She gasped at the shock of cold air against her skin, moaning in relief and delight when Wyatt cupped her breasts with his gloved hands.

Squirming, she pushed back against him, involuntarily lifting her breasts more fully against his palms.

"Bruises from…that? Oh, God. That feels…" Words escaped her.

Wyatt's hands moved, the friction of leather over her nipples making her stomach tighter.

"Feel good?"

His low chuckle against her neck sent shivers of delight racing up and down her spine.

"Hayes and I have a lot to teach you about loving. Something tells me you'll be a very responsive student."

His hands slid to her hips, holding her to him as though she wanted to get away.

"I love exploring you. I love your passion. I love all those wonderful sounds you make and the look of surprise in your eyes at the pleasure you get from my touch. I want to learn every inch of you with my fingers…my lips…my tongue."

Savannah shivered, longing to experience the pleasure his softly spoken words promised. She knew, though, that she would be better off not knowing what she would be missing when she left. She'd already miss so much and wondered if she'd ever be able to sleep through the night again without Wyatt and Hayes invading her dreams.

"That…you know…can never happen again."

One gloved hand made its way between her thighs, making her cry out as a leather-covered finger slid over her clit.

"It's going to happen again, honey. A lot. So, what do you think of your new home?"

The swift change of subject caught Savannah by surprise. Blinking, she tried to focus on the landscape surrounding them, but no matter how hard she tried, she couldn't douse her arousal.

The air blowing over her nipples made them tighten almost painfully, making her crave his attention there even more. Her pussy clenched, the need to be filled with his cock so strong that her stomach tightened, the muscles quivering beneath his hand.

She couldn't get enough air into her lungs, the cool air filling her overheated body with every panting breath. Her mind screamed at her to cover herself, but her body had other plans, her back arching to thrust her breasts out in invitation.

"What are you doing to me?"

She didn't recognize the raw huskiness in her voice as her own, but it seemed to please Wyatt very much.

He gathered her closer and sighed, sliding his fingertips over her abdomen and making her stomach muscles quiver.

His hand made a slow journey to the fastening of her pants and slid inside. With devastating slowness, he moved his hand lower, his gloved fingers parting her folds.

"I'm loving you, something I plan to do at every opportunity."

She grabbed his forearm, crying out at the too-light stroke to her clit.

Travelling just as slowly, his other hand moved to caress her breast, stroking lightly over her heaving chest.

She squirmed on his lap, excited, and gasping for air. She stilled when Wyatt cursed and pressed the bulge at the front of his pants against her. Weak with pleasure from his attention to her clit and nipple, she slumped against him.

"Wyatt, we shouldn't do this. It's wrong."

It didn't feel that way, though.

In his arms, she felt desirable. She felt important. She felt safe.

She'd always dreamed that one day she would find someone she could feel safe with, the way Maggie felt with Eb and Jeremiah.

As a young girl, she'd wished for a man she could trust—someone she could rely on.

They'd been nothing but childhood dreams, daydreams of a little girl, and then a young woman, one who spent too much time alone.

Nothing could have surprised her more than meeting not one—but two—men she trusted and respected, and that made her feel safer than she ever had before.

Nothing—except falling in love with them.

She hadn't been ready for it, and certainly hadn't given a thought to desire. She hadn't realized how much a kiss could affect her, or anticipated what it would be like to be on the receiving end of so much attention.

She had no experience with affection and never realized just how eagerly she would lap it up.

She had no experience with this kind of love and feared she would become lost in it. She already felt helpless against it and was very much afraid that she would never find the courage to turn her back on it and walk away when she needed to.

Sliding his hand from her breast, he turned her in his arms, his hand firm between her thighs. Laying her back over his forearm, he bent over her.

His eyes seemed to glitter from beneath the brim of his hat, the affection in them sharpened with lust and what appeared to be a glimmer of anger.

"Does this feel wrong, Savannah?" He moved his finger in a circular motion over her clit, smiling in arrogant satisfaction when she whimpered.

Her heart raced, her body both tightening and yielding in anticipation.

Fisting her hand in the front of his thick coat, Savannah stared at his lips, needing to feel them on hers as much as she needed her next breath.

"Wyatt, nice women aren't supposed to do this."

Wyatt's gaze lingered on her breasts, making them feel swollen and heavy, before his eyes, full of amusement, lifted to hers.

"You look pretty nice to me. Beautiful, in fact."

Stroking her clit, he smiled at her moan, his gaze moving slowly up and down her body. "The most beautiful woman I've ever seen."

The appreciation in his eyes made her *feel* beautiful. No one had ever looked at her the way Wyatt and Hayes looked at her—a look that made her feel feminine and desirable. Looking up at him through her lashes, she swallowed heavily.

"That's not what I meant."

Wyatt continued to stroke her clit, a light stroke designed to drive her crazy. His eyes narrowed to slits as they moved over her squirming body, a muscle working in his jaw.

"We're getting married as soon as the preacher gets back to town."

That warm swell of pleasure began again, one that she'd already discovered would lead to the wave of release she'd come to crave.

Her clit throbbed beneath his finger, burning as the pressure inside her built.

She took a deep breath, struggling to say what she needed to say.

"I'm not marrying you. Or Hayes. Or anyone. Ever." Maybe if she said it enough, she would eventually be able to convince herself.

The dangerous glint in Wyatt's eyes matched his low, smooth tone.

"You *are* a bad girl. You give your body to me, but you won't let me have the rest. We'll have to do something about that."

Outraged at his arrogance, and more than a little unnerved by his teasing threat, Savannah tried to push against him, only to cry out in alarm at his quick move. She grabbed at his shoulders, trembling at the feel of his hand at her waist as he lifted her to a sitting position again in front of him.

Staring out at the land in front of them, Wyatt kept a supporting arm around her. With slow deliberation, he removed his right glove and curved his fingers around her breast, stroking her skin with just his fingertips, almost absently, as if he couldn't keep his hands off of her.

"This will be our home. We start work on the house tomorrow. Most of the wood has already been cut and is just beyond those rocks over there. Of course, it won't be a house as grand as the Tylers', but it'll be ours. While we're in town getting married, you can pick out some of the things you want for it."

Bending, he nudged her head to the side and nuzzled her neck, staring down at where his finger circled her nipple.

"Hayes and I don't have a lot of money, but we'll take good care of you, Savannah. We'll protect you and provide for you and make a good life here."

Savannah's low moan sounded loud in the silence. Her clit still tingled so badly she couldn't stay still, and his attention to her nipple only made it worse.

"I already told you. I'm not staying, and I'm not getting m— married."

His low chuckle broke off abruptly, becoming a groan.

"You keep rubbing that bottom against my cock, you're going to make me explode in my pants before I can turn you over my lap and show you one of those spankings you're so afraid of."

Savannah gasped at the sharp pinch to her nipple, rubbing her thighs together at the jolt of heat that settled between them. Arching her back, she threw her arms up and around his neck, rubbing against him and giving herself over to his touch.

Imagining what it would feel like to do such a thing when they were alone in a bedroom and both naked, she turned her face to rub against his strong jaw. Breathing in the scent of him, she moaned again, cursing the fact that she didn't seem able to resist him.

Why had she made that promise to Maggie?

"Wyatt, we can't do this anymore. I'm not staying. Please understand."

Bending his head, Wyatt brushed her lips with his warm, firm ones.

"Always so polite, even when your body's trembling with need. I don't want to hear any more talk about you leaving, Savannah. You're marrying Hayes and me, and you're staying here if I have to tie you to my bed."

"No!" God, she wanted to.

Savannah yelped when, in a quick move, Wyatt lifted her to him.

Bending her over his arm, he took a cold nipple into his hot mouth, sucking gently while caressing it with his tongue.

Grabbing onto his shoulders, she writhed on his lap, bucking against the wild hunger building inside her. Alarmed at the feel of cold air on her bottom and the tops of her thighs, she fought harder.

"What are you doing?"

With her pants at her knees and caught at the tops of her boots, she could no longer kick with any force. She cried out again in shock and sharp need when he released her damp nipple from his mouth, allowing the cold breeze to blow over it.

Startled by the sensation, she grabbed at him in panic, fighting to hold on to him as he turned her over, draping her across his lap with apparent ease.

"Wyatt! What in damnation are you doing? Pick me up right now. Do you hear me?"

Wyatt's warm hand sliding over her bare bottom filled her with trepidation, but it was the cold intent in his tone that really alarmed her.

"Darlin', if you keep yelling, everyone at the ranch will be able to hear you. Why on earth would I let you go when I've got you just where I want you?"

Savannah stilled, looking around to make sure they were still alone, the threat of a spanking sending her into a panic. "You can't be serious! You're not really thinking of spanking me, are you?"

The thought of it both terrified and excited her. The fear she understood. The excitement she didn't understand at all.

She tightened her bottom cheeks against the hand that kept moving over them, feeling his gaze on her there. Holding on to his leg, she moaned again, startled when his other hand slid over her breast, the feel of leather cool and decadent against her tender flesh.

Wyatt chuckled softly, bending close. "I told you that I would, Savannah. You know that I'm a man of my word."

He ran his fingers over the backs of her thighs and over her bottom, sending streams of sharp awareness to her pussy and clit.

"I want you to believe that I mean every word that I say to you. You're frightened of this, and I want you to see that it isn't what you think it is. The only way to see that is to experience it. I also want you to have an idea of what will happen to you if you ever, *ever*, put yourself in any kind of danger. This is a rough place to live, and I can't have you being careless. You're everything to us, Savannah. I can't let anything happen to you."

Drawing on years of experience in dealing with her uncle, she kept her voice calm, a feat harder to accomplish than she'd anticipated. With her uncle, she fought fear and disgust. With Wyatt, the layer of fear excited her and filled her with anticipation, making her want to curl into him instead of running away.

She didn't know what kind of person that made her, but didn't want to think about it too closely.

Clearing her throat, she looked away. "Wyatt, I believe you. You don't have to prove anything to me."

"I think I do."

Before she could form the words in an attempt to reason with him, he tugged at her nipple with one hand while using the fingers of his other to part her folds.

"Christ, you're beautiful."

She forgot what she wanted to say, the words dissolving in the heat of lust. Self-conscious at being outside and exposed in such a way, she couldn't deny that another part of her reveled in the appreciation glittering in his eyes as they moved over her. The air blowing over her wet slit and beaded nipples sent another wave of longing through her, reminding her just how completely she lay open to him.

"W–Wyatt, we can t–talk about this."

"Later."

His clipped tone gave her a moment's pause, the cold snap of it filling her with equal parts apprehension and lust.

The U.S. Marshal who even the most dangerous outlaws feared now held her practically naked, and in the most compromising situation she'd ever been in.

She'd wanted him before, but the hunger in his touch and in his tone took her way beyond *want* to something she truly didn't understand.

She just knew she wanted more.

She pushed herself against his leg in an effort to lift herself, but he took the hand from her breast and pressed it against her lower back.

"Wyatt, let me up."

"No."

Savannah cried out as a sharp slap landed on her bottom, the sting even more intense on her cold bottom than it should have been.

Furious and embarrassed that a spanking could give her such pleasure, she wiggled furiously in an effort to get away.

She couldn't believe the things he did to her, or how desperately she wanted more.

Tears of mortification and frustration stung her eyes, tears she hurriedly blinked away. Expecting him to hit her again, Savannah tried to cover her vulnerable bottom, but Wyatt brushed her hand away and caressed her, spreading the heat until it settled between her thighs.

"You snake. You sidewinder! You—ow!"

"Calling your husband names isn't nice."

"You're not my husband, and you never will be!"

Another slap landed. "Yes, I will be. Now stop complaining and pay attention. I want you to feel what I'm doing to you."

Startled that lust began to override anger, she struggled to recapture the fury.

"I am paying attention to what you're doing to me. I *am* feeling it, you brute. You're hurting me. I thought you were different. You're just like other men. Worse, because you made me believe you. I thought you said women would be—oh!"

He slid a finger into her pussy, the shock of it cutting off her outburst.

Without meaning to, she moved, rocking her hips in a desperate attempt to take more.

Withdrawing his finger with a speed that left her pussy clenching, he chuckled at her curses of frustration. Another slap landed, this time on the other cheek.

"Temper. Temper."

Wyatt held his hand over the place he'd just slapped, reaching down to caress her breast again.

"Your pussy's soaked, and you keep tightening on my finger. The heat from your spanking is spreading, making you warm down there. Feel it, Savannah. Let yourself feel things you've never felt before. Let me show you."

Wiggling, she moaned. "You're no gentleman."

When the next slap landed, Savannah squirmed at the heat, knowing that he didn't hit her nearly as hard as he could have.

The realization that he didn't mean to hurt her robbed her of some of her anger.

Again he laid a hand over the place he'd slapped, this time caressing it and spreading the heat outward.

"Figured that out, did you? I never claimed to be a gentleman. A gentleman would never stand a chance out here."

The inability to prevent him from doing anything he wanted to do to her gave Savannah something she'd never before experienced. His strong hold and forcefulness allowed her to feel things she'd never felt before, things she would never have allowed herself to experience if they hadn't been forced on her.

Fascinated at the intense pleasure, she still couldn't get past the embarrassment of getting so aroused at this kind of treatment.

"Stop hurting me, damn you!" Chagrined at the breathy quality in her voice, instead of the forcefulness she'd tried to exert, she slapped his leg in frustration.

Wyatt laughed softly at her half-hearted resistance, his voice like warm honey flowing over her senses. "Be honest with yourself, Savannah. You're not in pain. I would never hurt you, Savannah. This isn't about pain. It's more of a way to get you to think about your actions. There'll be consequences for putting yourself in danger. I would never survive if anything happened to you."

The underlying desperation in his voice astounded her.

His finger slid deep into her pussy and slowly withdrew most of the way before sinking into her again.

"I need you too much to ever take a chance of losing you."

Rocking her hips, she moved on his finger, biting her lip to hold back her moan of pleasure at the friction her movements caused.

Her breasts swelled, sharpening her awareness of them, the cold air blowing over her nipples making them harder and more sensitive. The need inside her became darker and more decadent, a primitive need she didn't understand.

Wyatt delivered another slap, this time lower on her bottom, almost to her thighs.

"Damn, honey. You like that even more than I'd expected. The way your soft pussy keeps clamping on my finger makes me wish it was my cock inside you."

Running his hands over her bottom, he sighed. "Unfortunately, that's going to have to wait."

Shaking with need, Savannah parted her thighs as much as she could, crying out when he pressed at a spot inside her that made her mindless with pleasure.

He was right.

She wanted him to take her. She needed him to fill her with more than just his finger.

Furious at his control, she kicked at him. "Take me, then, damn you."

Wyatt groaned, his cock jumping against her hip. "No. That's the punishment part of your spanking. No matter how much you want it, I won't take you."

With a groan, he moved his hand over her again, his fingers clenching on her bottom.

"It's punishing both of us."

Savannah had no idea what he was talking about. She just knew that she couldn't stand much more of this.

She fought harder than ever, bucking on his lap, furious that he chuckled and slapped her bottom again.

The decadent sizzling between her thighs made her crazy. She pumped her legs, closing them and trying to rub her clit against his hand in an effort to get some relief, but he thwarted every effort she made.

"You snake! You—oh, God. Oh, God."

Gulping in air, Savannah froze at the feel of Wyatt parting her bottom cheeks and exposing her forbidden opening to the cool air— and his heated gaze. Exposed in the most intimate way she could imagine, she shuddered, unable to hold back her cries.

Wyatt circled her puckered opening with a fingertip, making her jolt.

She couldn't believe he touched her there, and lay frozen, stunned at the tingling that made her aware of that part of her as never before. Her own vulnerability shocked her so much that she couldn't even seem to process all of the sensations racing through her.

Wyatt pressed slightly at her opening, his body tight and tense against hers.

"So tight. With some attention and a lot of patience, your tight little bottom will give all of us as much pleasure as your sweet little pussy does."

She tightened against the finger that circle her puckered opening, alarmed at the pinpricks of pleasure his soft caress created. Embarrassed that she couldn't stop clenching, she tried to twist away, yelping at the sharp slap that landed on her already heated flesh.

This one intensified the sensation, making her bottom, pussy, and clit all tingle hotly. Her body tightened, her breath coming out in quick pants, not easing even when he removed the threatening finger.

"You're not serious!"

"I'm *very* serious about pleasing you."

Withdrawing his finger from her pussy, he pressed it against her bottom hole, the slick juices he'd gathered allowing him to slip the tip of his finger inside.

Savannah cried out in surprise, taken aback at the sting and the too-intimate penetration, shivering in fear and desire as he pushed past the tight ring of muscle to press a little deeper.

It hit her suddenly how little she knew this wicked aspect of him, but she'd never in her wildest dreams imagined anything like this. More complicated and much naughtier than she'd suspected, he was a force to reckon with in more ways than she'd expected.

She respected him for his strength of body and mind, but she hadn't anticipated his passion to be just as strong, nor had she imagined how sinful and decadent his passion would be.

Shaken by her inability to handle her own response, Savannah knew she didn't stand a chance of handling *his*. Angry at herself for thinking, for even a moment, that she could have this kind of love, Savannah slapped at his leg, forcing back tears.

She would never have believed that something so naughty and domineering could excite her so much, but Wyatt apparently did, which told her he knew more about her body than even she did.

"That's enough. Let me up. You're a brute and a snake. You try to convince me that you're different than other men, but you're not. You're mean and use your strength against me."

Wyatt stilled, the threat in the air unmistakable. With an abruptness that made her dizzy, he lifted her against his chest, one hand tangling in her hair to hold her face to his while the other remained between her thighs.

"My strength *protects* you!"

His eyes narrowed to slits, a muscle clenching in his jaw. He looked every inch the fierce lawman whose reputation for being ruthless spread far and wide. He slid a finger over her clit, using the perfect amount of pressure to keep her teetering on the edge but not allowing her to go over.

It proved his mastery over her body more than anything he'd done so far, increasing her sense of vulnerability.

She moaned against his chest, worried that she would never be able to satisfy such a man.

"I hate what you do to me. You know how to please me, but I know nothing about pleasing you."

Unexpectedly, Wyatt smiled.

"You'd better not know any more than what Hayes and I teach you!"

Savannah cried out again when he took her mouth in one of his slow, blazing kisses, a cry he swallowed as he moved his finger over her clit, pushing the one in her bottom a little deeper.

Her pussy and bottom pulsated, the sizzling awareness in both openings like nothing she'd ever experienced before. His too-light touch had her lifting her hips to get more pressure against her clit, eliciting cry after cry from her as her movements also shifted the finger in her bottom.

Alarmed, aroused, and shaken, she pushed against him, breaking off their kiss. Breathing heavily, she had to swallow before speaking, her entire body shaking so hard she had to hold on to Wyatt for support.

"You can't touch me there."

Wyatt tilted his head, his eyes hot as they raked over her body. Lifting a brow, he smiled, a smile filled with wicked intent.

"You trying to tell me you don't like the way I touch you?"

Frustrated and irritated at his arrogance, she wished she had the strength to resist him. The second he lifted his finger from her clit, though, she struggled in his arms, lifting her hips in an effort to get him to touch her there again.

"No! Don't stop. Damn you. You know I meant the—oh!"

He pressed steadily, slowly sliding deeper into her bottom and moving his finger to caress her inner walls.

"I knew there was a passionate woman under all that cold distance."

Taking a shuddering breath, Savannah closed her eyes, unable to meet his gaze.

"I can't. Oh, God!"

Wyatt slid his thumb over her clit, making her jump and taking a little more of his finger inside her.

"You're close to coming already."

"No."

"Yes, you are. It's not nice to lie." He lowered his head and brushed her lips with his. "I love it when you're like this, but it's not enough. I want more."

She bit her lip when he intensified his strokes to her clit, but still couldn't hold back her cries as the shimmering heat became more intense.

"You're inside me." She couldn't believe where he penetrated her, or how extreme it made her arousal.

Withdrawing slightly, Wyatt stared down at her, his eyes so dark and full of emotion it left her breathless.

"Only the tip of my finger. I know enough about a woman's body to know how much you like this. Those breathless whimpers make me crazy to have you. You cry out your pleasure at even the slightest caress of your clit. Those sweet little cries make my cock so hard it hurts. Your juices are wetting my hand because this soft pussy wants to be taken. Imagine how it'll feel when Hayes and I take you together."

His deep, rumbling voice vibrated from his wide chest, as strong and full of purpose as the man himself. His hooded gaze held hers, sharpening as he stroked her clit again, once again keeping his touch too light to send her over, but making sure she remained on the razor-sharp edge.

Fighting for the release that Wyatt kept just out of reach, Savannah gripped the front of his coat as he drew out one whimpering moan after another from her. Her bottom grasped at his finger as though trying to draw it in deeper, something that shocked her to her core.

She wanted it, though. She wanted him to push deeper and take anything he wanted from her and ease the tremendous need that he'd created.

When he touched her this way, she became a different woman—one of need and fire—a woman she hardly recognized.

"You c–can't take me at th–the same t–time."

His eyes flashed with something dark and sinful, something that pulled at her and encouraged her to follow him down the decadent path he'd forged, the promise of wicked pleasure too irresistible to ignore.

"Yes, we can, and if your reaction to what I've done to you is anything to go by, you're going to love it."

Keeping his horse at a very slow walk, he led them into a section of trees and stopped, the movements of the horse working her bottom on his finger.

It went deeper than before, pressing relentlessly into her and making her bottom hole sting.

"Wyatt, please! It stings. It's too deep. Oh, God!"

She couldn't bear another minute of this incredible need, shaking so hard that her teeth chattered. She wanted so badly to fight him, but couldn't. Even the shock of being penetrated so intimately and the fear of the burning sting couldn't keep her desire from growing.

Wyatt laughed softly, a deep, intimate sound, full of wickedness.

"I'll make a deal with you, honey. If you don't come hard with your tight little ass gripping my finger, I won't touch you there again. But if you come, we're going to explore you some more and prepare you to take us together."

He withdrew his finger just enough to tease her opening, before slowly working it inside her again.

"You're so tight, and so amazingly hungry for love." He brushed her lips with his as he increased the strokes to her clit.

"It's not surprising, though. I'm sure you haven't had very much tenderness or affection in your life. Come for me. You know you can't hold off much longer. You were made for lovin', darlin'."

His command over her body frightened her, filling her with a vulnerability she couldn't afford. She'd vowed never to let a man control her again, and yet here she was, allowing Wyatt to control her with her own body.

"I won't."

Wyatt placed his thumb over her clit and began to stroke, firm, intent strokes guaranteed to drive her wild.

"You will. There's nothing more arousing to a man than a woman who can't resist his touch. You'll learn to come whenever and however I touch you."

"I won't!"

Panicked at the possibility that he spoke the truth, Savannah bit her lip in an effort to hold back the orgasm she could feel approaching, but she didn't have a chance. She bucked as the tingling in her clit exploded, the pleasure so intense it made her dizzy. Her body bowed, the waves of pleasure making her cry out again and again.

Her bottom closed on his finger, squeezing it tight, making the sensation of being filled there even stronger. Her cries echoed as she stiffened and arched into the hand between her thighs. The action lifted her breasts high, offering him everything she had to offer.

She could do nothing else.

As the sublime pleasure crested, she let go, knowing at that moment that he could have done anything to her that he wanted to and she would have been a more than willing participant.

He held her firmly, his hold keeping her safe as he steadied her, letting her experience all the pleasure his touch gave her without worry.

He was a warm, solid wall—a rock—in a world that spun out of control.

As the last shimmers of pleasure faded away, Savannah bit her lip, shivering as Wyatt's finger slipped from her bottom. Her face burned with shame that she'd allowed him to see, such a naughty side of her, one she hadn't even known existed.

With more gentleness than she would have believed, he lifted her against him, giving her another of those mind-numbing kisses that left her hot and trembling.

He poured passion into it, but also caring, letting her feel his need for her while bringing her safely back to earth again.

Brushing her lips with his, he crooned to her, his intimate tone deep and soft.

"You are so incredibly beautiful. I love the way you fall apart in my arms. I wake up in the middle of the night reaching for you, and wishing that you were already my wife."

Kissing his way up her jaw to her ear, he held her close.

"Now that I know the passion in you, I won't sleep at all. I need you, Savannah. I love you, and I'll spend the rest of my life showing you how much. Don't be afraid of the pleasure. Don't be afraid of us."

* * * *

By the time he lifted his head, tears filled her eyes.

Tears of surrender.

Tears of vulnerability.

Tears of failure.

Tears of love that she couldn't allow herself to show.

Wyatt pulled her pants back up before helping her to a sitting position, his eyes tender as he reached for the buttons of her shirt.

"Come on, honey. Let me get you dressed. You're cold."

Furious and mortified that she'd responded so completely while he hadn't even broken a sweat, Savannah pushed his hands away and reached for the buttons herself, her face burning as she watched him slip his glove back on.

"It's a pity you didn't think about that before you had your way with me."

Wyatt stiffened, gripping her chin and turning her back to face him.

"If I had my way with you, Savannah, you would know it. Seeing and hearing you come excites me more than anything else in the world, and in case you hadn't noticed, my cock's hard as a fucking rock, but I'm not taking you. Not sinking my cock into that slick pussy is the hardest thing I've ever done, so I wouldn't push it right now if I were you."

Insulted and angry that, despite Wyatt's claim to be aroused, he seemed to be in perfect control of himself, Savannah yanked her chin from his grip and finished fastening her shirt.

Drawing on years of experience, she carefully schooled her features and turned her head to glance up at him, pulling her coat closed against the chill that settled over her.

"I would tell Eb what you did to me, but it would only upset Maggie. I can't wait to leave here."

Wrapping an arm around her waist, he pulled her back against him and started back the way they'd come.

"Eb would hold a shotgun to my head and demand that Hayes and I married you right away. It sounds like a good idea, honey. It'll save Hayes and me a lot of time and aggravation."

"Aggravation?" Swallowing her fury, Savannah stared straight ahead. "That's what I am to you? Aggravation?"

Wyatt's voice went cold again, his words clipped.

"Yep. You know you're going to marry us, but you want to be coy about it. You like sex but pretend not to. If you didn't have feelings for us, you wouldn't have given yourself to us, but you deny it. Aggravating."

Struggling to keep all emotion out of her tone, she shrugged.

"You're the one who's aggravating. Won't take no for an answer and think you can control me by doing things like…that."

His cold laugh filled her with foreboding.

"Darlin', I *can* control you with that, but I have no desire to. I want a wife, Savannah. You know that."

"Well, you'll never have the chance to do anything that *sinful* to me again."

"Oh, you're going to have that done to you again. Many times. I told you that if you came while I had my finger inside that bottom, I would do it again. Next time, though, it'll be my cock filling you."

Chapter Five

Pleased with himself and with life in general, Wyatt set down his fork and swallowed the last bite of his apple pie.

"That was delicious, Savannah. Are you sure you don't want a piece of this pie? It's the best I've ever eaten."

Full of pride in the woman he would soon marry, and nearly bursting with happiness, Wyatt sat back, unable to keep his eyes off of her.

Only her flushed cheeks told him she'd noticed.

Even though she'd approached him as soon as they got back this evening to invite them to a private supper with her that she'd cooked herself, she'd managed to avoid almost all eye contact with both of them.

Until she got over her nervousness, he and Hayes would need to be patient.

He took her invitation as a good sign, though. After this afternoon, he'd have bet good money that she would have tried to avoid them. It appeared she'd been more taken in by their play that afternoon than he'd imagined.

He smiled in her direction, convinced that her desire to be alone with them meant that she'd decided that the three of them belonged together. He worried that she hadn't eaten much of the fried chicken she'd prepared. Nerves probably kept her from eating, and he wanted to get her to relax so they could talk.

"You're a very good cook. Hayes and I will be the envy of every man here."

His chest swelled at her obvious attempt to show them what a good wife she would make.

He could have told her that he didn't care if she couldn't cook at all, although after the meal he'd just eaten, he probably would have married her for her cooking alone. Sitting back, he rubbed his full stomach, having eaten one of the best meals he could remember.

Hayes frowned and sipped his coffee, staring thoughtfully at Savannah, as he'd done for the last several minutes.

"You've hardly touched your dinner. I know you're nervous about marrying us, but there's no reason to be."

Savannah blushed and glanced up, meeting their eyes for the first time in almost a half hour.

"Actually, I invited you here to talk, but neither one of you will believe that I'm not marrying you and I'm not staying."

Hayes leaned forward, the tension in him apparent.

"Actions speak louder than words, Savannah. You still haven't given us any good reasons."

"It's none of your concern."

Taking one of Savannah's hands in his, Hayes pulled her closer.

"You're very quiet tonight. I know what Wyatt did to you earlier today."

Wyatt hid a smile as the blush that colored Savannah's cheeks darkened, his cock jumping at the surge of desire.

At her look of surprise, he lifted a brow and regarded her steadily, wanting for her to understand the way things would be between them right from the start.

"When it comes to you, Hayes and I have no secrets. We'll both be your husbands, Savannah. You'll have two men to care for and protect you."

Savannah's serene smile sent a cold chill down his spine.

"Lucky me."

Ever since she'd invited both him and Hayes to eat at the house, she'd been very subdued and even downright polite. He'd suspected nerves and shyness had made her quieter than normal, but now he wondered if it might be something else—especially since she couldn't quite hide the defiant gleam in her beautiful eyes.

He watched her carefully now as she gathered dishes and left the dining room. Still watching the doorway, he leaned toward Hayes, keeping his voice low.

"Something's wrong. I don't like it. I'm probably too suspicious, but I get the feeling she's up to something."

Hayes sipped his coffee, staring in the direction Savannah had gone.

"After we're married, she'll settle down. She's trying to show us what a meek wife she can be. She'll soon learn that the last thing we want is for her to change. We'll give her some time to adjust. She's just a little skittish."

Maybe because he felt the same way and had been listening for it, Wyatt heard the uncertainty in his friend's tone.

Hayes shifted in his seat and took another sip of his coffee, smothering a yawn.

"Damn, I'd hoped to have a chance to do a little snuggling with her tonight, but if she's this skittish, I don't want to scare her. We'll just have to keep her calm until Saturday. Once we're married, everything'll work itself out."

Hayes frowned and turned to Wyatt.

"I haven't been able to stop imagining how she looked draped over your lap. She liked it, huh?"

Wyatt smothered his own yawn, surprised at the fatigue that came from nowhere.

"Hell, I'm so full, I'm falling asleep. We're not going to be able to eat like this every day. Desire doesn't need fat sheriffs."

Hayes smiled slightly, lifting a brow. "We'll make sure Savannah helps us work it off."

Wyatt and Hayes both came to their feet as Savannah came back into the room. Smothering another yawn, Wyatt grimaced as his cock came to attention. It didn't seem to matter if he was tired or not, his cock appeared to be ready for Savannah at any given moment.

"Thank you for the dinner, honey. We'll be by in the morning to take you to breakfast."

"I'm looking forward to tomorrow morning."

The look on Savannah's face might have fooled someone who didn't know how to spot a lie, but it didn't fool him for a minute.

Hayes stiffened beside him.

"You don't look too disappointed to see us go."

Something flashed in Savannah's eyes, something that looked a lot like amusement, before she quickly masked it. Shrugging, she turned away to stare out the window.

"It's not as though we won't see each other again soon. You're living in the bunkhouse, aren't you?"

Hayes glanced at Wyatt, frowning. Turning his attention back to Savannah, his eyes sharpened.

"For now. Until our house is ready. Wyatt said he showed you where it would be this afternoon. We start building tomorrow. With everyone chipping in, it should only take about a week."

Wyatt knew the two of them would be spending every minute they could there in order to see that the house was ready by next Saturday. They'd already ordered a bed and would pick it up when they went to town, and they'd let Savannah pick out the rest of it later.

The bed, though, they would need right away.

He couldn't wait to get Savannah naked and under him again. The next time he took her, it would be as his wife.

She would belong to him in every way.

On their wedding night, and every night afterward, he would have her completely naked, a bounty for him to explore.

The throbbing of his cock got even worse as he imagined her legs held high in the air and his face buried between them. He blinked, finding it harder and harder to keep his eyes open. Damn, he was more tired than he'd thought. He didn't want to make any mistakes with Savannah when they were so close to making her theirs. Unable to shake off the fatigue, he figured it would be better to leave now than to accidentally say or do something that would scare her away.

Moving closer to her, he stroked a finger down her soft cheek.

"I don't know what's bothering you, Savannah, but we'll talk about it in the morning."

Even through his fatigue, he couldn't miss the look of relief in her eyes.

To add insult to injury, she moved away, patting his arm and moving to the back door, opening it wide.

"That's fine. I have some sewing to do that Maggie hasn't been able to finish."

Apparently Hayes didn't like to be dismissed any more than Wyatt did.

With a bit-out curse, he tugged her away from the door and pulled her close, bending his head to take her mouth in a punishing kiss.

Leaning against the door to block the view of anyone who might be passing, Wyatt watched in fascination as Savannah struggled to get closer to Hayes, his cock getting harder by the minute.

He'd never considered himself the kind of man who would get excited while watching another man make love to the woman he considered his, but damned if his cock wasn't about to burst through his pants as he watched Hayes and Savannah now.

Knowing Hayes would be every bit as much her husband made a huge difference.

It became obvious from the start that both he and Hayes wanted her, and the relationship between the three of them had begun to take shape before he'd even realized it.

Fascinated by her hesitation before reaching for Hayes, something he knew his friend couldn't have seen, he fought the urge to close the distance between them.

Intrigued, he watched Hayes and Savannah together, noticing things he might have missed if he'd been the one kissing her.

From his vantage point, he could see her move restlessly, rubbing her thighs together. He'd bet his horse that her clit felt swollen and desperately wanted attention and that her thighs were damp with her juices.

His mouth watered with the need to taste her. He wanted to bury his face between those creamy thighs and feast on her until she came over and over against his tongue.

He smiled, thinking about the look on her face when Hayes used his mouth on her and wondered it if would affect Hayes as much as it did him.

He winced, inwardly cursing as his cock stirred again, and he smothered another yawn. He didn't know what the hell was wrong with him tonight, but suddenly he could hardly stay awake.

His cock, however, had other ideas. He had a feeling it would be another long night.

Hayes lifted his head, his breathing harsh.

"We've got to get married soon."

He walked out without another word, leaving Wyatt alone with Savannah.

Wyatt stared after him, knowing exactly how his friend felt. He'd kissed Savannah often enough to know that Hayes fought not to rip her clothes from her and sink into her.

When she took an unsteady step backward, he hurriedly reached for her, his reaction slower than normal. Feeling her body tremble against his, he pulled her closer. He pressed his lips to her silky hair, struck once again by her frailty.

His cock jumped again at the dazed look in her eyes, the need to make this beautiful woman his burning inside him like a hot brand.

"Hayes is right. We have to get married soon. I want you in my bed. In my life. I want you to be the first thing I see every morning and the last thing I see every night."

Savannah blinked as though coming out of a trance, her eyes flashing as she pushed away from him.

"Don't say things like that to me."

Irritated that she could adopt that cool distance with such ease, Wyatt yanked her to him, a little alarmed that he almost missed.

"Don't take that tone with me. I saw the way you tried to climb up Hayes. You don't have to pretend with us."

Savannah's eyes went wide, her expression one of outrage, her show of emotion pleasing him immensely. She took a deep breath and let it out slowly, and to his frustration, adopted that schoolmarm expression that never ceased to infuriate him.

"I'm sure you're mistaken."

Rubbing his eyes, he sighed and released her as he came to another realization, one he should have come to before.

"You keep saying I shouldn't touch you and that things we do are sinful. I know you were raised by that poor excuse of a preacher, but we're getting married. It isn't sinful to—"

"Have two husbands?"

That cold, sarcastic smile made him want desperately to turn her over his lap—or fuck her until she didn't have the energy to defy him.

"Damn it, Savannah. It's not like that."

"I think you'd better go."

Having the door closed in his face before he even got to kiss her wasn't how Wyatt had planned to spend the evening. Things had started out so well, but had somehow gone wrong.

He'd misjudged her—a mistake he couldn't afford to make.

His assumption that she'd agreed to marry them had obviously been wrong.

It didn't make sense, though, for her to invite them to dinner just to refuse them.

She was up to something, but for the life of him, he couldn't figure out what.

So tired that it took tremendous effort just to put one foot in front of the other, Wyatt decided that this wouldn't be the best time to sort it out. He barely resisted glancing back at the house and went to join Hayes and the Tylers where they stood talking.

Rubbing his eyes, he promised himself that as soon as he got some sleep, he'd get to the bottom of whatever bothered Savannah—and get rid of the cold knot that had formed in his stomach the day she left Kansas City—a knot that had never quite gone away.

* * * *

It took every ounce of willpower Hayes could muster to keep from running back to the house and laying Savannah right in the middle of the dinner table and making a meal of her.

He could still taste her and had to resist the urge to lick his lips as he tried to concentrate on what Eb was saying. Noticing that Eb and Jeremiah both stared at him expectantly, he struggled to remember what they'd been talking about.

He remembered suddenly that Eb had been telling him who he would be sending to help him and Wyatt with the house. Nodding once, he glanced toward the closed back door.

"I appreciate the help. We want to get Savannah settled."

An obviously exhausted Maggie leaned against Jeremiah and frowned up at him.

"Are you sure Savannah said she would marry you? She wouldn't even discuss it earlier. Not that I'm not thrilled, but she was acting strange."

Maggie's yawn proved to be contagious.

Smothering yet another yawn, Hayes avoided Eb's narrowed stare and kept his eyes on Maggie.

"Savannah's ready. This afternoon, Wyatt took her out to see where her new home will be, and I think it must have really made her think. She said she can't." He waved negligently, dismissing anything that would keep Savannah from him. "But she can't give us a reason. She cooked a delicious dinner for us, probably to show us what a good cook she is."

Hayes sighed and glanced toward the house. "She must have been nervous, though. She was really quiet."

He smiled at Maggie. "I think she was reluctant to have two husbands at first, but seeing how happy you are with Eb and Jeremiah probably helped change her mind."

Uneasy at the way Maggie avoided looking at him, he lifted his gaze to Jeremiah's, raising a brow.

Jeremiah shook his head and smiled, pulling Maggie closer.

"Apparently Maggie won't tell you, but she's going to have to learn that all of us men have to stick together in order to make this work. If Savannah's as quiet as you claim, you might have a problem."

Eb touched his shoulder, his eyes full of concern.

"Do you feel all right?"

In deference to Maggie, Hayes bit back his curse.

"Yeah. No. I don't know. I can't seem to stay awake." He turned to watch Wyatt walk unsteadily toward them.

"Wyatt seems to have the same problem. We probably ate too much."

He rubbed his eyes and shook his head. "It's not as though we're not used to being up all night. Maybe I should head into the chow house and get another cup of coffee."

Eb drew a deep breath and let it out slowly.

"I hope the doc gets here soon. We need one around here. Maybe you're getting sick."

Jeremiah pulled Maggie back several feet.

"Don't give anything to Maggie. We've got to watch out for the babe."

Maggie pushed out of his arms. "Don't be ridiculous. I can't stand this anymore. Hayes, did you or Wyatt do anything—say anything—to make Savannah mad?"

Thinking of what Wyatt and Savannah had done that afternoon, Hayes shrugged, not about to share intimate details of their relationship with anyone else.

Maggie straightened, fisting her hands on her hips and stared at Wyatt. "When you left this afternoon with her, didn't you say something about—oh, my God! You didn't actually try to *spank* Savannah, did you?"

Jeremiah wrapped an arm around Maggie and hugged her against him.

"It's none of your business. Come on. Let's get you inside before you get chilled."

When she started to struggle, he merely lifted her into his arms and strode away with her, carrying her across the yard, up the back steps, and into the house, but not before giving Eb a censuring look.

Once Jeremiah had Maggie inside and closed the door behind them, Hayes turned back to Eb, crossing his arms over his chest.

"I know you mean well, but don't meddle in our dealings with Savannah. I know you're looking out for her, but you know damned well how we feel about her. She was real quiet today, but she went out of her way to make us a nice supper and made sure we had some privacy. That tells me she's made up her mind to marry us. We'll take over caring for her now."

He hated like hell explaining himself, especially regarding a woman he would marry, but felt it necessary. He wanted to make it clear that as much as he appreciated that the other men would be watching out for her when he and Wyatt weren't around, Savannah was *theirs*.

He sure as hell wouldn't take kindly to any interference in the way he handled her.

He loved her. He wanted her like he'd never wanted another woman. Only her soft touch and calming voice had kept him from breaking the laws he'd sworn to uphold and killing the man who'd dared to bruise her.

Her uncle had a lot to answer for, and his own inability to lock the reverend away for beating Savannah still infuriated him.

The reverend, as her guardian, had the right, and there hadn't been a damned thing he and Wyatt could do about it.

Here, things were different, and if the reverend showed up, there would be a far different outcome.

She belonged to them, and both he and Wyatt would do anything and everything in their power to keep her from being harmed.

He'd gladly kill any man who touched her—including her uncle.

Eb nodded once and started to turn away. Pausing, he turned back and smiled coldly, eyeing both him and Wyatt in a way that made Hayes stiffen.

With his hands on his hips, Eb cocked his head, gesturing toward the house, his eyes hard and as cold as ice.

"I've been protecting Savannah for a long time now, and there's one thing I've learned. It never hurts to have other men you can trust to keep a woman safe. You can't always be there. I know you don't want my advice, and I have half a mind to walk away without telling you what I know, but the women's safety is my main priority."

Rubbing a hand across the back of his neck, he sighed.

"Wonder why you're so tired? If you knew Savannah well enough, you would know that when she's quiet and subdued, she's up to no good. She put something in your food. Something to make you sleep. That's why she invited you to the house. The two of you must have really pissed her off. What did you do, spank her? Tell her that she was marrying you no matter what?"

Hayes avoided looking at Wyatt, not about to let Eb know that he was right. What happened between them and Savannah was nobody's business. Struggling against the jealousy caused by Eb knowing things about Savannah that he didn't, and his own pride, he felt his temper snap.

"And just how would you know she would do such a thing?"

Eb's jaw clenched.

"Because I'm the one who showed her how to do it. Let me tell you a few things about Savannah's uncle."

Chapter Six

Picking the last of the vegetables, Savannah knelt in the garden, jolting at the shout from somewhere behind her. Recognizing it as Eb's shout of encouragement to Phoenix as the other man worked to break a wild horse, Savannah let out a breath and forced herself to relax.

The suspense of wondering when Wyatt and Hayes would appear and retaliate made her increasingly jumpy, until she couldn't stand it anymore.

Deciding to see if she could find out what they had planned for her, or when they'd be around, she started toward the chow building, where she knew Duke would be fixing supper.

During the short time she'd been here, she'd learned that, although he seldom spoke, Duke knew almost everything that went on at the ranch.

Crossing to the chow building, she scanned the yard for Wyatt and Hayes, both depressed and relieved that she didn't see them. Hearing sounds coming from inside, she opened the door and went in, relieved to find the place empty except for Duke.

Turning from where he stirred something in a large pot, he nodded.

"Ma'am."

Savannah nodded back, a little surprised at the cold glint of anger in his eyes, especially since he'd been so nice to her ever since she'd arrived.

"Hello, Duke. I...um...haven't seen Wyatt or Hayes for awhile." To avoid meeting his eyes, she poured herself a cup of coffee she didn't want.

He looked at her strangely, his frown accenting the scar down his cheek, making him look even scarier.

"They're building your new house. They were in a strange mood, those two. Hardly talked to anybody, and even growled at a couple of the ranch hands on their way out. Must've been something they ate."

Embarrassed that Duke obviously knew about what she'd done, Savannah shrugged and said nothing.

The lump that formed in her throat surprised her.

She'd been trying to turn them away since the moment she met them, and couldn't get them to listen to her. Now that they avoided her, she should have been happy.

Leaving here, though, didn't have the appeal it once did.

Knowing she had to anyway, she should have been relieved that Hayes and Wyatt didn't appear to want her anymore. It would make leaving much easier, and she would be able to relax and enjoy herself with Maggie for the rest of the time she had here.

She should be happy.

Instead, the numbness, the sadness, the anger, and the hurt felt an awful lot like grief.

Blinking back tears, she lifted her gaze, surprised to find Duke staring at her. Forcing a smile, she turned away.

"So, what are you making for supper?"

Her mouth watered at the smell of apple pie scenting the air, and she watched with interest as Duke removed several cast-iron Dutch ovens from the fire and set them aside.

Unsettled at his anger and the uncertainty of Wyatt and Hayes's absence, she said the first thing that came to her mind.

"Maggie loves apple pie."

It didn't surprise her at all that his features softened.

"I know. That's why I'm making them. She's a special lady. It takes one to be able to make two husbands happy."

The implication that she wouldn't measure up wasn't lost on Savannah, who nodded and headed for the door, inexplicably hurt.

"I'm sure she'll appreciate that. I've got some chores to take care of before Maggie wakes up from her nap. Sorry to have bothered you."

She started out, ignoring him when he called out her name. She jolted when his hand curved around her upper arm, not even aware that he'd moved.

Not having a choice, she'd remained just inside the door, ignoring the curious stares from a few of the men standing just outside the door.

"What?"

To her surprise, Duke moved closer, not stopping until he stood only a few feet away.

"I would be nervous, too, if I were you. Your men know what you did. If you were mine, I'd turn you over my knee and paddle your bottom until you couldn't sit down."

Keeping her head straight, she glanced up at him from the corner of her eye, alarmed at his size. Up close, he seemed as big as a mountain. He stood taller than the other men, but she hadn't realized just how huge he was.

Swallowing heavily, she took a step back, lifting her chin. "I have no idea what you're talking about."

His cold smile scared the hell out of her.

"Yes, you do. I wouldn't take that tone with them if I was you. Lying is only going to get you into more trouble."

Looking away, Savannah shrugged, her stomach clenching. "I'm not in any trouble at all. Your rules don't apply to me. I'm leaving just as soon as Maggie has her baby. Besides, it doesn't look like either Wyatt or Hayes is interested in me anymore anyway. Now, if you'll excuse me, I promised Maggie I'd tend to the garden."

Walking back across the yard, she once again looked for Wyatt and Hayes, trying to convince herself that the cold, hard knot in her stomach would go away.

She took a deep breath and let it out slowly, reminding herself that she'd gotten exactly what she wanted. As soon as Maggie had her baby, she could leave here and head south, riding toward the life she'd been dreaming about for years.

Ignoring the heaviness that settled in her chest, and aware that several pairs of eyes sharpened on her, she kept her head lowered and headed for the back door. She bent to pick up the basket of vegetables she'd left beside the garden, the basket she'd forgotten to take to Duke.

"I'll carry that for you."

Startled, she looked up into the hard, cold eyes of Hawke Royal, one of the Indians who worked on the Circle T.

"Thank you, but that's not necessary." She lifted the basket, intent on getting inside, and away from prying eyes, as quickly as possible.

Lifting an arrogant brow, he took the basket from her anyway.

"We take care of women around here."

Sensing that more than just carrying a basket lay behind his remark, Savannah kept walking.

"So I've heard. Sometimes, though, women don't want men telling them what to do."

"Women need the protection of men."

"Not all of them."

"All of them."

She quickened her steps, anxious to get away from the intimidating Indian.

"Your men aren't at all happy that you tried to poison them. None of us are."

Savannah whirled. "I didn't try to *poison* them!"

Hawke lifted a brow, clearly skeptical. "No?"

"No!" She sighed, looking away. "Look, I really don't want to discuss this with you. Eb's lecture and Duke's censoring looks are about all I can take."

"You deserved both. Eb told us why you did it."

Savannah turned back, looking up at him through her lashes. "He shouldn't have. It's nobody's business."

She'd never appreciated being the subject of gossip in a small town. It appeared that even on a ranch as large as the Triple T, everyone knew everyone else's business.

Blade inclined his head. "I can understand why you'd think that way. Except for my brothers, I'm a loner myself. It's different here, though, and hard to get used to. Here, we're all connected. We have to count on each other to survive and to protect the women. Eb said you just wanted a little time and space for yourself. I can understand that, too."

Smiling faintly, he lowered his already low voice. "Tell the truth. If Eb hadn't caught you, you were going to run, weren't you?"

Clenching her jaw against a surge of anger, Savannah glared at him. "No. I promised Maggie that I would stay until she has the babe. I gave my word."

Hawke's brow went up again. "Good for you. You're not the coward I thought you were." His lips twitched. "So you really did it just to get them to leave you alone? They must have really made an impact on you for you to be so desperate to get away from them."

Not knowing how to respond to that, Savannah shrugged and changed the subject, turning the tables to talk about him instead.

"How did you learn to speak English so well?"

Hawke's eyes became shuttered, his expression harder than she'd ever seen it. "Our mother was white. Phoenix, Blade, and I are half-breeds."

Savannah inwardly winced at his tone, uncomfortable that she'd inadvertently touched on an obviously sore subject.

"Oh."

To her surprise, Hawke grinned, his smile taking her breath away. "You're a woman so you're naturally nosy and want to know more, but just don't know how to ask without opening yourself up to being asked questions about *your* past."

Furious at being so easy to read, she cursed under her breath and spun back toward the house.

Once they reached the back door, Savannah turned and yanked the basket out of his hands.

"You know what the trouble is with the men around here?"

If possible, Hawke's eyes narrowed even more.

"What's that?"

"They're too arrogant for their own good."

Hawke's eyes lit with amusement, and a good bit of that arrogance that set her teeth on edge.

"With good reason. You're too used to city boys who act tough when they don't know the first thing about protecting what's theirs. Wyatt and Hayes do, and they'd both die to protect you."

"I'm not theirs."

Alarmed that her voice broke, Savannah rushed into the house, furious at the tears that burned her eyes.

Setting the vegetables on the big wooden table, she took a deep breath and let it out slowly, furious at herself for being hurt by Wyatt and Hayes's obvious abandonment.

"Something bothering you?"

With a gasp, Savannah whirled and, if not for Jeremiah's fast reflexes, would have knocked the basket of vegetables to the floor.

"I wish you people would stop sneaking up on me!"

Jeremiah blinked once before a slow smile tugged at his lips.

"I came in through the back door while you were working in the garden. I even spoke to you, but you were lost in thought and didn't hear me. You got something on your mind you want to talk about?

Afraid those sharp eyes of his saw too much, she turned away. "Yes. I can't wait until Maggie has her baby so I can get out of here."

Jeremiah had the nerve to laugh.

"I can't wait until Wyatt and Hayes get a hold of you and make you pay for putting something in their food to make them sleep."

Gritting her teeth, she glared up at him through her lashes. "They wouldn't have known if Eb hadn't told them."

Jeremiah tapped the underside of her chin until she lifted it.

"Eb finally told me why he taught you to do that. He told Wyatt and Hayes, too. He figured that after what you did to them, they had a right to know. You're a brave woman, Savannah—braver than I suspected. I know you had a good reason for putting your uncle to sleep so he didn't bother you, but you won't get away with doing that here. Wyatt and Hayes are so mad that they've been afraid to come near you."

Savannah stamped her foot, furious and mortified. "He had no right to tell them that! He had no right to tell anyone that. Maggie doesn't know, does she?"

Jeremiah gripped her shoulders, his smile full of tenderness and understanding.

"No, honey. Maggie doesn't know. There's no point. But surely you see that Wyatt and Hayes have a right to know that the woman they're going to marry was almost raped by her uncle. If Eb hadn't shown up that night—hell. I don't even want to think about it."

Savannah shoved at him, turning away.

"It's none of their business! I'm not marrying them or anyone else."

"I'm afraid you're mistaken about that. You're definitely marrying us."

Savannah spun toward the open doorway, her heart leaping into her throat at the sight of a furious-looking Hayes standing there.

"Damn it. If one more person sneaks up on me, I'm going to scream."

Hayes came forward, not even glancing in Jeremiah's direction as he bent and put a shoulder to her belly and lifted her kicking and screaming over his shoulder.

"You're already screaming, honey, and you'll damned well be doing a lot more of it before I'm through with you."

Chapter Seven

Using every curse word she'd ever heard, Savannah hung on to Hayes as he all but dragged her out the back door and to his horse, where a stone-faced Wyatt waited.

Savannah had never been so scared in her entire life, which said a lot considering how life had been with her uncle. She looked back in time to see Jeremiah come out the back door.

He stopped to lean over the porch railing, his arms folded over his chest and one booted foot crossed over the other.

"Jeremiah, damn you! Help me."

He straightened, spinning to catch Maggie who flew out the door, clearly upset.

He lowered his head and said something to her that Savannah couldn't hear before straightening and heading toward her, Maggie trailing right behind him.

Struggling not to show fear, Savannah stood her ground, more than a little surprised that Hayes merely held her arm and waited for Jeremiah to approach.

To her shock, Eb appeared from somewhere behind her.

"Problem?"

Savannah whirled as much as she could with Hayes holding on to her arm.

"Of course there's a problem. Hayes and Wyatt want to beat me!"

At the last second, she looked around, mortified at the number of ranch hands who witnessed the entire thing.

One steely look from Hayes had them turning and walking away.

Reaching out a hand to Maggie, he pulled her close, his sharp eyes raking over her in concern.

"Settle down, darlin'." After taking in Hayes's cold expression, he met Savannah's gaze.

"I don't blame them for that. They're your men, and you played a pretty mean trick on them. If Maggie did that to me, her bottom would be red for a week."

Maggie pulled out of Eb's hold, a trace of panic in her eyes.

"What's going on? What are you doing to Savannah?"

Crossing his arms over his chest, Eb eyed Savannah intently.

"I guess that depends on Savannah. She can't get away with what she did. What if she needed their protection?"

Savannah lifted her chin. "I don't know why you're so mad about it. You're the one who taught me how to do it, and you said there wouldn't be any danger."

"There was a reason I taught you that, and I meant there would be no danger to *him*. What you did the other night made it damned near impossible for Wyatt and Hayes to protect you properly."

Lifting a brow, he looked even more intimidating.

"Of course, I can't have anyone doing something like that in my town. It's usually up to Jeremiah or me to handle, but since Hayes and Wyatt are the new sheriffs, and since you're their woman, it's their right to handle you."

"I'm *not* their woman!"

She could actually feel Wyatt's and Hayes's stares boring into her. Keeping her face averted, she fisted her hands at her sides. "Please don't let them do this to me. I really can't marry them."

Eb inclined his head.

"If that's the way you want it, fine, but that's between you and them. They've stated their claim on you and you've accepted it, Savannah."

With a look at the others, he took Savannah's arm and pulled her to the side, his eyes full of tenderness.

"Honey, I know you're scared of their anger, but Wyatt and Hayes both love you very much. If I believed, for one minute, that either one of them would ever hurt you, I'd interfere."

Bending, he kissed her forehead. "Both Wyatt and Hayes are good men—but I think you know that already. They're scared of losing you, honey, and those men don't scare easily."

Nodding, Savannah looked over her shoulder to see Wyatt and Hayes both watching her intently. Even from this distance, she could see how stiffly they held themselves.

"I'll talk to them." Turning back, she reached out to touch Eb's arm.

"I really wish I could stay. I'd love to be a part of what you're all building here. I can't believe you'd do all this for Maggie."

Eb lifted his gaze, looking over her shoulder to where his wife stood with Jeremiah, the anxiety on her face apparent.

"There's not much I wouldn't do for that woman."

Meeting her gaze again, he smiled. "And there's not much Wyatt and Hayes wouldn't do for you. Talk to them, Savannah. They'll do everything in their power to make this right for you."

Not daring to look at any of them, Savannah allowed herself to be led to back to where Hayes and Wyatt stood.

Eb stopped with her directly in front of them and lifted her chin. "Talk to your men."

Closing her eyes against the fierce possession in theirs, Savannah nodded.

Hearing Maggie's sigh of relief from behind her, Savannah knew she'd made the only choice she could make. She'd talk to Hayes and Wyatt about it later, when they were alone, and get them to understand why she couldn't stay.

The hunger inside her stirred at the flash of need in Hayes's brilliant green eyes and Wyatt's much darker ones.

Hayes held out a hand, raising a brow as Savannah hesitated before placing hers in it.

"We need to talk."

Eb met both men's eyes squarely.

"If either one of you hurts her, you'll be thrown out of the town by the rest of us, and she can stay here where she'll be safe."

Hayes clenched his jaw, his eyes full of rage. "I'd kill any man who hurt her."

Savannah blinked, not having expected such a thing. Whirling, she gripped Eb's arm.

"Are you serious?"

Eb scowled at her, putting his hands on his hips as though fighting the urge to shake her.

"What have we been saying all along? Did you think we were lying about the strength of our need to protect the women? It's important to us, Savannah. Very important. We can't have a town or any kind of civilization here without women. Of course, we have to protect them. Wyatt and Hayes are very much aware of that, and it's an important part of their jobs. They wouldn't even have considered coming here to make a life with you until they were assured that everything possible would be done to protect you."

Ashamed of herself for taking their claims so lightly, she still bristled at the thought of getting spanked.

"If you're so determined to keep us from getting hurt, why in tarnation are you so hell-bent on spanking us?"

Sliding a hand under her hair, Wyatt tilted her face back.

"To protect you. To keep you from getting too relaxed about what's around you. We're not in the city anymore. We want you to think about everything you do and stay sharp."

Leaning closer, he brushed her cheek with his lips. "It keeps you from getting too lazy about your safety. Call it a reminder— something to remember when you're about to do something that might put you in danger. Tell the truth. Did that spanking I gave you the other day cause you more *pleasure* or *pain*?"

Remembering the way it had felt to be naked, and with his hands running over her, Savannah couldn't hold back a moan.

Wyatt straightened and smiled, a slow, wicked smile full of remembered pleasure.

Eb chuckled from somewhere behind her.

"I guess that's that."

Savannah heard more than saw the others move away, leaving her alone with Hayes and Wyatt. Still aroused at the memory of Wyatt's hands on her, she had to clear her throat before speaking.

"Now that we're alone, I need to talk to you. I really can't stay here."

Hayes wrapped an arm around her waist, lifted her against him, and started for his horse.

"We're going to be even more alone in a few minutes, and we're going to talk about what you did to us the other night."

He tossed her onto the back of his horse and followed right behind her, settling her on his lap before starting off. His hooded eyes held the promise of retribution, along with the dangerous combination of anger and desire.

"Among other things."

Chapter Eight

Turning toward the pond, Savannah wrapped her arms around herself and stared out, her nerves stretched to the breaking point.

Neither one had said a word on the way here, but the tension emanating from both Wyatt and Hayes spoke volumes.

Part of her wanted to run to them, to have them hold her close and tell her everything would be all right, but the dozen or so feet between them seemed like a mile.

She wanted to have a chance to explore all the passion their eyes promised, to spend the rest of her life taking care of them as much as they claimed to want to take care of her.

She wanted to be held in the darkness, to feel safe when she closed her eyes at night.

She needed to be needed—to be wanted for herself.

Right now, though, the emotional distance between them seemed insurmountable, but she didn't doubt that they would somehow manage to change that.

It hadn't escaped her notice that Wyatt and Hayes wouldn't allow her to hide behind the wall she'd long ago erected between her and everyone else. Each time she swallowed emotion and only allowed the cool politeness she'd used with her uncle to show, Wyatt and Hayes plowed through it, not satisfied until they'd gotten to the real woman underneath.

They wanted *her*—the real woman.

For the first time in her life she felt valued, and not for the favors she could do.

She felt alive.

Another part of her figured it would be better if Wyatt and Hayes decided against marrying her. She could leave here and live her life the way she wanted to.

She wouldn't have to worry about her uncle coming for her ever again. He could find her here, but he'd never find her in Texas.

Seeing a movement out of the corner of her eye, she glanced in that direction, stiffening even more when she saw Wyatt move closer.

He settled himself on a large flat rock near the water and leaned forward, his legs spread, his laced fingers dangling between them. He appeared relaxed and calm, but his eyes told a different story.

Sharp and dark, they glittered with something that looked suspiciously like possession.

As much as the inner voice inside her fought at the thought of being possessed, Savannah couldn't deny the pleasure and inner warmth that went hand in hand with it.

Clasping her hands together, she glanced at Hayes and found herself caught in his penetrating stare, struck by the intensity of the anger and need in his eyes. Careful to keep her voice low and even, she turned to face him squarely, fighting the urge to shuffle her feet.

"I think you need to come to terms with the fact that I can't stay."

Hayes lifted a brow, his expression one of cold arrogance, much like he'd worn almost constantly in Kansas City.

"I think you need to come to the realization that we won't let you leave. You're ours, Savannah. You've already given yourself to us by words and by deed. Strip."

Shaken by his tone and the icy intent in his eyes, Savannah gasped and took a step back.

"What did you say?"

He sounded so cold and distant, but the hunger in his gaze as it moved slowly over told her he was anything but.

Crossing his arms over his chest, Hayes leaned back against the trunk of the tree behind him, his stance making him appear larger than life. "You heard me. Get those clothes off. We're going to settle everything once and for all, and I don't want there to be any misunderstandings, and I sure as hell don't want anything in my way."

She didn't know this side of him and in this mood, he would be too unpredictable to anticipate.

It made her even more nervous when Wyatt went to his saddlebags and produced two blankets.

His lips curved in what appeared to be a semblance of a smile as he walked over the uneven ground and took his seat again.

"It's a nice day, but you can wrap one of these around you once you get those clothes off. Keep the boots on so you don't hurt your feet."

Hayes stared at her breasts as he moved slowly toward her, not stopping until he stood only a few feet away. "It's warm out, with just enough of a chill in the air to make you more aware of your nakedness. I want the breeze blowing over those pink nipples. I'm sure they're already hard, but the cold will make them even harder— and more sensitive. Now strip, or I'll do it for you. If I do it, though, your clothes will be in tatters and you'll have to wear the blanket back to the ranch. Take off the shirt first."

Shivering at his cold tone, Savannah took a step back, stopping abruptly when she almost slipped on the wet stones.

Hayes whipped out a hand to catch her, holding her against his hard body for several heart-stopping seconds, before pulling away to look down at her.

"You fall in that pond and I'm going to beat your ass raw. Lose the shirt."

With a large hand, he gripped her upper arm and pulled her to the tree he'd been leaning against, a dark brow going up.

"Last warning."

Savannah shook off his hand, knowing that she could only because he allowed it. "If this is how you're going to treat me, can you blame me for not wanting to marry you?"

Hayes nodded and went to his own horse.

"Something we're going to settle before we leave here. Are you going to take off that shirt, or am I?"

Need and fear made a potent combination, one that left her shaking so hard her teeth chattered.

Her fear didn't stem from thinking they wanted to hurt her.

Whatever they had planned for her had nothing to do with pain and everything to do with pleasure. She could see it in their eyes.

Her fear came from the unknown. Not knowing what further decadence they had in store for her had her trembling in anticipation, every inch of her skin sensitized with awareness. Not knowing if she could handle it terrified her.

Knowing how completely she responded to them, and the sense of connection she experienced with them each time they touched her, scared her even more.

Whether they decided that they still wanted to marry her or not, her heart would be broken. Before she left town, however, they could make her fall in love with them even more, making the hurt even worse.

"What are you going to do to me?" She gulped heavily as he turned, her stomach tightening when she saw he held a coil of rope. "What are you going to do with that rope?"

She took a step back, and then another, crying out in surprise when she encountered an immovable object.

She hadn't even heard Wyatt move.

His arms came around, trapping her against him. Nuzzling her neck, he chuckled softly.

"Let me help you out of this shirt before Hayes loses his temper. If you give him what he wants, he might just go a little easier on you—something you might want to remember for the future."

Hayes stopped several feet in front of her and looked up toward the top of the tree. With an expert flick of his wrist, he sent one end of the rope sailing over a thick branch several feet over her head.

Savannah shivered as Wyatt unbuttoned her shirt, parted and lifted the ends. Holding her hands above her head, he made quick work of tying her wrists together with her shirt, leaving her breasts bared and her unable to cover herself.

Hayes took full advantage, his eyes raking over her and making her tender nipples bead even more.

He'd been right about how exposed she would feel with the cool air blowing over her breasts, but she hadn't anticipated having her arms lifted over her head. It lifted her breasts and made them even more sensitive, the position adding a vulnerability she'd never experienced.

The feel of the abrasive rope touching her hands made her jump and try to pull away, but Wyatt overpowered her, keeping her arms held high and pulling the loop in the rope tight around her wrists.

"What do you think you're doing? Untie me right now!"

Reaching around her, Wyatt ran the tips of his callused fingers over her beaded nipples, the delicate friction sending shards of tingling heat racing through her veins, heat that seemed to all concentrate at her slit.

"The material of your shirt will keep your wrists protected from the rope no matter how hard you struggle."

Hayes tugged the end of the rope he held, pulling her arms higher, his eyes narrowing as he stared down at her breasts.

"And you *will* struggle—but not because you want to escape." Reaching out, he tapped a nipple, sending another jolt of delight to her already overloaded system.

The reminder that he and Wyatt could do anything they wanted to her breasts increased her sense of vulnerability.

His eyes glittered with the knowledge of her helplessness.

"It'll be because you're going to want to come so badly, you'll be struggling to get closer."

"Bastard!"

Scandalous Desire 115

She tugged against her bonds, but Hayes held the other end of the rope firmly. Being exposed outdoors with Wyatt had been exciting and dangerous, but it hadn't been anything like this.

Her love and need for both of them changed everything.

She knew to her soul that she was as safe as she wanted to be with them.

They didn't say it, but their caring and love for her shone in their eyes. Startled to realize how much she wanted to give in to them, she reminded herself of the trouble her uncle would make.

The town and everything they wanted to build would be destroyed before it ever got started.

She had to resist what she'd discovered to be the most important thing in the world.

Love.

"Let me go. I don't know what you think you're doing, but it's not funny."

Hayes never took his eyes from hers as he tied the rope off, securing it to the trunk of the tree.

"I'm not laughing, Savannah."

Wary of his mood, Savannah looked over her shoulder, searching for Wyatt. She spotted him leaning against the trunk of the tree Hayes had tied her to, his arms crossed over his chest.

He gave her a slow wink. "Oh, I'm here, darlin'. You belong to both of us all right, but it's Hayes's turn. Sometimes we'll make love to you, or like now, play with you, separately. Sometimes together. Either way, we'll both know what the other did to you."

Hayes brought her attention back to him by running a finger over her breast, using his fingertip to circle, but not quite touch, her nipple.

"There'll be no secrets between us. This wouldn't work if there were. So, you want to tell me why you put something in our food that put us to sleep?"

Biting back a moan, she arched toward him, trying to get him to touch the aching tip. Frustrated that he managed to avoid it, she tugged at the ropes, wondering why the strong sense of helplessness excited her so much when she'd fought her entire life not to be helpless.

"I'm sorry for that, but you asked for it. Hayes!"

She watched in fascination as he lowered his head, calling out his name at the feel of his warm breath on her nipple. She couldn't hold back a gasp when his tongue flicked over it, her sharp intake of breath becoming a cry when the cool breeze blew over it. The dampness he'd left behind made it even colder, a sensation that made her nipple bead even tighter and sent a fresh rush of pleasure to her pussy.

With his mouth poised just inches from her nipple, he circled the other, avoiding her attempts to get his mouth on her again.

The cool patience of a lawman gleamed in the eyes he raised to hers.

"I'm waiting for an answer, Savannah."

Rubbing her thighs together did nothing to ease the throbbing ache that settled there, an ache she would bet he knew about.

He and Wyatt always seemed to know what her response would be to everything they did to her before she did.

She'd never expected to meet men as strong and unwavering as the Tylers, but Wyatt and Hayes had shown themselves to be that and more.

Their patience appeared to know no bounds, and the tenderness and desire for her weakened her knees.

If she had been able to stay, she knew she would have spent the rest of her life asserting herself, and loving every minute of it. The challenge of standing up to not one, but two determined husbands would keep her on her toes.

She could do no less than keep them on theirs.

Hayes tapped a nipple, frowning.

"I'm waiting, Savannah."

Reminding herself that she had to stand firm against them if she was to have any chance at all of leaving here with her dignity, she fought the wave of longing his touch created.

Throwing her head back, she thrust her breasts out, close to begging.

"Because I wanted to be left alone, damn it."

Hayes rewarded her by giving her nipples the attention she'd been dying for, rolling them between his thumbs and forefingers.

"Don't ever do it again. We can't protect you that way, and we sure as hell have no intention of walking away from you."

Before she could reply, he bent and took her nipple into his mouth, swirling his tongue around it and heating the cold tip.

Crying out at the sharp contrast, she stood on her toes, arching her back and struggling to get closer. She couldn't hide anything this way, certainly not how much she wanted them.

Letting them see would only give them more ammunition to use against her. Hoping to hide her desire behind anger, she clenched her jaw, hoping that they would only see irritation in her eyes.

"Why are you doing this to me? Why can't you just take me and be done with it?"

If he took her the way he had that night in Kansas City, she could hide her face and they would never know.

"Because I want to get your attention, and make sure you're not going anywhere. I want to talk to you and get some answers, but you seem hell-bent on avoiding us. I also notice that, although you don't lie, you don't answer or commit to something. You just stand there and let us think everything is settled, when it's not."

Remembering the first time they'd brought her out here to the pond, when she'd done that very thing, she felt her face burn, crying out again when Hayes straightened and tapped her other nipple.

"You just told Eb that you were going to marry us, and as soon as he walked away, you changed your mind."

She shivered when he walked around her, the tips of his fingers running over her breasts, her belly, her shoulders, her back, everywhere, sensitizing every inch of skin he touched.

"There are rules, Savannah."

That cold tone sent a shiver up her spine, one that he intensified by running his finger up the center of her back.

"Rules you *will* follow."

His hands moved slowly around her, tickling slightly as his fingertips moved over her waist. His lips brushed over her raised arms as his fingertips moved over her belly, making the muscles there quiver as he reached for the fastening of her pants.

"Rules made to keep women safe. Rules to keep men from acting like savages around them. Rules made to entice other women to come here. You'll abide by those rules just as much as we will. We won't beat our women, but a nice spanking to warm that bottom and a little play will go a long way in getting our message across."

His demeanor changed in a heartbeat, becoming brisk and hurried as he moved around to stand in front of her. He yanked her pants to the top of her boots, cursing as he worked them off. A few tugs later, he managed to get them over her boots and straightened. Tossing them to hang over the rope by his shoulder, he took a step back, his eyes glittering hotly as they moved over her.

"You're subject to those rules. You'll obey them, and we'll enforce them for everyone, but especially with you. I don't know what's going on in that head of yours, but I'm not about to let you make a mistake that could get you killed. You shouldn't be alone out there, and you know damned well that you love us or you wouldn't have given yourself to us in the first place."

With a booted foot, he slid her feet several inches apart and placed both feet between them so she couldn't close her legs.

"Damn, woman, you frustrate me. You're as unpredictable as a brush fire."

Savannah shrugged, secretly thrilled.

"A woman doesn't like to be too predictable and boring."

As soon as the words left her mouth, she recognized them as her mother's. A wave of depression washed over her, dousing her desire like a cup of cold water. To her surprise, Hayes seemed to notice immediately.

His eyes sharpened and narrowed on hers, the concern in them almost her undoing. To her further shock, he started to reach for her before fisting his hands at his sides, his eyes hooded as they moved over her.

"I have a feeling being bored is the last thing I have to worry about with you. A moral, passionate woman who goes out of her way to help others, and who's brave enough to face the world alone and then take on two husbands. Wyatt and I are lucky men."

Wyatt grinned. "And we're about to get luckier."

Out of the corner of her eye, she watched him go back to his saddlebag and return with a small tin in his hand. Recognizing it, she shivered as he moved behind her, the feel of his rough clothes on her bare skin renewing her awareness.

"What are you going to do with that salve?"

The feel of the cool air blowing over her damp folds sent another wave of longing through her, her need apparent in the moisture that he gathered when he slid his fingers between her thighs.

"You're wrong about me. Don't make me into something I'm not. I can't stay in Desire. Oh!"

She gasped as Hayes slid a finger into her, clamping down on it as her need for him took over. She started to rock her hips, moaning at the sensation of his finger moving inside her. Staring into his eyes, she knew where she belonged. Just seconds before, her desire had waned, but one touch from either of them could stoke the flames and reignite embers she'd thought had gone cold.

"Damn you. How do you do this to me? It's not fair. You're stronger and—oh, God!"

The brush of Wyatt's clothed body against her nakedness as he moved in behind her made her feel even more exposed, but the rough hands he placed over the cheeks of her bottom sent her arousal soaring.

Pulling her cheeks apart, he touched her forbidden opening, and no matter how hard she clenched the cheeks of her bottom, she couldn't close against him.

His lips moved against her hair, his deep voice almost a whisper.

"You're a lot more powerful than you think, darlin'. Hayes and I can't even sleep at night because we're thinking of you. You walk across the yard in those damned pants and my cock gets hard as a rock."

Savannah stilled, filled with trepidation at the slight pain as Hayes closed his teeth over a nipple. She found it even more amazing that the danger excited her, the thrill of being naked outside and being so defenseless against whatever Hayes and Wyatt decided to do to her.

Hayes withdrew, sliding his slick finger over her clit, his eyes flaring at her strangled cry.

"We're going to get her ready. Not yet, though. I'll tell you when. I've got a few more things to discover before that."

Chuckling softly, Wyatt removed his finger and slid his other hand up to cover her breast.

"I guess it's only fair that you get what you want this time since I got to spank her."

Hayes smiled, a wicked smile filled with sinful intent. He aimed his words at Wyatt, but his eyes remained steady on hers.

"Yes, you said she liked it. We already knew our little Savannah had fire. I'm anxious to see how far we can push her." His eyes sharpened and narrowed to slits.

"She likes this. She likes being vulnerable and exposed. She likes the things we do to her. I don't think she really understands that hurting a woman isn't the way to get her attention. It's through pleasure and just enough danger to keep her on edge."

Relieved, and oddly disappointed that Wyatt had removed his finger, she stared up at Hayes, mesmerized by his glittering eyes.

"The way you make me feel is sinful. I've never felt like this with anyone else before."

Rolling her clit between his fingers, he ran his other hand over her hair.

"You ever do and you'll get your ass paddled so hard you won't sit for days. Putting bruises on you is sinful, Savannah. Beating you and forcing you to be a slave is sinful. We're just two men who want to marry you. We want to pleasure you—and we sure as hell want to make sure you don't get yourself hurt or killed."

Frustrated that she couldn't use her arms to pull him closer, Savannah groaned.

"By tying me to a tree?"

Hayes slid his fingers through her folds and into her, stroking her inner flesh, his body stiffening when she cried out and clamped down on him.

"Don't try to tell me you're not enjoying this. Your thighs are soaked with your juices, and only my restraint is keeping you from coming. You'll remember this, Savannah. The next time you even think about doing something like that to us again, you'll remember this."

With a low curse, he released her and reached for the fastening of his pants. His hands shook as he yanked them to his knees, his eyes swirling with need and possessiveness.

Savannah couldn't help but look down, her breath catching when she saw the size of his cock, hardly able to believe she'd taken such a huge thing into her body. It looked so hard and threatening, so big around she didn't even think she could get her hand around it.

Thinking about holding his cock in her hand made her long to touch it.

She wondered what he would think of her if he knew how desperately she wanted him.

Shaking uncontrollably, she rubbed her thighs together, stopping abruptly when Hayes stepped forward again and reached for her, taking her bottom into his hard, warm hands and lifting her against him.

Feeling his warm, firm body against hers, she wanted to cry. It seemed like forever since she'd been held like this.

She hadn't realized just how much she needed to be held by him again.

Wrapping her legs around him, she closed her eyes on a moan as his cock jumped against her center, rocking her hips against the hard length of it.

Memories of how it felt inside her came crashing back.

The heat. The passion. The feeling of being cherished.

She wanted it all again so badly she would have given almost anything to stay.

Anything except the future happiness of the people she loved.

With a strong arm at her back, Hayes pulled her closer, his eyes glittering with need as his hold effectively stopped her squirming.

"No. You're going to come with my cock inside you."

With his hands on her hips, he moved her back slightly and thrust into her with one smooth motion, filling her with his amazing heat.

She stilled, the shock of being filled so completely making it impossible to move. Her pussy walls clenched repeatedly as she struggled to adjust to the size of him, his hard cock forcing her inner walls to yield.

He held himself still, his jaw clenching as he searched her features, his body tense as though poised to withdraw if she needed him to. Holding her to him with one arm, he ran the fingers of the other through her hair.

"Easy, honey. I won't move until your body accepts me."

Nothing he could have said or done would have convinced her more that, although he and Wyatt appeared to be in charge, she actually held all the cards.

Relief, love, desire, and an unbelievable sense of freedom washed over her, the combination making her light-headed. Feeling more powerful than she'd ever felt in her life, she looked up at him through her lashes and dug her heels into his tight bottom to keep him inside, inadvertently taking him even deeper.

"I'm not delicate."

If he withdrew from her now, she wouldn't be able to stand it.

Having him inside her, being surrounded by his and Wyatt's heat and strength and held as if he never wanted to let her go, felt like she'd always imagined coming home should feel.

She clenched on him again, fascinated that each time she did, his cock jumped inside her and his eyes flashed with need.

She'd never been wanted like this before. No one had ever paid attention to her this way before, as though every word she spoke, every move she made was important.

She could no longer avoid it. When she left here, it would be with a broken heart.

Suddenly, the need to store up as many memories as she could was of the utmost importance.

Staring into his eyes, she tightened on him again.

"Take me."

His eyes narrowed, gleaming with something dark and mysterious, but so hot she found it difficult to breathe. Adjusting his hold, he wrapped an arm around her lower back and reached up behind him to release the rope.

"You're delicate, and your refusal to see it is going to give me many sleepless nights. Put your arms around my neck and keep them there."

Doing his bidding, Savannah lifted her still-tied wrists over his head, leaning back against Wyatt.

Brushing his lips over her shoulder, Wyatt slid his hands around her to cup her breasts, rolling her nipples between his thumbs and forefingers.

"My cock's about to burst through my pants. I want her ass, Hayes."

Hayes dug his fingers into her buttocks, squeezing the fingers close to her vulnerable opening, exposing it even more. With his hooded gaze holding hers, he withdrew almost completely and then surged deep again, his eyes flashing when she whimpered.

"No, not tonight. I want to get her used to feeling us in both openings at the same time first. Stretch her just a little. Make sure you use a lot of salve. I don't want to hurt her."

If Savannah had ever heard a scarier, or more erotic thing in her life, she didn't remember it.

With a groan, Hayes withdrew and thrust deep again, the muscles in his shoulders bunching and shifting, his hold firm as she jolted.

Her legs and arms stiffened at the feel of Wyatt's finger touching her puckered opening, her toes curling inside her boots. Her strangled cry echoed through the trees, and she pushed against Hayes's arms in an involuntary effort to lower her legs.

The instinctive need to protect herself had her struggling in his hold, whimpering at the strange sensation of a generous amount of salve being spread around and slightly into her bottom.

"No." Adjusting his hold, Hayes slid his hands to her thighs, keeping her legs raised.

"Wyatt told me how much you liked your spanking and having that tight bottom played with. Tonight, we're going to take it a little further. He's going to use his finger to open that bottom hole a little and fuck it with his fingers while I'm fucking your pussy with my cock."

Savannah froze, shaken by the way Hayes spoke to her and the edge in his voice, but also at their wicked intention.

He'd never used that kind of language before, and he'd never had that barely contained growl in his throat when he spoke to her. His hands became rougher, his movements less smooth as he withdrew and slid deep again.

Wyatt groaned from behind her. "Damn, I want to do everything with her. I never thought much of spanking a woman, but there's something to be said for having a round naked ass over your lap. She squirmed and spread her legs wider and was soaking wet. You got her?"

Savannah jolted in surprise and panic when Wyatt's finger pressed against her puckered opening and forced its way inside. Letting out a cry, she squeezed tight in an attempt to keep him out, even while part of her wanted him so desperately to do it.

Wyatt wouldn't be denied, holding her with an arm around her waist and pushing his finger deep.

Since Hayes no longer had to hold her up, he ran his hands over her upper thighs, delivering several sharp slaps before sliding his palms over her sides and up to her breasts. His hands moved constantly, slapping her thighs just enough to keep them hot, before returning his attention to her nipples again.

Sometimes he pinched the sensitive tips and sometimes he merely circled them with a callused finger, his lips curving when she fought to get him to touch her.

The entire time, though, his cock slid slowly, steadily in and out of her pussy, each thrust sliding his cock over her inner walls and making them quiver.

"Yeah, Savannah. You like to play, all right. Makes a man want to see how far he can push you."

Unable to help herself, she clenched on Hayes with each stroke, which also served to grip Wyatt's finger as it pressed relentlessly into her ass.

Chills raced up and down her spine at the decadence of having her bottom breached, the feel of it much stronger than what he'd done to her the other day.

It made the cock inside her feel even larger, a sensation that intensified each time she clenched.

Her clit throbbed with the need for attention, and the infrequent brushes against Hayes's abdomen didn't give her the relief she craved.

She trembled everywhere, her whimpered pants growing louder and more desperate as the pressure inside her continued to build.

Hayes chose that moment to circle her nipple with his finger, not touching her where she needed it most. Even though she knew it amused him, she couldn't prevent her instinctive move to get closer, gasping when it shifted the angle of the finger Wyatt used to press against the inner walls of her ass.

"It feels so wicked."

Wyatt lifted her arms from around Hayes's neck and brought them over his, settling her arms around his neck and leaving her breasts totally exposed and vulnerable again.

"Let's see how wicked we can be."

Hayes groaned, his hands tightening on her hips as he began to thrust faster.

"Hell, woman. For someone as innocent and cantankerous as you are, you sure as hell have a body made for sin."

Savannah shook from her head to her toes, the too-full sensation of having both her pussy and bottom filled sending her into a frenzy. When Hayes withdrew, Wyatt pushed his finger deep, only to withdraw again as Hayes thrust back into her.

Her breasts, now totally exposed, drew their almost continuous attention. She shivered each time their fingers moved over them and down to her belly, only to retrace their path and slide up to her neck and shoulders. Her stomach muscles quivered beneath their touch, only to tighten when Wyatt moved the finger in her bottom, or when a light pinch to her nipple sent more of that incredible heat to her clit and made her clench on both of them.

It felt incredible.

Crying out, she arched her back, rocking her hips to move against them. Her movements took them deeper and spurred them both to greater heights.

Each groan Hayes emitted got deeper, his hands moving with increasing purpose over her skin.

The arm Wyatt wrapped around her slid higher and he began to tug at her nipples.

"You're so damned beautiful. And ours."

The tingling heat raced over her skin, gathering at her clit until, between one breath and the next, the pleasure inside her exploded.

Clamping down on both of them, she stiffened as the wave inside her crested. Pushing back against Wyatt, she lifted her breasts into his hand.

She didn't recognize the strangled whimper as hers until it stopped and she realized she couldn't catch her breath.

She couldn't imagine a better feeling than this, as though every single inch of her body burst with pleasure at exactly the same moment.

Hayes groaned, his gaze lingering on her breasts, the possessiveness in it making her feel cherished and incredibly feminine.

Beautiful.

"Pinch her nipple harder."

Savannah couldn't tear her gaze away from his as Wyatt moved the finger in her bottom, his fingers punishing as they closed on her nipple. Sucking in a breath at the unexpected pain, she tried to pull away, but he'd already released it.

Stunned by the jolt of heat to her already overloaded system, she clamped down on both of them, crying out again as the pleasure she'd thought had crested rolled over her again.

With a harsh groan, Hayes plunged deep, his fingers digging into her hips as he closed his eyes and threw his head back, his release sending hers even higher.

The delicious sensation seemed to last forever.

"I don't want it to end! It's so wonderful."

Wyatt gathered her close, his voice barely recognizable.

"You'll have it again, as much as you want. We all will. We can't lose this, Savannah."

As the indescribable pleasure finally released her from its grip, she gazed at Hayes, fascinated that the hard, cold lawman deep inside her and holding her so fiercely could find such pleasure with her.

Wyatt nuzzled her neck from behind, his groan drowning out her whimper as he withdrew from her bottom, teasing her sensitive opening.

With the last shimmers of delight still warming her, Savannah tightened her legs around Hayes and rocked against him, a giggle escaping at the wary surprise in his eyes.

She couldn't tell which one of them was more surprised by her giggle. It had been so long since she'd really laughed that it felt strange to her. Snapping her mouth closed, and filled with unease, she lifted her eyes to his, taken aback by the teasing glint in his narrowed ones.

"You want to play, honey?" Sliding his hand over her hip, he reached with a work-roughened thumb to caress her clit, his lips twitching when she gasped at the jolt to her too-sensitive flesh.

The light of anticipation in his eyes and the edginess in his tone gave her a thrill, his expression making it plain that he would welcome such play.

"Like that, do you?"

Savannah couldn't hold back a smile, delighted that she could bring out this side of him, a side she would bet few knew about.

She never would have believed it if she hadn't seen it with her own eyes. The yearning for more made it impossible to resist teasing Hayes again.

"No."

Both brows went up, his eyes gleaming with challenge.

"I thought you didn't lie. I may have to spank you for that." His lips twitched, making the threat more erotic than menacing.

The memory of Wyatt's spanking made her already sensitized and slick bottom tingle with anticipation. Rocking her hips as desire flared and warmed her again, she moaned at the tug to her nipple from Wyatt's strong fingers, snuggling against him.

"You'd better not. Look what happened last time."

Using his thumb to stroke very lightly over her clit, Hayes smiled, a cool smile filled with erotic intent.

"Are you threatening me?"

Smiling at his incredulous tone, Savannah rocked her hips, delighted with the way his hands clenched on her body and the flash of heat in his eyes.

She actually felt dizzy with excitement and a happiness that warmed her from deep inside. Never in her life did she expect to be able to tease a man, especially one like Hayes.

She'd never imagined that playing with a man she loved could be so fun—and exciting. Looking up at him through her lashes, she adopted the innocent expression she'd worn for most of her life—an expression Eb, Jeremiah, and Maggie would have recognized right away.

"You're the sheriff and a lot bigger and stronger than I am. I would *never* threaten you."

With narrowed eyes, Hayes withdrew from her and set her on her feet, his eyes never leaving hers as he righted his clothing.

"Is that a fact?"

With a soft laugh, Wyatt lifted her still-tied wrists from around his neck.

"That sounded a lot like sarcasm to me."

Now that Wyatt had released her, she had to reach out, placing her hands on Hayes's chest for support, while out of the corner of her eye, she watched Wyatt move to the pond and bend to wash his hands.

Looking up at Hayes, she thrilled at the feel of the hard muscle bunching and the rumble of his chest beneath her palms. Clenching her fingertips into the firm muscle, she leaned closer, her breath catching at the feel of his shirt against her nipples. Looking up at him through her lashes, Savannah shifted restlessly under his scrutiny, wondering what devious thoughts lay behind those gorgeous eyes of his.

They taught her things about herself that she didn't feel comfortable with, things that made her wonder if she knew herself at all. Her uncle had told her that she was her mother's daughter from the time she could remember.

Wondering once again if the need for intimacy with more than one man ran through her veins made her suddenly cold.

"Will you untie me now? I want to get dressed."

Hayes's eyes sharpened as he moved around to stand behind her, his fingertips over her belly making her stomach muscles twitch.

"No."

Wyatt approached, moving to stand in the place Hayes just vacated. Glittering darkly, his eyes narrowed as he stared down at her. He unfastened his pants and yanked them down to his thighs, drawing her gaze downward. Fisting his cock in one hand, he used the other to lift her wrists over his neck.

"There's no shame in liking what we do to you. You're ours, Savannah. It's all right for us to enjoy each other."

Releasing his cock, he lifted his hands to cover her breasts, the shock of cold drawing a gasp from her.

"Wyatt, your hands are freezing from the pond!" No matter how she twisted, she couldn't get away from the fingers he used to roll her nipples.

Wyatt's slow grin was her only warning before he lowered one of his hands and sank a cold finger into her pussy.

"Are they? I guess I'd better warm them."

With a cry, Savannah came to her toes, falling against him.

"Wyatt!"

From behind her, Hayes ran his hands up and down her sides.

"In case you're wondering, you're not anything like your mother. Yeah, we know all about her. You're a warm, passionate woman, one who needs more than just sex. You need men who love you—men who will give you all the affection you need. God knows you've had very little in your life. And, you're not getting dressed yet. We still haven't settled that we're getting married on Saturday."

"S–Saturday?" Shivering under his hands, she rolled her hips, fucking herself on Wyatt's cold finger, something that apparently fascinated him.

Tightening his hands on her waist, Hayes touched his lips to her shoulder.

"Yes, Saturday. You committed to it in front of others, but then as soon as we're alone, you tell us you don't want to get married. I'm not letting you play games with us, Savannah."

He ran his hands over her hips and to her bottom.

"Not that kind of game, anyway."

Savannah's skin tingled everywhere he touched, her body becoming languid and slumping even more against Wyatt. Even weak with need, she couldn't stop clenching on the now warm finger inside her pussy.

"I told you I can't stay, but you won't listen. I told you…ah…that I don't want to belong to anyone."

Wyatt withdrew his finger from her pussy with a speed that left her inner walls clenching. He lifted her against him, and with one smooth stroke, he impaled her on his cock, lifting her legs to wrap around his waist.

"Too late. You already belong to us and you know it. As much as you want to fight it, it's there and there's no getting away from it—or us."

Fisting a hand in her hair, Wyatt tilted her head back, his eyes dark with anger and need.

"You're ours, Savannah. I'd kill any man who touched you. We belong together and you know it, and we can live here the way we want. We'd be happy here." His cock jumped inside her as he moved his hips, not stopping until he drew a moan from her.

Surprised by the desire that raged through her so soon on the heels of being taken by Hayes, Savannah clamped down on the cock filling her, trying to ignore the awareness that he'd already created in her bottom.

"No. If I stay, your town would be ruined."

Wyatt stilled, glancing over her shoulder to where Hayes stood. "Why?"

It embarrassed her to tell him, and she didn't like talking about the life she'd left behind, but knew they wouldn't give up until they knew.

"My uncle. He sent me a telegram while I was in Tulsa. He knew where I would be going and told me if I didn't come home within a month, he would come and drag me back."

Hayes slid his hands up to cup her breasts, toying with her nipples. "No one's *dragging* you anywhere."

Struck by the ice in his lethal tone, Savannah turned to look over her shoulder at him, shivering at the look of deadly intent on his face.

His eyes darkened dangerously, his scar on his cheek moving as a muscle worked in his jaw. "If he tries to take you, he'll pay. He'll have to come through me to get to you, Savannah, and that won't happen. I thought you understood that."

Shaking her head, Savannah gasped again as her movement shifted Wyatt's cock inside her. "He's more evil than you know. I don't want to talk about this now."

Whimpering at the slight tug of her sensitized nipples, she moved on Wyatt, shocked that she took him so deep. With a cry, she sank her fingers into his hair, knocking his hat to the ground.

"Please."

Hayes ran a slow hand over her bottom, somehow making an affectionate gesture seem threatening. Running his teeth over her shoulder, he slid the other hand up her body, the backs of his fingers lightly stroking the delicate underside of her breast.

"Please what, Savannah? Please give you the pleasure you're already learning to expect? Please fuck you? Please paddle this soft ass for playing games with us and for knocking us out with that stuff you put in our food?"

Savannah wanted it all, and only years of keeping her needs to herself kept her from blurting that out. She shouldn't want like this. She shouldn't *need* this way. Every inch of her body tingled with awareness and heat, heightening her senses, her already sensitive body aroused to a razor-sharp edge.

Her pussy felt stretched and hot around Wyatt's cock. Her clit demanded attention, but the pleasure gained by rubbing the too-sensitive flesh against Wyatt proved to be too sharp to bear.

Frustrated at the inability to move enough to get that delicious feeling again, she bucked against Wyatt.

"I can't do this. Let me go!"

"Never." Hayes's voice rasped over her ear, making her shiver.

A second later, a sharp slap to her vulnerable bottom had her crying out, stilling in shock. The slight pain almost immediately spread, becoming a diffused heat that made her entire slit hot and tingly.

Her breasts seemed to swell against Wyatt's chest, her nipples tight and in need of attention. Her bottom hole, still slick from salve, clenched at emptiness, her inner walls still quivering with awareness at Wyatt's recent play.

She needed to be filled there.

The realization that something so intimate and forbidden could be so incredibly exciting alarmed her, but with that alarm came the recognition of how much she trusted them and how very much she wanted to please them.

And give them the submission they seemed to all revel in.

Hayes reinforced her sudden insight by circling a finger around her puckered opening, making the tender flesh tingle and tighten.

"No more arguing. I want your promise—right here, right now—that you'll *never* put anything like that in our food again. We have to be able to protect you, and I won't put up with your tricks to avoid us."

With her eyes closed, Savannah threw her head back against Hayes's strong shoulder. She desperately wanted to rock her hips, but the threat of the finger which began to press at her bottom hole kept her from moving.

Remaining still had to be the hardest thing she'd ever done.

The finger disappeared, followed almost immediately by another slap. Another cry broke free, one more of surprise than pain. A nervous moan followed when he pressed his finger against her again, applying even more pressure.

She wanted it inside her so badly that it took incredible willpower not to press back against him.

"I promise. I won't do that ever again. Please. Take me. Don't play with me this way. It's mean."

She wanted to come. She *needed* the relief from this torment. She needed her ass filled again. She wanted it stretched and full and came close to begging Hayes to take her with his cock.

Only fear of trying to take something that large into her bottom kept her silent.

Hayes applied more pressure. "You gonna marry us?"

"I can't—ah!"

Wyatt withdrew and surged deep.

"Because of your uncle?"

"Yes. He'll ruin everything. He'll spread the word about this town and come down preaching about hellfire and damnation until—yes!" Her words came out in a rush as she squirmed helplessly between Wyatt and Hayes.

Hayes wrapped an arm around her waist and pushed his fingertip into her bottom, using pressure against the sides of the tight ring of muscle to stretch her there and making it sting.

"Your uncle doesn't stand a chance. This town is closed to outsiders, and it's our job to keep it that way. He won't get to you, Savannah."

Whimpering, she pushed back against Hayes, taking a little more of his finger, making the cock in her pussy feel even larger.

"It's not me I'm worried about. It's you…the town. He'll ruin it all. The things he said after the Tylers left…" Her words came out in quick, panting breaths, cutting off altogether when Hayes thrust his finger deep.

Wyatt's slow, smooth thrusts came faster, his cock spearing inside her with more force than before.

"That's enough. We take care of what belongs to us, you most of all." Tightening his hands on her hips, he moved her on his cock, surprising her with his strength. His movements also moved her on the finger impaling her bottom, a finger that pressed with unrelenting pressure against her inner walls.

Even though she'd already experienced it, the sensations raging through her still shocked her so much that she couldn't move.

It didn't seem to matter because Wyatt moved her however he wanted to, moving her on his cock with increasing speed and strength.

Before she knew it, her body started to gather again, the pressure building toward the release she knew they would give her. Her clit felt huge and tingled in the way she'd come to expect when her orgasm got close.

She never seemed to be able to hold it off, no matter how hard she tried. Every slide of their hands over her skin, every groan or encouraging word, even the heat of being spanked added to her pleasure and made them impossible to resist.

She couldn't hold back her response from them any more than she could hold back water from a dam. She yearned for their touch and the pleasure they could give her with every fiber of her being. Staring into Wyatt's eyes and with Hayes whispering erotic promises against her ear, she knew her response to them was more than just physical.

The thought of refusing them, of walking away from them, became unbearable.

Hayes scraped his teeth over her neck, growling as his hand tightened around her waist.

"No matter how far you run, you'll never get away from me."

He stunned her by removing his finger, yanking it from her bottom with a speed that stole her breath. Even though Wyatt's cock filled her pussy, their play with her bottom had awakened her there, and now that part of her craved their attention so badly she wanted to cry.

Sliding the hand from her waist to her breasts, he bent to scrape his teeth over her shoulder, the gesture somehow both threatening and affectionate. His fingers closed lightly over her nipple, his intention clear.

"And we both know how to take very good care of you in all ways. You had us fooled, you know? Trying to mislead the sheriff will get you thrown in jail. I could tie you naked to the bars, and no one would be the wiser."

"I d–didn't mislead you. You made assumptions about m–me. You saw what you were supposed to see. Just like everybody else."

Wyatt's expression became hard and tense as he slowed his thrusts.

"We're supposed to know you better than anyone else does. That sweet and innocent woman we fell in love with in Kansas City turned out to be someone quite different than we expected."

His words sent a chill through her, and she had to swallow before meeting his gaze.

Trying not to clench on him, she stiffened as Hayes closed the fingers over her nipple, pinching it just hard enough to shoot arrows of heat to her slit.

"And you figured out I'm just like my mother after all, and not the kind of woman you should marry."

Struggling to keep her hurt from showing, she clenched on Wyatt, her body making demands even as her mind screamed to push him away.

Hayes chuckled softly against her ear, sending more of those irresistible shivers up and down her spine. Pressing a hard finger against her bottom hole again, he slid a thumb over her nipple.

"We figured out that underneath that cool, polite shell was a warm woman who isn't afraid to fight for what she wants—a passionate woman who responds to everything we do to her. How about two fingers in that tight ass, honey? Then Wyatt can let you come."

The pinch of her puckered opening being stretched wide curled her toes. "It's too much. Oh, God. I'm so full."

Hayes groaned, the hands on her breast becoming even more demanding. "Wait until we both have our cocks inside you. Damn, honey, you're tight."

Wyatt's groan sounded even more tortured as he took her with short, forceful thrusts.

"I can't hold off anymore. Too good."

His fingers dug into her as he took her in earnest, the friction of his cock over the inner walls of her pussy even more intense as his cock jumped and seemed to swell inside her.

Low groans and whispered words of sex poured over her from both sides, the affection in their tones even now warming her from within. Surrounded by their heat, penetrated in both openings, and with their words of praise and encouragement surrounding her, Savannah knew she'd never be happy anywhere else.

Hayes pressed against the inner walls of her ass, groaning and clenching the hand covering her breast.

"I can't wait to take this ass. Damn, you're responsive. So sweet. I want you naked and in my bed every night."

Her body tightened, every muscle quivering. The fullness in both openings made her more aware of her slit than ever, as though nothing mattered except Wyatt's cock and the devious fingers Hayes pushed inside her.

Her body no longer felt like her own, trembling in their arms and jerking uncontrollably.

Wyatt groaned and surged deep, his voice like broken glass.

"Yes, darlin'. Just let go. We've got you. Hell."

Her cries sounded desperate and wild and nothing at all like her as her body gathered and, like a dam breaking, the pressure inside her burst free.

Her legs dropped, becoming stiff and jerky as her orgasm washed over her in huge, pleasure-filled swells. Grateful that Wyatt and Hayes held her securely, she couldn't hold back her cries as her body tightened, making her bottom burn around the fingers Hayes stroked slowly in and out of her.

They murmured to her and to each other, their hands running over her easing her gradual descent.

Wyatt's eyes raked over her body, his expression hard and unrelenting.

"Never letting you go. Never! You'll stay if I have to tie. You. To. The. Bed."

Each thrust accompanying his words seemed to fill her more than the last.

Hard muscle tightened all around her as Wyatt thrust deep and groaned, his big body shuddering against hers.

"Christ, I'm going crazy just thinking about that."

His cock jumped as he came inside her, his groan hoarse and even more desperate sounding than before.

As she held on, Hayes leaned over her, covering her back from behind and cocooning her in warmth. With slow deliberation, he withdrew his fingers from her bottom, leaving it prickling with awareness.

"I'm not a man who likes to talk about feelings, so pay attention because I may not ever say it again. Just because you don't hear the words very often doesn't mean I don't feel them. I love you, Savannah, and I'm not a man who loves lightly. I want to marry you and spend my life with you. I can't make it any plainer than that."

Kissing her hair, he straightened and reached out to untie her wrists, catching her against him as Wyatt withdrew from her and set her on her feet.

"I'll do everything in my power to keep you here, but if I can't, I'll follow you."

Surprised that they dressed her, Savannah held on to Wyatt's shoulders, blinking back the tears that stung her eyes, tears caused by her weakness and their gentleness as they cared for her.

"My uncle and his friends would ruin everything you're all trying to build. I couldn't live with that."

Hayes stopped her beside his horse, mounted, and reached down to pull her up in front of him in a show of strength that impressed the hell out of her.

"If we can't handle people like your uncle, we wouldn't last long here anyway. Haven't you noticed how the men in Tulsa sidestep us? They don't know what to make of us, so they shun us. Half the women look at us with interest and the other half spit on the sidewalk when we walk past. Maggie's well protected every time we go there, and you will be, too."

As they started out, Hayes pulled her close, his big hand spread over her belly.

"We may have already made a baby with you."

The thought of carrying their child filled her with joy. Bubbles of happiness burst throughout her, making her almost giddy.

"If you don't get that look off your face, I'm taking you again."

Turning to meet Wyatt's grin, she couldn't hold back a smile.

"I know Eb and Jeremiah both think of Maggie's baby as their own. Would the two of you feel the same way?"

Wyatt blinked, frowning. "Of course. Hayes and I will share everything concerning you, Savannah. We'll be a family. I know it'll take some time to get used to—for all of us—but we've seen the results. It's worth it."

Letting herself slump against Hayes, she smiled again when his arm tightened around her. They rode in silence for several minutes, both men apparently lost in their own thoughts.

Not long after the ranch came into view, Savannah turned to look up at Hayes's stonelike features.

"If you want to marry me so much, why did you avoid me after I put the stuff in your food?"

If possible, his expression became even harder.

"Because Eb told us what happened between him and your uncle—and what your uncle tried to do to you."

Stiffening, Savannah stared straight ahead. "He had no right to tell you that."

Cursing, Hayes caught her before she could fall.

"It's our right to know the threats to you, Savannah."

Careful not to look at either of them, Savannah rubbed her arms against the chill that went through her.

"So you had to think about whether or not you still wanted me after learning that my uncle wanted to make me his whore?"

With a jerk of the reins, Hayes brought his horse to a standstill, his hands clenching.

"Say that word in reference to yourself again, and you'll get a spanking that'll keep you from sitting for months."

Gripping her jaw, he turned her to face him.

"Only the thought of leaving you kept me from riding all the way back to Kansas City and killing him. I was too furious to be around. Wyatt and I spent the day trying to come to grips with the fact that your own uncle tried to rape you."

From behind, Wyatt slid a hand over her hair.

"It made us crazy, Savannah. We were so enraged, we were scared to touch you. We sure as hell didn't want to do anything that would remind you of your uncle."

Incredibly touched, Savannah reached up to cup Hayes's strong jaw.

"Nothing you could do could remind me of him."

She stiffened at the sound of a rider approaching, sucking in a breath at the arm that tightened around her middle as Hayes used his other hand to draw his gun and turn his horse, shielding her with his body.

Wyatt let out a breath. "It's Phoenix."

Blade's younger brother called out to them about the same time.

"You have Savannah with you?"

Hayes turned his horse back and started forward. "Yes. Why?"

"Maggie's having her baby. She wants Savannah. Hurry. She's been calling for her for over an hour."

Chapter Nine

Still wiping her hands, Savannah walked out onto the back porch, surprised to see that the sun had risen.

Also surprising was the number of men who'd gathered, some sitting on the porch, some standing around the yard. They all straightened, rushing toward her as she came out.

Hayes reached her first.

"Well? We heard crying."

Despite the fact that she was so tired she felt as though she could sleep for a week, Savannah grinned.

"It's a healthy baby boy."

Amid whoops and back slapping, Hayes and Wyatt led her to a seat and before she knew it, Duke came forward and placed a plate of hot food on her lap.

"Maggie all right?"

Savannah smiled her appreciation, for the food and for his concern for her friend.

"Maggie's fine. Just tired. I'm sure she's going to be hungry, too, in a bit. She worked hard."

Duke nodded. "Already got a plate hot for her. Just waiting for the bosses to come down."

Without thinking, Savannah leaned into the hand Wyatt threaded through her hair.

"One of them should be down soon. They're fascinated with little Ace and can't wait to show him off. Ah, there's one of the proud papas now."

Smiling as the others all gathered around Jeremiah and the newest addition to the ranch, Savannah picked up a biscuit and started to nibble on it, too tired to make the effort to eat anything else.

Washing it down with some of Duke's strong coffee, she sat back, enjoying watching a group of such hard-nosed cowboys brought to their knees by the sight of a newborn baby.

The sun warmed the large porch, while the house protected it from most of the brisk wind, leaving her pleasantly warm and drowsy.

Absently listening to them, she closed her eyes and leaned back, a little surprised by the wistfulness she heard in their voices. Their whispered words of congratulations and concern for Maggie swirled around her and seemed to come from farther and farther away.

The hand in her hair began a slow and gentle massage that worked wonders on the headache that she hadn't realized she had until now.

Jolting at the slide of hands under her, she snapped her eyes open to meet Hayes's.

"W–What—"

He lifted her high against his chest, turned and sat down again, holding her on his lap, his big body blocking out the rest of the wind and making her even warmer.

"Sh. Come on and eat a little something, and then you can go to sleep."

* * * *

Wrapping his arms around Savannah, Hayes adjusted her to a more comfortable position against his chest, savoring the feel of having her in his arms.

His cock stirred at her nearness, a fact that no longer surprised him, but for now it remained a pleasant arousal. Pushing her damp hair back from her forehead, he smiled down at her, knowing just how quickly a look from her could turn mild need into a raging hunger.

Letting his gaze move over her face, he took in the dark circles under her eyes and the paleness of her skin. Concerned at the fatigue fogging her eyes, he loaded a spoon with the beef stew Duke had made from the plate Wyatt held.

"You didn't even feel Wyatt take the plate from you before you spilled it. You're exhausted, darlin'."

Her eyes, dark and clouded with sleep, opened slightly.

"Just a little tired. Did you see the baby? He's beautiful. The whole thing was amazing. Poor Eb and Jeremiah. I think they wished they could have the baby themselves. They kept apologizing for all the pain they put Maggie through."

Taking in Wyatt's worried frown, he tapped Savannah's lips with the spoon, his stomaching clenching at the thought of seeing Savannah in pain.

"I think I can understand that. Come on. Eat a little something and then you can get some sleep."

Aware of the other men watching, Hayes lifted his head, keeping his expression cold and daring them to make some remark about the way he was taking care of Savannah. He didn't care what they thought. Savannah was his, and she damned well needed to be cared for.

Duke watched closely, his eyes filled with pain and memories. Meeting Hayes's eyes, he inclined his head.

"Women need to be coddled now and then. Lets them know they've got someone to count on—someone who's paying attention."

Shocked that the other men nodded in approval, Hayes shared a look with Wyatt and gave his attention to Savannah.

"Come on. Duke'll be upset if he finds out you didn't eat his stew."

Alarmed at her paleness, Hayes put the spoon to her mouth again.

"You've gone too long without eating, and you didn't get any sleep last night."

Savannah smiled, a weak smile that tugged at his heart and brought all of his protective instincts to the surface.

"I'll bet you stayed up all night, too, didn't you?" She opened her mouth around the spoon, looking up at him while she chewed.

Hayes stilled, taken aback by the surge of protectiveness and possessiveness that feeding her created inside him. At that moment, he knew he wouldn't be satisfied until she belonged to him in every way it was possible for a woman to belong to a man. He wanted her with a fierceness that went far beyond a desire for sex.

He wanted to protect her, to take care of her in ways he'd never even considered. He wanted to make her happy, wanted her to come to him whenever she had a problem or just when she felt sad. He wanted the right to be the one to deal with her anger, and wanted her to fight with him when she felt the need.

He wanted to know all of her secrets, those of her mind and her body.

Seeing her this way, tired, disheveled, and out of sorts, he realized he loved her far more than even he'd suspected. It went beyond just caring for her and wanting to share his life with her. It went beyond lust.

He'd spent the entire night picturing her heavy with the child he and Wyatt would plant inside her, if they hadn't already. A sense of destiny, of finding exactly what he hadn't even realized he'd been looking for, came over him, and he knew then that his life had changed forever.

He wanted to have it all from her. He needed to give her everything he was.

Pride in her filled him, just as strong as his love.

She was his, and he would die to keep her safe.

"Hayes?"

Snapping back to the present, Hayes dipped the spoon back into the stew, struggling to remember what they'd been talking about.

"Eat. You're tired. I managed to get a little sleep last night. Marshals learn to sleep whenever and wherever they can."

He held the spoon to her mouth again, aware of the attention from the other men.

"Open."

Savannah smiled up at him, making his heart swell. He'd learned long ago that a smile from her could brighten his day, but this was different.

His heart swelled with love for her, along with a strong sense of responsibility.

Looking up, he saw the worry in Jeremiah's eyes and understood why the other man kept looking up toward the bedroom where Maggie lay.

It didn't surprise him when Jeremiah left with the baby after only a few minutes and headed back inside, yelling over his shoulder that he would be back for Maggie's plate.

Everything Eb and Jeremiah wanted to do here and every one of the rules they'd set in place now made perfect sense. Just thinking about all the sorts of danger that Savannah could face every day sent a chill down his spine.

Hell, no wonder Eb and Jeremiah wanted to tie Maggie to the bed. No wonder they watched her like hawks and why it was so important for her to understand that she had to obey the others when it came to her protection.

Christ, he broke out in a cold sweat, just imagining the ways she and Savannah could get hurt.

"You're lying."

Hayes met Savannah's drooping eyes again and refilled the spoon. "Lying about what, darlin'?"

He shot a glance at Wyatt, unsurprised to see that his best friend seemed even more fascinated by Savannah than usual.

"I'd bet that neither one of you slept at all last night."

He leaned into the hand she laid on his cheek, not caring about the other men's stares.

"Careful. Calling your husband a liar is a good way to get yourself turned over his knee."

Savannah wrinkled her nose. "You're not my husband, and I thought you only gave a spanking if I put myself in danger." She took another bite and closed her eyes as though the effort of keeping them open proved to be more than she could manage.

"Besides, a woman shouldn't get spanked for speaking the truth." She curled into him, her loose fist against his chest.

Hayes frowned as her words slurred, and he dropped the spoon in the bowl, handing it to Wyatt.

"You're right, honey. Nothing wrong with speaking the truth."

Looking up at Wyatt, he settled back in the chair.

"She's asleep. We'll let her sleep for a while and make sure she eats something when she gets up."

Duke, who'd settled in a chair a few feet away, nodded. "I'll keep something hot, but it looks like she might just sleep until supper." He paused, as though weighing his words. Sitting forward, he kept his voice low.

"You take care of her real good. I worried when I first came here and heard about the rules set up for the women. Figured they weren't much better than laws anywhere else. Not the same at all, though. Women need to be taken care of, no matter how much they might object. Tiny little things, aren't they?"

He came to his feet, all six and a half feet of him.

"Guess I might stay after all."

Keeping his voice at a whisper, Wyatt lifted a brow. "Didn't know you were planning to leave."

Duke stretched, the muscles in his arms and chest rippling at the movement. Shrugging, he met the gazes of several of the other men as they went past, obviously on their way back to their chores.

"Depended on what happened with the women." He waited until the last of the ranch hands left the porch before glancing at Savannah.

"Women are tough in some ways and so frail in others. Scary. They sure as hell need men to protect them."

Something in Duke's tone caught his attention.

"You sound like you speak from experience."

Duke stared out over the yard in silence, the grief on his face unmistakable. He didn't speak for so long that Hayes figured he didn't plan to answer.

Hayes turned his attention back to Savannah, laying a hand over her waist and wondering if she already carried his child.

"Had a wife once."

Hayes looked up, not sure if he'd heard Duke right.

"Did you say you were married?"

Duke kept staring out at the yard, his face a mask of grief and despair.

"Yeah. Shy little thing. Got into some trouble in town with a couple of outlaws who were robbing the bank. I came running from the livery when I heard her scream. He held a gun to her head and was dragging her away. I tried to convince him otherwise. That's how I got this, from one of his friends."

He gestured toward the scar that ran from his temple to his jaw and then pointed toward Hayes's own scar.

"You know how that feels."

Hayes clenched his jaw, imagining how he would feel if another man threatened Savannah.

"Mine was a bounty that pulled a fast one. Hasn't happened since. What happened to you must have been hell. What happened?"

Duke shrugged. "I was young and too inexperienced and took a knife to a gunfight. Never did care for guns." Sighing, he turned, looking from Hayes to Wyatt to Savannah.

His eyes lingered on her features, but Hayes had the feeling he didn't see them at all, his mind filled with memories of his dead wife.

"Bastard took my knife from me and cut me. Then, he shot me and took her. Found her body three days later. Such a little thing. Didn't have a chance at all." His voice broke and he looked away, moving across the porch. "I'd better get started on supper."

Watching Duke go down the steps and cross the yard, Hayes pulled Savannah tighter against him, easing up when she whimpered in her sleep.

Wyatt ran a hand over Savannah's hair, lifting it abruptly when she stirred.

"Hell, no wonder he's so cold. No man should have to go through that. I can't imagine having something like that happen to Savannah. Look at her. She's so tired. Jeremiah said she did great last night, keeping everyone calm and making things easier for Maggie. He said he and Eb weren't ready to see Maggie in that kind of pain."

Sitting back, Wyatt stared after Duke.

"Can't believe he went through that."

"And promised himself he'd never marry again."

Hayes and Wyatt both lifted their heads as Hawke Royal appeared from around the side of the house, making his way toward them.

The eldest of the three Royal brothers glanced at Savannah as he paused at the bottom of the steps and leaned against the railing. The brief flash of wistfulness in his hooded eyes disappeared almost as soon as it appeared, surprising Hayes that it had shown at all.

Taking the knife from its holder at his waist, Hawke studied it thoughtfully, turning it back and forth and letting the sun glint off the blade.

"Never saw anyone as good with a knife as Duke. It took me close to a year, but I got out of him in bits and pieces that after his wife was killed, he practiced every day." He put his own knife away, his lips twitching. "Carries at least a dozen with him at all times."

Hayes lifted a brow. "Is that a fact?" He carried knives himself, but usually only four or five.

Wyatt settled back in his seat, toying with Savannah's braid.

"Kind of understand why he doesn't want to care for a woman again, but speaking from experience, it doesn't seem we have much of a choice. Can't imagine my life without her now."

Hayes nodded, understanding just how empty his life would be without Savannah.

"I don't know what I'd do if anything happened to her. I understand now why Eb and Jeremiah worry so much. Anything could happen. Hell. It gives me chills just thinking about it."

He ran a hand over her arm, his chest tightening when she sighed and snuggled closer.

"We'll keep this town safe. We'll uphold the rules and run all troublemakers out of town. We'll just have to hope it's enough."

He looked up, staring toward the building Duke had gone into.

"Who knows? Maybe with all the women Eb and Jeremiah are sending for, Duke will find a new wife. It'll do him good to have a woman again."

Hawke's expression hardened.

"Not all of us want a woman in our lives, but we'll help protect yours."

Hayes shared a look with Wyatt, wondering if the big Indian realized just how much of his hunger for a woman of his own showed.

"You saying you're not interested in having a wife to come home to?"

Hawke straightened, stiffening. "No sense in wanting something you can't have. No woman is going to want to tie herself to a half-breed. I'll just help Blade and Phoenix protect their women."

Wyatt raised a brow. "Aren't they half-breeds, too? If you don't think a woman would want you, what makes you believe they'll marry?"

Hawke glared at him over his shoulder.

"It doesn't seem to make any difference to them. They're too damned hardheaded to accept the truth."

Turning, he walked back the way he came.

Wyatt waited until he left before turning to Hayes, his lips twitching. "Talk about hardheaded. I'd love to see him brought to his knees by a sweet little thing."

Hayes cradled Savannah closer when she shivered in an effort to warm her. He turned to ask Wyatt to go get her a blanket, just as Eb came through the door with one. Between them, they covered her and Hayes settled back, smiling when she burrowed as close to him as she could possibly get.

"Thanks. I should really take her up to bed, but—"

Eb grinned tiredly.

"But you're not quite ready to let go of her yet." He stared after Hawke, his eyes dark with concern.

"You're right about him being hardheaded. I hope one of the mail-order brides knocks his knees out from under him."

Hayes laughed, careful not to wake Savannah.

"I'd pay money to see that."

Eb turned back to him and grinned again.

"Lot of people said the same thing to me about two U.S. Marshals not too long ago. Didn't think two such hard, cold men would be taken in by a woman."

Before Hayes could reply, Eb's expression became somber, worry and fury swirling in his eyes.

"Got a telegram from Pa. The Reverend Perry bought a train ticket and left Kansas City, but not before being joined by a posse of his friends who are just like him. He's on his way here."

Hayes smiled coldly, adrenaline racing through his veins at the chance to end this thing and begin his life with Savannah. "Looking forward to it."

Chapter Ten

After making sure that Maggie and the babe slept soundly, Savannah walked outside and stretched. Lifting her face into the warm sun even as she pulled the shawl closer against the cool air, she made her way across the yard, looking forward to a cup of Duke's strong coffee.

It had been several days since Maggie gave birth, and they'd fallen into somewhat of a routine.

Each day, her desire to be a part of such a place, to have the love of two men unlike any she'd ever met before, grew stronger until she could no longer imagine a life anywhere else.

Texas seemed farther away every day.

Even though she knew both men had been working hard every day to finish their house, she couldn't help scanning the yard for Wyatt and Hayes. Not expecting to see either one of them, she paused as Hayes straightened from the fence he'd been leaning against and turned toward her.

Sucking in a breath at the sight of him, Savannah pulled the shawl closer and stood frozen in place, wondering if she'd ever get used to the heightened awareness and hunger each time she saw him.

With the aura of danger surrounding him, and a tall, muscular figure that she saw in her dreams, Hayes stood watching her, his eyes searching. With his hands on his hips and his hooded gaze raking over her, he made an imposing sight, one that she would remember her entire life.

Struck by his presence, she could only stare at him, hardly able to believe such a man would want her.

As always, need welled inside her, but she'd begun to notice a change in her desire for both of them.

It stemmed from much more than just physical need. Bolder now, and more intense, the need now merged with emotion and strengthened, becoming far more potent than ever.

Her skin tingled now with the need to feel his hands on her, to be held against him. She yearned for his kiss and for the soft tone of voice meant just for her.

Staring into his eyes, she felt the familiar flutters in her stomach and the familiar tingling of her nipples and clit. Her pussy tightened in anticipation, releasing her juices to coat her thighs.

Her heart raced with love and excitement, beating so hard she wondered sometimes how it didn't jump right out of her chest.

A gust of wind blew her hair in her face, momentarily blocking her view of him, and she brushed it aside impatiently, not wanting to miss a thing.

Grabbing it in her fist, she held it back, her pulse tripping at the emotion in his hooded gaze.

Her breath caught at the love and desire shining in his eyes, something she wondered if she'd ever get used to. Ever since the day Maggie had her baby, Wyatt and Hayes had looked at her with an intensity that hadn't been there before.

While neither had touched her in any intimate way since then, their eyes seemed sharper than ever as though neither one of them wanted to miss a single thing.

Hayes held her gaze for what seemed like forever before lowering it, allowing it to rake over her, leaving a trail of heat in its wake. Holding out his hand, he met her eyes again.

"Come here, Savannah."

Shivering at his silky tone, Savannah started forward before she'd even decided if she would or not.

Once she did and saw the flash of love and satisfaction, nothing on earth could have prevented her from closing the distance between them.

Hayes reached for her, wrapping a hand around her wrist and tugging, catching her as she fell against him.

Burying her face against his chest, she breathed in the scent of him, the scent of leather and sunshine, a scent she would have recognized in the dark.

Blinking back tears at all she would be missing, she wrapped her arms around his waist, snuggling into him as his arms tightened around her.

Running a hand over her hair, Hayes bent, touching his lips to her temple.

"I woke up reaching for you, and you weren't there. I don't like waking up without you beside me. I've never even spent the night with you, but I reach for you in my sleep."

Savannah blinked back tears, figuring there would be no point in telling him that she reached for both him and Wyatt through the night. Each time she encountered cold bedcovers instead of a warm body, she woke up feeling even colder and emptier.

Choking back a sob, she held on, struggling to compose herself. In an effort to ease the tension, she poked at his hard belly.

"I thought you didn't like to talk about your feelings."

Hayes stilled.

Gripping her shoulders, he held her slightly away from him, his eyes sharp as they searched hers.

"Tell me what's bothering you."

Savannah blinked, wondering how he saw through her so easily, and then smiled at the arrogance that was so much a part of him.

"Most people would have asked me if something was wrong instead of demanding that I tell them."

One of his hands slid up from her shoulder to cup her neck, his thumb tracing the line of her jaw. Holding her gaze, his eyes continued to search hers, the trace of concern in them making her nervous.

He saw too much, and paid far too much attention to her for her to be able to hide anything from him for long.

It made her uneasy, especially after spending her life with no one giving her even a second glance, taking her distance at face value.

Hayes didn't.

"I'm not most people, and I don't have to ask if there's something wrong. I can see it. What is it?"

Tomorrow was Saturday.

Neither Wyatt nor Hayes had made any reference to it for the last few days, but it was there.

They should have been getting married tomorrow, and in a perfect world, they would have.

Savannah's world was far from perfect, a fact she'd had to come to terms with a long time ago.

Forcing a smile, she shrugged and lowered her lashes to avoid his scrutiny.

"I'm just tired and hungry."

His strong fingers gripped her chin, lifting her face to his and searching her features.

"You're lying. You want to try again?"

Scared that he would see the truth, Savannah tried to pull away, but Hayes twisted her hair in a big fist, effectively keeping her there.

"Damn it, Hayes. Let go of me."

"Tell me."

His features appeared to be chiseled from stone, his eyes sharp and hooded. "You might as well learn right now that I won't tolerate lying from you. Ever. Spit it out right now, Savannah."

Savannah had learned to read people early in life, and her experiences with Wyatt and Hayes had taught her a lot about them. Her mind raced with possibilities, finally reaching one that would give him the truth, while at the same time hiding what she needed to hide.

Allowing her eyes to well with tears came easy.

"Oh, Hayes. My uncle's going to show up here and cause so much trouble. He's already made a mess of my life, and now he wants to ruin everything here. I can't even sleep thinking about it."

As she'd expected, Hayes's expression softened, and he gathered her close. Rubbing her back, he held her.

"Don't worry about your uncle. He's in Tulsa right now. He knows that we're going to show up there to get married tomorrow, so he's waiting. He's got a room in the hotel, along with four of the friends he brought with him."

Surprised that he knew so much, Savannah stilled.

"How do you know all that?"

Hayes chuckled, patting her bottom. Straightening, he pushed her hair back and smiled.

"It's my job to know. I don't want you worrying. We'll take care of him when we get there, and then we'll meet up with the preacher. I don't want you to worry about a thing. Your uncle isn't worth the time you spend worrying about him."

Wrapping an arm around her waist, he urged her toward the chow building. "Come on and let's get some food in you, and then you can go back to the house and sleep a little while Maggie's taking her nap. You'll feel better. Then, after supper we can show you your house."

"It's finished?"

Hayes opened the door and ushered her inside. "It will be by tonight. Tomorrow after we get married, we'll pick up the bed. You can order the rest of the furniture later."

Savannah smiled in greeting at several of the men inside, leaning toward Hayes and careful to keep her voice at a whisper.

"You ordered a bed?"

"Damned right. I've taken you on the ground and standing. I want you in my bed where it's soft and there's more room."

He grinned wickedly. "Starting tomorrow, there's no need to get dressed afterward. I can cuddle up to your warm naked body all night long."

Savannah said nothing, knowing she would choke if she tried.

She wouldn't be here tomorrow. She'd already said good-bye to Maggie, and would be leaving here today.

Chapter Eleven

In the hurry to take care of her uncle, Savannah left the ranch right after breakfast and rode straight to Tulsa, stopping only long enough to water her horse.

The knots in her stomach had grown with every mile of her trip here, her eyes wet with tears for the first half of her ride.

She missed Wyatt and Hayes already and kept looking over her shoulder, with both dread and anticipation of finding them closing in on her.

Thinking about facing her uncle and his friends didn't worry her as much as what Wyatt and Hayes would do when they got the note she'd left for them.

Riding the rest of the way, she'd come to the startling realization that she didn't fear her uncle's wrath anymore.

His anger couldn't hold a candle to the fury she would have faced if she saw Wyatt and Hayes again.

Riding in complete darkness for the last several miles sharpened Savannah's senses even more, making her jittery and jumpy and tightening the cold knots in her stomach until it hurt.

By the time she arrived at the outskirts of town, she rode with one hand on the butt of her gun.

She kept her eyes moving, her awareness of her surroundings heightened in a way they hadn't been while she'd been in Desire. She realized how much she'd trusted others to keep her safe and trusted their instincts, while she'd hardly paid attention to her own.

After years spent on guard, she'd relaxed around them, probably a lot more than she should have.

With the realization of how alert she had to be from now on, Savannah straightened in the saddle and made her way to the livery. Leaving her horse there, she went out, careful to stay in the shadows as she made her way around the building to the other side, the one closest to the hotel.

Trying to appear as nonchalant as possible, she paused, searching the street for any sign of her uncle and his friends.

One friend in particular—one who she wanted to keep away from Hayes and Wyatt at all costs.

A man who'd killed and was proud of it—a man who apparently idolized her uncle and made a deal with him to take care of a little girl so he could ride off with her mother.

Savannah hadn't seen him since the day he'd taken her mother away, laughing and smiling as he loaded her and her bags onto the buckboard.

Her mother hadn't even turned and waved, leaving Savannah crying on the porch, her uncle's firm grip on her shoulders the only thing keeping her from running after her.

She'd never seen her mother again.

Blinking back tears, she pushed aside the gut-wrenching emptiness of being abandoned.

The suddenness of that empty feeling left her knees shaking, along with the knowledge that Wyatt and Hayes had systematically been filling that empty place inside her and she hadn't even realized it.

She had to go back.

She *would* go back to the only people in the world who meant anything to her. She couldn't let her uncle destroy the rest of her life as he'd destroyed it so far. She deserved to be happy.

She'd found love, and she wanted nothing more than to go back to Wyatt and Hayes and embrace a life she never could have dreamed of.

First, though, she had to deal with her uncle.

Straightening her shoulders, she couldn't stop smiling at the renewed sense of purpose that filled her. Just thinking about Wyatt and Hayes strengthened her. With them in her life, she could face anything.

She pushed away from the side of the building, keeping her hand on her gun as she made her way toward the steps that led to the hotel she'd stayed in only a few weeks earlier.

It felt like a lifetime ago.

Knowing that her uncle would have already finished his evening meal, she ignored her own growling stomach and started toward the front door of the hotel. Only willpower kept her stride steady when she saw the five of them sitting on the front porch, just seconds before she heard the deep voice of the man she hated almost as much as she hated her uncle.

As she'd expected, Ronny Callister saw her first.

She knew, because she'd been watching him, knowing him to be the most dangerous in the bunch.

He smiled in that way he had that she supposed he thought was charming.

"Well, if it ain't the runaway whore. I guess you *are* just like your mother. Maybe I should have come back for you after your mother died."

Fighting back nausea, Savannah stopped, leaning against the post in what she hoped appeared to be a relaxed pose.

Forcing a smile, she glanced at her uncle as he came to his feet, but kept her attention on Callister, thankful that the lamps lit outside the hotel made it possible to see him clearly.

"If it ain't the two-bit outlaw. You kill any more men to take their wives, or are you just killing women when you get tired of them?"

Pleased by the anger that flashed in Callister's eyes, she kept him in her line of vision and nodded in her uncle's direction, not bothering to hide her disgust. "Hello, Reverend. I heard you were looking for me. What do you want?"

She glanced briefly at the others, who crossed their arms over their chests, adopting looks of disapproval, but none of them had the courage to say anything. Realizing they were the harmless windbags they'd always been, she dismissed them, concentrating on her uncle and Callister.

Her uncle got to his feet, his face already red.

"Savannah Perry, what on earth were you thinking? You're coming home with me on the next train, and I don't want to hear a word about it."

Savannah couldn't help it. She laughed.

"Hell, I remembered you as being scarier than that. Must be the company I've been keeping. Next to them, you seem much smaller."

Straightening to her full height, she stood toe-to-toe with her uncle for the first time in years. She grinned, enjoying the feeling of power immensely.

"Yep. Definitely smaller. I'm not coming home with you. Kansas City's your home, not mine, and I won't ever be going back there again. You have a nice trip back, though."

Turning, she kept Callister in her sights, realizing her mistake almost immediately. She barely bit back a gasp when her uncle reached out a hand and grabbed her forearm, sinking his nails into her.

Surprising at his strength, she winced before she could hide it, furious at herself when he smiled coldly.

"Don't take that tone with me, young lady. You're going back to Kansas City with me if I have to tie you up and drag you with me."

Callister came to his feet, his hand resting lightly on the gun he wore at his hip.

"And I'm here to make sure your friends don't cause any trouble."

"Too late. Trouble's already here. Get your hands off my woman."

Surprised at the voice that came out of the darkness, one she barely recognized as Wyatt's, Savannah stopped struggling against her uncle's hold and turned toward the direction Wyatt's voice had come from. Her heart leapt when he stepped forward into the light, his expression hard and unrelenting.

She'd heard Wyatt angry before, but she'd never heard quite that tone. Even though it hadn't been directed at her, a chill went up her spine, the menace and deadly intent in it unmistakable.

Seeing him standing there with a gun in each hand, his legs braced slightly apart, Savannah sucked in a breath. She found it hard to believe that the man in front of her was the same man who'd given her such pleasure. She couldn't believe that the same hands that spanked her, hands that held her so tightly to him as he took her, were the same hands holding guns on five men right now.

Some part of her had known he was a dangerous man. After all, he was a U.S. Marshal.

She just hadn't seen him in action before—and she'd underestimated just how brave and deadly he could be.

Knowing she had to do something fast, Savannah took advantage of her uncle's surprise and yanked her arm from his hold, moving clumsily down the steps as she turned to face him again.

Unable to deny that she felt much safer with Wyatt at her back, she sucked in a breath when Callister's guns cleared his holster. Holding out a hand toward Wyatt, she kept her eyes steady on the outlaw's.

"It's all right, Wyatt. My uncle understands that I won't be going with him."

Not wanting Wyatt to be taken unaware, she raised her voice to make sure he could hear her.

"The one on the left is Ronny Callister. He's killed quite a few men, but never gets convicted. He kills the husbands of women he wants and gets the women to testify on his behalf, telling the judge that he was with them at the time of the murder."

Savannah shrugged, turning to glance at Wyatt. "I guess that part's true."

Facing Callister, she jumped when Wyatt spoke again, his voice coming from much closer than it had before.

"I know all about Callister, but I don't think your uncle realizes that Callister plans to take you with him long before you get to Kansas City."

Her uncle's friends, all but Callister, sat back down, obviously shaken. Longtime friends, they usually backed her uncle in everything, but evidently not when on the wrong side of two loaded pistols.

Giving each of them a dirty look, her uncle glanced at his dangerous friend, his eyes full of unease.

"Don't be ridiculous. Ronny wouldn't do such a thing to me."

Callister said nothing, waiting until her uncle turned back to her before shooting Savannah a smile—one filled with evil intent.

Oblivious, her uncle raised his voice to be heard by the crowd who'd gathered, clearly in his element.

"Well, looks like we got a standoff. Of course, since Savannah is my niece, she'll be coming home with me where she belongs."

Another man came forward, one she'd seen in town a few times before. Drawing his gun, he stepped up behind Wyatt.

"I recognize you. You're one of those troublemakers in *Desire*. I think the lady needs to go with her uncle and you need to go back to—"

His words stopped abruptly at the sound of a gun cocking right behind him, one drawn and cocked before she could even get hers out of the holster.

Hayes stepped out from the shadows, tapping the man who held a gun to Wyatt against the side of his head with his gun.

"Drop the pistol. Savannah, step closer to Wyatt."

The demand in his voice couldn't be ignored.

The other man dropped his gun into the dirt at the same time Savannah moved, holding her gun at her side.

Another man stepped out of the shadows, and then another.

"I think you men ought to move on. It appears the lady's kin is here to take her back where she belongs. The men in Tulsa stick together."

Another voice sounded, one she recognized from the Tyler ranch, just seconds before Hawke Royal appeared from around the side of the hotel closest to her.

"The men of Desire stick together, too, and we protect our women. Savannah's one of ours."

In her entire life, Savannah had never felt as if she belonged somewhere as much as she did in that moment.

She smiled gratefully at the scowling Indian, noting that her uncle's eyes kept darting between them.

Her uncle, though, didn't appear to give up easily. "Savannah, if you go with these men, you're going to hell. You need to come back home with me, and everything'll be just like before. The children there need you. The people there need you."

Savannah tried not to think of the nice people she'd left behind. She would miss many of them, especially the children she read to, but she knew she could never be happy there again.

"This is what *I* need. I'm happy here."

When Blade Royal came around the other side of the hotel and Will Prentice and Adam Marshall, two of the ranch hands she'd met only briefly, came up behind Wyatt, even Callister looked uneasy.

The other three men with her uncle looked like they wished they were someplace else.

Hawke and Will pumped shells into the chambers of the shotguns they held on Callister, their hands steady as they stared down the barrels at him.

"Savannah, get over here right now." Wyatt's voice held an edge it hadn't held before.

The lawman who feared nothing was scared—for her.

Dropping her arm to her side, she started toward him, keeping Callister in her sights.

"No."

Callister moved faster than she would have expected, firing his gun as he ran toward her, knocking her uncle down as he passed him.

Savannah froze as the sounds of several shots being fired in rapid succession filled the air, feeling her gun jerk in her hand.

She saw the look of shock on Callister's face right before he clutched his chest, but she saw nothing else as a hard body slammed into her from behind, sending her to the ground.

Hard.

She heard shouts as men came out from everywhere, but with Wyatt on top of her, she couldn't see a thing.

"Stay still, Savannah. Christ. Are you hurt? Don't move."

Crushed under his weight, Savannah struggled to get enough air.

"I can't breathe. Let me up."

"Is she hit? Move. Let me see her."

Recognizing the panic in Hayes's tone, Savannah pushed against Wyatt, taking the time to run her hands over his warm chest as she did.

"I'm not hurt. Just let me up. Oh, God."

She looked up in time to see her uncle pushing the lifeless body of Callister off of him, not quite steady as he came to his feet.

Wyatt and Hayes alternately hugged her to them and pushed her away, turning her and running their hands over her.

"She's not hit. Hell, I slammed her hard. Be careful."

Hayes groaned and pulled her close, burying his face in her hair as chaos reigned all around them.

"Nothing seems to be broken, but there's not enough light to see her. Get her inside so we can check her out. I'll take care of things out here."

Will Prentice stepped forward, his eyes full of concern as they moved over her.

"Is she all right?"

Hayes rubbed her back. "I don't know. Wyatt's going to take her in while I deal with the sheriff. Holster your gun, Savannah."

Savannah looked down, just now remembering that she'd fired a shot. Looking up into Wyatt's concerned face, she dug in her heels when he tried to pull her toward the hotel.

"Wyatt. I fired a shot. Oh, God." She looked at where Callister lay unmoving, his blood dripping down the steps of the hotel porch.

"I killed him. Oh, God. I killed a man."

The horror of what she'd done seemed to drain all of her energy. Her knees went numb, and she could no longer keep herself upright. Collapsing, she didn't even have the strength to grab for Wyatt.

Thankful that he caught her, she looked up into his face, seeing his mouth move, but the roaring in her head made it impossible to make out what he said.

She looked down at her hand, surprised to see that she no longer held the gun. She wanted to ask what had happened to it, but couldn't find the words.

Lifting her head, she stared in the direction of where Callister had lain, but saw nothing and thought she'd gone blind for a moment, until she heard a voice and realized that Will Prentice wore all black and blocked her view of the steps of the hotel.

Wyatt's curse penetrated the fog surrounding her, and she found herself lifted into his arms.

Closing her eyes against the dizziness, she became more aware of the voices around her, some she recognized from the ranch and others she didn't.

Even with her eyes closed and her face buried into Wyatt's coat, Savannah saw nothing but the shocked look on Callister's face when she'd killed him.

* * * *

Wyatt kept his body between Savannah and her uncle as he carried her into the hotel.

Will led the way, pointing to a group of chairs in the lobby. "Why don't you sit there with her? I'll scrounge up some rooms."

Nodding his thanks, Wyatt sat, holding Savannah close. Closing his eyes, he saw her again, putting herself between him and Callister and drawing her gun. He knew the vision would give him nightmares for weeks to come.

Pushing her hair back, he fisted a hand in it to pull her head back from his chest. "Honey, can you look at me?"

She'd been too quiet ever since the shooting, and it scared the hell out of him. The tears wetting her cheeks scared him even more.

"Savannah?"

Holding on to his coat, she lifted her pain-filled eyes to his.

"I killed him. I killed Callister."

Wyatt smiled and began to rock her. "No, you didn't. He's alive and on his way to the jail right now. The doc'll see to him, and he can spend the next several years behind bars."

Savannah blinked and sat up, still weak enough to need his support.

"No. I fired. I shot him."

Will came back with a handful of keys. Kneeling beside her, he grinned.

"Honey, you couldn't hit the side of a barn. You shot out the lamp at the end of the porch. Almost hit me. Got some room keys. We'll all stay for the night and head home after the wedding tomorrow."

Wyatt bit back his jealousy when Savannah grabbed Will's arm before the other man could rise.

Her clumsy movements as she struggled to sit up tugged at Wyatt's heart.

"Are you sure? He's not dead? I didn't kill anyone?"

Will chuckled, glancing at Wyatt. "Just a lamp. Of course, it could have been because Wyatt knocked you down."

To Wyatt's horror, Savannah started to cry, her little body shaking and heaving with sobs.

"Oh, hell." Worried for Savannah, he cradled her close, absently noticing the stunned horror on Will's face as he straightened and backed away, holding out his hands as if he didn't know what to do with them.

"What did I say?"

Pleased with his knowledge of his woman and the way her mind worked, he smiled up at Will in relief.

"These are tears of relief that she didn't kill that bastard."

Savannah nodded against his chest and cried harder. "Th–Thank G–God."

After several minutes of rocking her, Wyatt frowned when her tears didn't ease. Worried that she would make herself sick, he met Will's look of helpless frustration, feeling much the same way.

With a conspiratorial smile, Wyatt continued to rub Savannah's back, loving the feel of having her in his arms.

"Of course I'm going to have to redden her bottom for this."

To his amusement—and relief—Savannah stilled, her sobs subsiding.

Hiding a smile, Wyatt sat back, sharing a look with Hayes, who rushed toward them.

"She deserves to be spanked for running away and for thinking she could face her uncle and Callister on her own."

Hayes opened his mouth to say something, but Wyatt shook his head, stopping him.

"She was hysterical because she thought she killed Callister, and then started crying buckets when Will told her she hadn't."

Hayes lifted a brow and nodded in understanding, but his eyes remained dark with concern.

"She should be crying at the thought of being turned over my lap. I don't know what kind of harebrained scheme she thought she was pulling, but not telling us about Callister was damned dangerous. Did she think we didn't know about him? She must not have a hell of a lot of respect for what we do for a living."

Aware that Savannah peered up at him, Wyatt kept his head lifted as Will handed a key to Hayes and moved away.

"It appears we're going to have to work a little harder to earn her respect. When I think of what could have happened to her if we hadn't realized she was gone almost immediately—what if we'd been too late? She put herself in danger instead of being honest with us from the start."

Hayes nodded. "I don't know what she hoped to accomplish by coming here alone, but she's going to learn that doing things like this won't be tolerated."

When Savannah pushed against his chest and sat up, her eyes sparkling with anger, Wyatt wanted to throw back his head and laugh in relief.

"Don't you take that tone with me, Hayes Hawkins. For your information, when I left Desire, I had no intention of coming back."

Surprised at that, Wyatt lifted a brow and tumbled her back against him and started to speak, but Hayes beat him to it.

Hayes knelt in front of her, running a hand over her thigh, his eyes narrowed. "Is that a fact?"

A knot formed in his stomach, not easing even when she eyed Hayes warily and pressed back against him in an apparent need for protection.

She had to learn that she couldn't get away with that. If they hoped to have any chance of keeping her safe, he and Hayes would have to stick together. A haze of red formed in front of his eyes. The danger she faced here had been enough to enrage him, but the thought of her leaving them for good sent his temper soaring.

"I'm not protecting you from Hayes. He's got a right to be angry. So do I. What the hell do you mean about not coming back?"

Savannah shrugged, looking over Wyatt's shoulder toward the front door as though hoping one of the men in the group gathered outside would help her.

"I didn't want my uncle to cause any trouble. Although they didn't say anything today, the men with my uncle know how to stir up trouble and turn people against those who don't think the way they do. They would have upset Maggie and wouldn't have been happy until they had everyone in Tulsa coming to Desire to *save* us. They would have ruined everything you're all trying to build. I told you that."

Wyatt took a deep breath and let it out slowly, determined to control his temper and keep her with them at all costs.

"We don't care what the people here think, and you had no right to leave without saying anything to anyone. It's a good thing Maggie told Eb what you were up to. What if we didn't get here in time? Why didn't you tell us about Callister? There's a damned Wanted poster of him in the sheriff's office."

Savannah's eyes went wide. "There is? How do you know that?"

Wyatt clenched his jaw and counted to ten. "What the hell do you think we do for a living, Savannah? It's our job to know these things. Didn't you think we checked? We've been in contact with the sheriff in Kansas City and with the train station. We knew who was with your uncle and when he left."

Savannah blinked up at him, looking far too fragile.

"You knew and you didn't say anything?"

Hayes tugged her arm, pulling her to her feet, and hauled her against him.

"We didn't want you to worry. It's our job to handle it. Now, about your leaving—"

"I'm not."

Wyatt ran a hand over her soft hair, hardly able to breathe.

"You're not? When did you decide this?"

She looked so adorable and vulnerable when she blushed that he wanted to stick her in his pocket and keep her there.

"When I got here. I realized that I wouldn't be happy anywhere else and that I wasn't going to let my uncle ruin my life any more than he already had. Are you sure Callister's not dead? There were so many shots. Did I hit him?"

Hayes chuckled and lifted her against him.

"No, you hit the lamp. Who taught you how to shoot anyway? You scared the hell out of Will."

Savannah's face turned even redder.

"I only missed because Wyatt knocked me down. How many times did Callister get shot?" Her eyes widened. "Did my uncle get shot, too? I saw him push Callister, but—"

Wyatt took her hand and started up the steps, struck again by how small it felt in his.

"Hayes shot Callister once in the shoulder, and Hawke shot him once the other. All the other shots were Callister's. Your uncle and his friends ducked and didn't get hit at all. Other than shooting my hat off, he missed with all of them. We *do* all know what we're doing, Savannah. Now, we need to talk about how much you deserve to be spanked for what you put us all through."

He had no intention of spanking her, but she didn't have to know that. After what she'd been through, she needed soft words and a lot of cuddling.

Smiling to himself, he started up the steps. He could always bring this up at a later date, and make sure she loved it.

To his horror, Savannah stopped after the first stair, wincing and lifting her face to his, her bottom lip trembling.

"All right, but I'm so sore. Can I take a bath first? You landed on me pretty hard and—"

Feeling like the brute she'd called him many times, Wyatt lifted her into her arms as carefully as he could and hurried up the steps, yelling over his shoulder for a bath for her.

"I'm sorry, honey. Where are you hurt? I should have known better. Damn, you're so delicate."

Hayes hurried ahead of them and opened the door, his expression lined with worry.

"I'll call for the doctor so he can look her over."

"No!"

Savannah held onto Wyatt's arm, looking up at him adoringly, making him feel ten feet tall.

"Please don't call anyone. I don't want anyone else here. Please? I'll be fine. I just need you and Hayes."

Hayes became a flurry of activity, unbuckling his holster and tossing it aside, whipping his jacket off and grabbing a blanket from the bed, wrapping it around Savannah as he sat on the edge of the bed and pulled her onto his lap.

"Don't you worry. No one else will touch you. Wyatt and I will stay right here with you all night."

Savannah lifted adoring eyes to Hayes, her bottom lip sticking out a little farther.

"Thank you so much. You and Wyatt are going to be the best husbands in the world."

Wyatt stilled, narrowing his eyes on the little minx. Her adoring smile and too-sweet tone were suspicious enough, but her last comment convinced him that she was doing her best to get out of a spanking.

He should have realized it sooner. Savannah wouldn't have complained unless she was bleeding from a dozen places or had a bone sticking out somewhere.

Wyatt studied her with Hayes, wondering just when his friend would realize that Savannah had already learned how to play them.

Shaking his head, he went to the door, knowing damned well Savannah would be sore as hell tomorrow after being slammed to the ground.

"I'm going to go check on her bath."

He couldn't stop smiling as he opened the door and went out. Hell, if she wanted to play him that way, he'd consider himself the luckiest man in the word.

Now, he just had to get her to admit that she loved him and life would be perfect.

Chapter Twelve

Yawning, Savannah stretched, feeling better than she'd felt in years. She paused in midstretch, frowning as she tried to remember when she'd *ever* felt this good.

She couldn't think of a single time.

Last night the intimacy between them had been deeper than ever, even though neither one of them had taken her.

"How are you this morning, honey?"

Savannah opened her eyes in time to see Wyatt slide, fully dressed, onto the bed next to her. She smiled, touched by the look of concern in his eyes.

"I'm fine. Wonderful even."

Wishing his clothes and the bedcovers didn't separate them, she ran a hand over his chest.

"I can't believe the things that you and Hayes did last night. I'm not used to be taken care of like that."

Running a fingertip over her collarbone, Wyatt smiled at her shiver.

"I think you're going to have to get used to it. It all goes together, Savannah. It's just like the night you helped Maggie deliver the baby. You were so exhausted that you couldn't even keep your eyes open."

He ran his finger lightly under her eye as if remembering the dark circles she'd had there.

"So tired. So strong. So fragile." With a sigh, he sat back, running his fingers over her arm.

Loving the feel of his hard body pressed against hers, she snuggled into him, lifting her face for his kiss, but instead of obliging her, he cupped her jaw, his expression somber.

"Wyatt? Is something wrong?"

Running his thumb over her bottom lip, he took a deep breath and let it out slowly.

Uneasy at his strange mood, she pushed away from him, pulling the covers higher to keep her nakedness covered while searching his features for some sign of whatever made him look at her like he'd been kicked by a bull.

"If you've changed your mind about getting married, just—"

Other than the flash of his eyes and the tightening of his fingers on her jaw, she had no warning of his intentions.

Ripping the covers from her hands, he tossed them aside, revealing her nakedness. The desperation in his touch alarmed her, even more so when he rolled on top of her, pinning her to the bed.

"Don't ever try to hide yourself from me again! Not marry you? I've been sitting here staring at you while you slept, trying to figure out how to tell you how much I love you, and how hard I'll try to make you happy. I've been worried sick about landing on you last night and wondering if I broke something that doesn't show."

His jaw clenched as his eyes moved over her body.

"Damn it, you've got bruises all over you. After I told you that we wouldn't hurt you—hell. Look what I did to you."

Savannah blinked as he cursed soundly, reaching for him when he stood abruptly. She missed and scrambled to her knees, shaken and incredibly touched that he would be so concerned about a few bruises.

Glancing down, she noticed a fairly large bruise on her hip where she'd landed and a few little ones on her legs, but nothing more.

"Wyatt! What are you talking about? You saved my life. I'd rather have a few bruises on my legs than a bullet in me."

Wyatt cursed and turned back to her, stilling when he saw her naked and on her knees.

"Damn, you're beautiful." Rubbing a hand over his face, he looked away. "I'm sorry, Savannah. I'm not good at this, and I'm messing it up. I can track outlaws. I'm a quick draw and excellent shot. I can fight with the best of them. I've been called cold, ruthless, heartless, and just plain damned *mean*."

Staring down at the floor, he rubbed his eyes, his shoulders slumping for the first time since she'd met him.

"I can pleasure you. I can protect you." Bleak eyes met hers.

"I just don't know if I can give you the tenderness that you need— the tenderness someone like you deserves. You're out of your element here. Just like Maggie. Look at you. Instead of being wrapped in silk and lace, you're getting married to us in pants and covered with bruises—bruises I gave you when I promised not to hurt you. Hell."

After the night of tenderness he and Hayes had both showed her, she couldn't believe he would even think such a thing.

Going on feminine instinct, Savannah kept her eyes on Wyatt's as she shuffled closer, hiding a smile when his eyes widened and then narrowed as they moved over her body.

"So, you think that I'm too fragile to handle a few bruises?" Trusting her instincts, Savannah ran her fingers lightly over the bruises and higher, stroking her abdomen and purposely drawing Wyatt's attention to her mound.

The delicious tingling she'd come to expect had moisture leaking from her to coat her thighs as his gaze lingered there as though transfixed.

Letting a pout creep into her voice, she slid her hands to the place between her breasts, surprised and delighted that touching herself in front of him seemed to arouse both of them. It also gave her a sense of power, something she'd never really felt before, even when on her own.

Curious to see how far she could go with it, she pouted. "Or maybe you just think I'm ugly when I'm bruised and you don't want me anymore."

A muscle worked in Wyatt's jaw as his eyes followed the movement of her hand.

"Yes. No. Of course not. I meant, uh, that I hated that I bruised you." He spoke in a monotone, obviously distracted. He licked his lips, meeting her eyes briefly before following the movement of her hands again.

Fighting her own arousal, and the memory of the way he'd licked his lips after using his mouth on her the night before, Savannah sighed as loudly as she could. It earned her a brief glance from Wyatt before he turned his attention back to her moving hands.

Teasing both of them, she arched her back and let her fingers wander.

"Eb and Jeremiah were still crazy about Maggie when she was heavy with the baby. I guess if a few bruises bother you, then you won't be able to stand looking at me when I'm fat."

Wyatt's eyes lowered to her belly, lingering there for several long moments, his expression of wonder tripping her pulse.

"I can't wait to see you that way. You could already be carrying our child."

The sound of the door opening startled her so badly, she yelped, reaching for the covers to hide her nakedness.

Recognizing Hayes, she breathed a sigh of relief and pressed a hand over her racing heart.

"You scared me."

Raising a brow, he said nothing as he shut the door behind him and glanced at Wyatt. He remained unmoving as though waiting to see what was going on, his eyes lingering on her uncovered breasts before gazing meaningfully at the covers she held in front of her mound.

Uncomfortable now, she sat on her heels and lifted the covers to her shoulders.

"Good morning, Hayes. Wyatt and I were just talking."

Leaning back against the door, Hayes crossed one booted foot over the other.

"Don't let me stop you. I just came to tell you that the preacher'll be ready in an hour, but this looks more important. He'll wait."

Wyatt took a step closer, drawing her attention to the bulge at the front of his pants, which appeared larger than it had been just moments earlier.

"Savannah's got bruises from me knocking her down. She thinks I think she's ugly because of them." Holding her gaze, he frowned. "At least, I think she does. I lost the thread of the conversation when she started talking about being with child while she was running her hands all over herself."

Hayes lifted a brow, his eyes twinkling. "Then this is definitely more important. Why would you think Wyatt thinks you're ugly?"

The dare in his eyes had her desire flaring, releasing more of her juices and making her nipples tingle. Coming back up to her knees, she covered her mound and ran the fingers of her other hand over her belly and up to the place between her breasts.

"He wouldn't kiss me. He didn't even smile at me."

Hayes whipped his head around to Wyatt, while Wyatt's gaze flew to hers.

Wyatt took a step closer, his eyes narrowing.

"Damn it, I was trying to tell you I love you. Why are you covering yourself?" He gestured toward the blanket she held in front of herself. "I want to see that pussy. I was going to tell you I love you and then kiss you, but you distracted me."

Hayes smiled.

"I'm distracted, but I still want a kiss." He straightened and came toward her, stopping abruptly when Wyatt stuck out an arm.

"Back off. I got a kiss from a warm, naked woman waiting for me."

Wyatt pushed him back, something Savannah hadn't thought possible.

"Too bad. I'm not finished."

To her surprise, Hayes grinned and took a step back.

Wyatt moved to the bed again and knelt at the edge, catching her when the bed shifted and knocked her off balance.

"I love you, Savannah." His eyes darkened with emotion as he held her close. "I probably won't always remember to say it, but I'm going to give you so much lovin', you'll never doubt it. Real lovin', not just sex. Sex is so much more now. Oh, hell, I sound like an idiot. I love you, dammit!"

Savannah could never remember seeing anything so endearing. That this big, tough sheriff could stammer and blush with insecurity about expressing his love for her just melted her heart.

Hayes smiled, winked at her, and backed away to sit in the chair by the door, the tenderness and yearning in his expression bringing a lump to her throat.

Wondering if she'd ever get used to giving her attention to a man she loved while another man she loved watched, Savannah smiled and reached for Wyatt.

Running her hands up and down his chest, she scooted closer, moaning as her body brushed against his, and lifted her face to his.

"I'll remind you to tell me you love me, and whenever you hurt me, I'll make you kiss it to make it better, the way you did last night. Now, I want my morning kiss."

Tilting her head, she arched into the hand running down her spine, thrilling at the play of his fingers over the small of her back.

"Or, are you going to be the kind of husband who doesn't kiss me before he leaves for the day?"

When he stilled, his expression unreadable, she stilled, wondering if she'd been too brazen.

Swallowing heavily, she pulled back, only to have him yank her against him.

"Wyatt!"

Using the hand at the small of her back to hold her to him, he lifted the other to the back of her neck, tangling it in her hair to lift her face to his.

"I like when you make demands. It does something to me."

Sucking in a sharp breath at the need that deepened his tone and made his eyes darken in that way that never failed to arouse her, Savannah slumped against him. Wrapping her hands around his neck, she rubbed against him, no longer surprised that the brush of his clothing against her nipples made her pussy clench with the need for him to take her.

Craving the feel of his cock inside her, she rubbed her thighs together and brushed her lips along his chin. Smiling at the feel of his cock pushing against her belly, she rubbed against it, delighting at his groan.

"What does it do to you?"

"It makes him addle-minded. That's what it does."

Savannah stilled, her bottom cheeks tightening in response to the threat in the hand Hayes slid over them. She tried to straighten, but Wyatt chuckled and kept her close, sliding a hand up to cup her breast.

Holding her gaze, he ran a thumb back and forth over her nipple, holding her to him when she slumped.

"I see your face, Hayes. Don't try to tell me that her bold little demands don't make you want to have her writhing under you until you've met all of them and more, until she's so weak and sated that she can't even think—let alone cause any trouble."

Savannah gasped. "Trouble? I—"

Wyatt covered her mouth with his before she could finish, slipping his tongue past her lips to tangle with hers.

Caught up in the spell of his kiss, Savannah tightened her arms around his neck, her head spinning.

Both he and Hayes seemed determined to drive her out of her mind, the light brushes of their fingertips moving over her skin making her jump and shiver. They touched her everywhere, so light and fleeting that by the time she felt it, they'd moved on.

She'd never released how sensitive the backs of her thighs were until Hayes gave her attention there. Moaning into Wyatt's mouth, she found herself pushing her knees outward in an involuntary effort to get Hayes to give her slit the attention it needed.

Instead, he chuckled softly and gave his attention to her inner thighs, making her clit swell with anticipation and her pussy and bottom clench with the need to be filled.

In the meantime, Wyatt held her up with a hand pressing at her back, the fingers of his other hand dancing over her breast and belly, making her nipples tighten and burn and sending shards of sizzling heat from her breasts to her slit.

The feel of Hayes's lips over the backs of her shoulders added to the heat until her knees started shaking and her toes curled.

When his fingertips worked their way higher, she let her head fall back, breaking off her kiss with Wyatt to get air.

Gulping it in, she let out a cry when Hayes tapped her clit, groaning when he shifted his attention to the cheeks of her bottom.

"No. Please. I need to come."

Her eyes flew open when Wyatt nipped her bottom lip. "We know you do, but you're not coming again until we're married and back home. You didn't really think you were going to get off so easy for running away from us and almost getting yourself killed, did you?"

A sharp smack on her ass made her jolt as Hayes straightened. Before she could recover, he'd slapped her other cheek.

"Get dressed. The preacher's waiting for us."

* * * *

Savannah was going to kill them in their sleep.

Eb and Jeremiah would understand, and she wouldn't have to go to jail because she would have killed the sheriffs.

It sounded logical, even reasonable to her and completely justified.

As she lay under the stars, with Hayes and Wyatt on either side of her, she planned the many ways she could do it, but found it hard to concentrate with her body screaming for release—a release the two of them had kept just out of her reach all day.

Wrapped around her from behind, Hayes slid a hand under her shirt and over her belly, working his way higher.

"Can't sleep, Mrs. Hawkins?"

Aware of the other men, those who'd come to town with Hayes and Wyatt sleeping only yards away, Savannah kept her tone at a cool whisper.

"I hate you."

Infuriating her further, he teased the underside of her breast right under her nipple.

"No, you don't. You love me, and I want to hear you say it."

Forcing herself to remain still, she closed her eyes, fighting the urge to roll back into his touch. She knew that Wyatt, lying on his back on her other side with his hand moving on her thigh, was wide awake and listening to everything.

"No. I hate you. You're mean, and I don't know why I ever married you. Are you sure I'm really married to both of you?"

Wyatt squeezed her thigh.

"You're definitely married to both of us. Don't doubt that for a minute. Hayes just happened to draw the high card, so you're wearing his name, but you belong to me every bit as much as you belong to him."

It had been a strange wedding, much like the one her uncle had performed, under duress, with Maggie, Eb, and Jeremiah.

Standing on either side of her, both men had promised to love, honor and cherish her.

The preacher hadn't looked at all surprised, not even when the men from the ranch had all gathered around them and stood as witnesses.

Afterward, they'd all been in a jovial mood, until an older woman spit on the ground at Savannah's feet as they walked past.

After that, the men had stayed close and they'd all been anxious to leave as soon as possible. After a meal at the hotel, they'd started back for home, stopping halfway to rest the horses.

Wyatt and Hayes had spent the entire day giving her meaningful looks, sharp reminders of the way they'd left her in turmoil that morning and keeping her arousal simmering throughout the day.

Suspecting that they did so to take her mind off of the insult she'd received in town, she'd resisted at first, but as the afternoon went on, she realized that Maggie dealt with the same prejudice. More importantly, she understood that the life she'd chosen came with consequences like that.

Having Wyatt and Hayes as her husbands was more than worth it.

By the time they stopped for the night, she was ready to scream, and it had only gotten worse since then.

Lying on top of their bedrolls and covered with blankets, Wyatt and Hayes never stopped touching her, their teasing caresses both arousing and angering her until she couldn't even think anymore.

Hayes seemed to enjoy her predicament, circling her nipple with a devious finger.

"It's a shame we're not alone. I would love to have that bare bottom of yours over my lap and paddle it good for scaring us that way. Do you know we beat you to town and couldn't find you? We looked everywhere and we were just about to split up to go looking for you when we caught you sneaking around the livery. Don't you *ever* think of doing something like that again."

He covered her mouth with his at the same time he pinched her nipple, smothering her cry as the white-hot stream of heat shot straight to her clit.

Taking her mouth with his in a kiss more demanding and possessive than any he'd ever given her, he rolled her nipple before releasing it and giving his attention to the other.

Wyatt anticipated her need to rub her thighs together, forcing his leg between hers to keep them apart. He made short work of loosening her pants and slipping his hand aside, bending close to whisper in her ear.

"I wonder if that's the kind of cry I'll hear when I take your ass tonight. You want to come, but neither one of us is going to let you."

Savannah sucked in a breath when Wyatt's fingers slid over her abdomen and lower, parting her folds. Moaning into Hayes's mouth, she bucked at the pinch to her other nipple, the heat from it making her clit burn as she started to come.

Both men seemed to realize it at once, backing off and holding her as she writhed beneath them.

Hayes lifted his mouth from hers, pushing her hair back from her face. Brushing her jaw with his lips, he and Wyatt worked together to push her pants to her knees.

"You're not coming until we take you together back home. Until then, though, we're going to play with you. We're going to make you so mindless with pleasure that you won't care what we do to you. Hold on to Wyatt."

Savannah did so without thinking, willing to do anything in the hope that she would be able to come before they could stop her.

Her breasts felt so swollen and heavy she couldn't stand it, and when Wyatt lifted her shirt to expose them, she didn't even balk. She wanted him to be able to touch them, and even under the blankets, the cool night air reached them and cooled her heated flesh.

A low fire made it almost impossible to see anything, especially as far away as they were from the glowing embers, but she appreciated the blanket that covered her. It still felt so naughty to be naked from her neck to her knees, and although anyone looking this way wouldn't see a thing, Wyatt and Hayes had total access to her body.

Determined to beat them at their own game, Savannah let herself go. She knew the kind of pleasure they could give her, and if she could just hide how close she came to release, they would send her over without meaning to.

Then she would get relief and they wouldn't. Imagining the looks on their faces when she came before they could stop her, she smiled in the darkness and snuggled closer to Wyatt.

"I love when you touch me. Your hands feel so good."

Rocking her hips, she tried to open her legs, but the pants tangled around her knees prevented it.

The hand Wyatt used to stroke her back stilled briefly before moving again. "I'm glad because I plan to have them on you every chance I get."

His low, gritty tone washed over her in the darkness, the need in it sending shivers through her. His touch became more possessive, his fingers moving over her skin with increasing demand.

Moving her hands on his chest, she was very aware of Hayes at her back, using his arm to pillow her head while the other hand traced circles on her belly.

Lifting her face, she kissed Wyatt's jaw. "Can I touch *you?*"

She wanted to laugh when he stilled again, but the hands running over her kept her need so sharp that a moan came out instead.

Wyatt covered her hands with his and pressed them against his chest. "You can touch me anytime you want, honey."

Hayes pressed his lips against her shoulder, running his fingers down her side to her hip.

"And while you're touching him, I'll be touching you."

Savannah worked to pull Wyatt's shirt up, wishing she could have done it with more finesse. Her fingers fumbled even more when Wyatt cupped her breast and ran his thumb back and forth over her nipple. Finally getting his shirt out of the way, she placed her hands over his chest, fascinated to find his nipples beaded like hers.

His sharp intake of breath delighted her and made her bolder. Snuggling closer, she put her lips against his warm skin and found his nipple with her mouth. The hand in her hair fisted, pulling her away, while the fingers of the other tightened on her nipple.

"Damn, that feels too good, Savannah."

Hayes removed his hand from her hip and fumbled with something behind her, cursing.

"What did she do? Damn it, we're so far away from the fire that I can't see a thing."

Wyatt groaned, loosening his grip and allowing Savannah to do it again.

"She put her mouth on me."

Hayes stilled. "Where?"

Running her tongue over Wyatt's nipple, Savannah wrapped a hand around his back to pull him closer, her breath catching when Wyatt rolled to his back, his fingers tugging at her nipple.

Wyatt groaned when she switched her attention to the nipple closest to her and ran her hand over his belly.

"She's kissing and touching my chest. Christ, don't get me thinking about that. Wait until you're on the receiving end of this."

Hayes leaned over her, using a firm hand from behind to part her thighs and slip his cock between them.

"Don't tell me you never think about having her take your cock in her mouth. I wouldn't believe you."

Savannah stilled at the feel of Hayes working his cock between her thighs, his efforts made easier because of the slickness there. To her surprise, he didn't slip his cock into her pussy, but kept it there.

Her head spun at his words and at the slow motion of his cock sliding through her folds, the friction of the hard heat against her pussy opening sending her arousal soaring.

Wyatt's hand tightened in her hair, pulling her closer, his stomach muscles taut beneath her hand.

"I don't want to think about it. She's our wife, for Christ's sake!"

Curious and intrigued by the tension in his furious whisper, Savannah lifted her head, holding on to Wyatt and arching her lower back in an effort to take Hayes's cock inside her, or at least to get the friction against her clit.

He thwarted her, his strong fingers holding her hips steady.

"Yes, she's our wife. That doesn't mean we can't do everything with her. She's ours forever now, and I plan to enjoy her to the fullest. I want that hot little mouth on my cock so bad I'm ready to come just thinking about it. Right now, I have my cock between her thighs and it's killing me not to sink into her."

Mindless with need, she rocked her hips as much as she could. She let her eyes flutter closed on a low cry when Wyatt reached under her with the one hand to tug a nipple, moaning when he used the other to undo his pants.

"Wyatt? Can I? Can I put my mouth on you there?"

He groaned. "Damned right. At least it'll muffle all those cries you're making so the others don't hear you."

Savannah knew she probably should have been alarmed when he shoved his pants to his knees and, with a hand fisted in her hair, pulled her head to his cock, but her own arousal and the obvious signs of his made his wicked demand even more enticing.

Unsure of what to do, she paused, sucking in a breath when Hayes pulled his cock out from between her thighs and pressed a hand to her back.

"Use your tongue on his cock. Suck it a little and take as much of it as you can into your mouth. He's going to love it."

The teasing in his hoarse tone told her that he was just as affected, his ragged breathing and groans becoming deeper by the minute.

Thankful for his advice and for his guiding hand at her back, she slid farther beneath the blanket and rolled onto Wyatt's legs. Feeling such hard muscle shift beneath her gave her a moment's pause, but his low groan and restlessness gave her the confidence she needed.

When the head of his cock touched her cheek, she reached for it automatically, surprised to find it so thick that she couldn't close her fingers around it. Fascinated by the velvety feel and amazing hardness, she ran her hand up and down the length of it, stopping abruptly when he hissed and another low groan rumbled from his chest.

His hand covered hers, moving it on his cock. "No. Don't stop. Keep going, Savannah. Take it in your mouth before you kill me."

Knowing that a big, strong man like Wyatt got such pleasure from her touch excited Savannah more than she could have imagined. It fired her own arousal and made it impossible to be still beneath the blankets. Wanting to make him as crazy as he made her, she did as Hayes told her and stuck out her tongue to touch it to Wyatt's cock.

His reaction was more than she'd bargained for.

His jolt almost knocked her off of him, his muscles rock hard and trembling with his apparent effort to remain still.

With a smile, she did it again, and again, using her tongue to explore him and fascinated by the smooth texture of his cock as much as his reaction to having her mouth on him.

She loved it, and for the first time, she really understood and embraced her femininity and understood the kind of power a woman could have over a man.

Inwardly cursing the fact that the others lay nearby, she promised herself that the next time she was alone with her two husbands, she would have them both screaming with pleasure.

She licked her way to the head of his cock, surprised at the salty fluid she found there, but more surprised at how much larger it was.

Wyatt jolted as though he'd been hit by lightning.

"Jesus. Holy hell. No, don't stop. Christ, Hayes, she's killing me."

Hayes chuckled softly from beside them.

"You're making more noise than she did. What's she doing?"

Excited by their play and determined to make both men putty in her hands, Savannah closed her mouth over the head of Wyatt's cock and began to suck.

Wyatt hissed sharply, both of his hands tightening in her hair.

"She's sucking me. I'm not coming in her mouth. Ever. I don't know how much more I can take. Fuck." Pulling her hair, he jerked her mouth away from his cock, his breathing as ragged as if he'd been running. Yanking her up his body with a strength that amazed and excited her, he took her mouth in a kiss that was a far cry from any kiss he'd ever given her.

Pure heat.

That was all she could think as he ravaged her mouth with his, plundering it with his tongue as though he couldn't get enough.

With his hands running up and down her back, he held her close, the hard bulge of his cock pressing against her lower belly.

She squirmed against him, frustrated that the friction of his shirt on her nipples and the feel of the rough blanket over her bottom only enflamed her more. With her pants tangled around her ankles, she couldn't spread her legs to wrap them around him and get the friction she needed against her clit.

The spasms in her pussy seemed relentless, growing stronger as the need to be filled became a living, breathing thing.

By the time he pulled her head back, breaking off their kiss, they were both out of breath.

Pulling her close, he squeezed the cheeks of her bottom. "You're going to kill me."

From behind, Hayes rubbed her back.

"I'm sure as hell not going to get any sleep tonight."

Wyatt rolled her to her back and reached for her pants.

"Come on, honey. Let's get you dressed so you can get some sleep."

With need still clawing at her, Savannah gripped his shoulders and tried to hook her leg around him, but she couldn't with him pulling her pants into place.

"Sleep? Wyatt, I can't sleep like this."

Wyatt finished and pressed a hand at her belly until she lay flat on her back.

"Sleep. My cock is hard enough to go through a board. I thought we could just play with you a little, but I should have known that as soon as we touched you, things would get out of hand."

Without even being able to see him well, she could tell he spoke through clenched teeth. It made her feel a little better, but not much.

Fire licked at her from all sides, consuming her with need and a hunger so strong she couldn't bear it. She wanted to taste Wyatt again, wanted—needed their hands on her. She needed relief and she needed it badly.

"I hate you. I hate both of you. You know what you do to me, and then you just leave me this way."

Hayes finished fixing his clothing and curled up behind her. "When we get home, we're not stopping until we're all too worn out to move. I swear, woman, I don't know how the hell I'm even going to be able to get out of bed and leave you in the morning."

Trembling with need, Savannah balled up her fists and hit both of them in the belly.

Before either one of them could do more than curse, she kicked both of them for a good measure, wishing she still wore her boots.

"To hell with that. You can't do what you did to me and leave me like this. If this is what you're going to do to me, I'm never letting you touch me again. You're mean and I wish I'd never married either one of you!"

Shoving the blanket aside, she started to get up, hoping a brisk walk would help her get rid of all this restless energy, but Wyatt tumbled her back.

Leaning over her, he held her wrists to the ground, his low whisper filled with tension.

"Damn it, Savannah." Bending his head, he blew out a breath. "I know. You're too inexperienced for this, but I don't want the others to hear you come. I'll make a deal with you. If you promise to be as quiet as you can and do what I say, I'll make you come and then at least one of us can get some sleep."

Hayes groaned and rolled to his side next to her. "Hell. My cock's pounding already. All right." He gripped Savannah's chin. "Just this time. In the future, if you do anything that puts your life at risk, I swear I'm going to tie you to the bed naked and torture the hell out of you."

The image of being tied to a bed and letting Hayes have his way with her caused her pussy to clench and more of her juices to flow from her. Her clit pulsed and seemed to swell even more. Not knowing what he would do if he knew what his threat did to her, she nodded furiously and swallowed heavily before answering.

"I can't take it. Please make me come. I can't stand it anymore. I'll do whatever you say."

Wyatt brushed his lips along her ear. "That's an interesting prospect. I like having you obey me. Maybe we should do this to you more often."

"I'll kill you in your sleep."

Wyatt released her hands and ran a finger between her breasts.

"I'll bet those nipples need attention. Do you want us to touch them?"

"God, yes." She fisted her hands at her sides, holding her breath in anticipation.

Wyatt's voice got deeper and cooled just a little.

"Then lift up that shirt and ask us nicely."

Savannah stilled. "I don't understand." Why didn't they just pull her shirt up and touch her the way they usually did?

Hayes ran a finger down her cheek and to her neck. "It means that if you want to be touched, you're going to have to ask for it. I like this, Wyatt. She's going to have to work for what she wants."

She knew that mischievous tone and wondered what lay in store for her. It seemed that they had something in mind, another of their wicked games.

Shaking with need, she would do anything they asked as long as they would give her the relief she craved. Trusting her husbands beyond anything, she reached for the hem of her shirt.

"If I do what you want, you'll make me come? You won't just tease me and leave me like this?"

Wyatt laid a hot hand on her belly.

"I promise, I'll make you come. You're in charge. You tell us what to do, and we'll do it. *But* you have to ask nicely."

Frowning in the darkness, Savannah rubbed her thighs together, knowing it would do no good at all, but unable to stop.

"I can't. You know what I need. Why can't you just do it?"

Thankful for the darkness that hid her burning face, she stroked Wyatt's chest.

"Please?"

Wyatt took her hand in his and rolled to his back.

"I guess you're not aroused enough to need relief. Go to sleep."

Gritting her teeth, Savannah reached for the hem of her shirt again. "I swear I'm going to kill you as soon as I get the chance."

Hayes chuckled. "For someone who would never threaten sheriffs, you're doing it quite a bit. The way you shoot, though, it'll never happen."

"I can shoot." Raising her shirt to her neck, she shivered as the cool air blew over her nipples. "There. It's up."

Wyatt rolled back. "And? What do you want us to do? You have to tell us, Savannah. We'll do whatever you want."

Taking a shuddering breath, Savannah closed her eyes. "Touch me."

Immediately, two hot, firm hands heated her skin, one low on her belly and the other a little higher.

"Not there, damn you!"

Hayes circled her belly button. "Be specific, Savannah." The underlying demand in his low tone told her he meant it.

Taking a deep breath, Savannah squeezed her eyes closed.

"Touch my breasts."

She'd never spoken like that in her life, but with Wyatt and Hayes as her husbands, she imagined she'd be doing a lot of things she'd never done before.

Wyatt clicked his tongue.

"I said you had to ask nicely."

"I hate you."

"I don't think so. Liars don't get what they want."

Savannah had always wondered why Maggie would even consider tying herself to two such domineering men, but Savannah understood now.

Their strength made her feel safe and very womanly, and she trusted that whenever she was with them, they would take care of her. It was an irresistible feeling, one she'd never thought to experience in her life.

Instead of their strength and presence overpowering her, it made her stronger, as if their strength was at her disposal whenever she needed it.

Drawing on it now, she shifted restlessly as the muscles in her stomach quivered.

"*Please* touch my breasts." It came out in a breathless whisper, one that had both men stiffening.

Wyatt cursed under his breath and covered her breast, his hand hot on her cool skin.

Hayes leaned close and brushed her lips with his. "You sound so good saying things like that. Very good. Anytime you want us to touch you, darlin', just talk like that."

To her frustration, although both men ran their fingers over her breasts, cupping them and teasing the tender underside, neither touched her nipples. No matter how much she writhed and arched into their caress, they avoided touching her nipples. She shivered beneath their touch, biting back a moan at the delicious torment.

"I hate you."

Bending close, Wyatt kissed her forehead. "Whatever you want, Savannah."

She would die if she didn't get some kind of relief soon.

"Touch my nipples, too. Touch me down there."

She pointed toward her slit, fisting her hands in their shirts when they each stroked a nipple.

"Slide your pants down."

Obeying Wyatt's demand, she fumbled clumsily beneath the covers to get her pants to her knees.

"I did it. Please, touch me the way you do to make me come."

Hayes bent his head, taking a nipple into his mouth. At the same time he covered her mouth with his hand, muffling her automatic cry.

Lifting his head, he cupped her breast again and brushed his lips against hers.

"What do you want? If you want a finger in your pussy, you have to say it. If you want attention to your clit, you have to say that."

Grabbing his head, she pulled him down and took his mouth as hungrily as he took hers. She froze when he stilled, wondering if she'd done something wrong, only to fall back with a moan when he took over, kissing her until she was breathless and weak. Their hands and the rough blankets on her bare skin only inflamed her further.

Lifting his head, Hayes nipped her bottom lip.

"Say it."

Long past caring about anything but relief, Savannah gulped in air and had to swallow before speaking. Tears stung her eyes as something inside her snapped.

"Please. In my pussy and touch my cl–clit. I love when you touch me everywhere. You make me feel so good. Oh, God, I love you both so much."

Hayes sucked in breath.

"That's it. When she says things like that she can have whatever she wants."

Taking her mouth with his, he let his other hand trail down her body to sink a finger into her.

"Get out of the way. I want her clit." Wyatt slid his hand over her belly, parting her folds and moving a finger over her clit. "I love you, too, wife."

The feel of his hot mouth drawing her nipple inside and the strokes to her pussy and clit sent her hurtling toward the edge.

She wanted to come so badly, but now that it slammed into her, she fought it, not wanting this incredible feeling to ever end.

Hayes changed the angle of his thrust, stroking the inner walls of her pussy and pressing against a spot inside her that made fighting it impossible.

The pleasure exploded from her clit, sizzling arrows of heat and delight that shot everywhere, consuming her body in ecstasy. Stiffening, she held on to Hayes, her body bowing and the muscles in her thighs closing and tightening on their hands.

It took every ounce of willpower she possessed not to scream.

As the strokes on her clit and in her pussy slowed, she began to tremble in earnest, and she felt the tight grip of her orgasm loosening its hold on her. Wyatt released her nipple from his mouth, pausing to run his tongue over it before lifting his head.

"Hell, woman, you turn me inside out. Come here. Let's get you dressed again so I can hold you."

Hayes broke off their kiss seconds later, a kiss she couldn't even remember participating in while she came.

"You held her last night. It's my turn to hold her."

Minutes later, drowsy and sated, she lay snuggled against Hayes with Wyatt at her back, and smiled. She never would have thought that two such magnificent men would not only marry her, but argue about who got to hold her.

Rubbing the two silver bands on her finger with her thumb, she sighed, blinking back tears when both men caressed her.

Hayes bent to kiss her hair.

"What is it, honey?"

Savannah patted his chest.

"Nothing. It just surprises me sometimes to realize that you really do love me. Despite the fact that you're both hardheaded and arrogant, I'm glad I married you."

Wyatt chuckled from behind her and kissed her shoulder.

"Of course we love you and you love us. You said it, and we're not letting you take it back."

Smiling, she let her eyes drift closed. "I said that in the heat of passion."

"One day we'll make you scream it out loud to everyone. Go to sleep, honey. You're going to need it."

Chapter Thirteen

As soon as they got back to the ranch, it quickly became apparent that they wouldn't be getting time alone with Savannah anytime soon.

Eb met them before they even got to the stables, his expression anything but friendly. "Did you get married?"

Hayes nodded and glanced at his wife. "We did. That's not what you came out here for, though. What's wrong?" He dismounted and went to help Savannah, but Wyatt had already reached her.

The tension in the air could be cut with a knife, and Phoenix was already speaking in low tones to his two brothers, his expression grim.

Eb shot a look at Savannah. "Go see Maggie."

Hayes barely managed to bite back his anger. Lifting a brow, he met Eb's gaze squarely. "Wyatt and I are standing right here. She's our responsibility now, remember?"

Eb smiled in Savannah's direction, his smile not meeting his eyes. "Sorry. Habit. Congratulations." He glanced back and forth between him and Wyatt. "We've got some trouble."

Wyatt touched his lips to Savannah's hair, his eyes cold. "Go see Maggie. Stay at the house. We'll come get you after we deal with this."

When Savannah frowned and opened her mouth, Hayes shot her a sharp glance, pleased that she snapped her mouth closed and nodded, obeying him immediately.

Pride in her swelled his chest, and he watched her go, knowing that if anything ever happened to her, he would never recover. Once she went up the back steps and into the house, he nodded toward Eb.

"What's going on?"

"Last night, there was a fire."

Hayes glanced at Wyatt, his heart racing. He knew damned well what a fire could do out here and whipped his head around, instinctively looking for any sign of one.

"It's out. Luckily, Phoenix and some of the other men smelled it and saw the light from it before it got out of hand. It looked like whoever lit it had no experience with campfires. Phoenix and the others must have scared them off because they left some of their belongings behind. Including this."

He placed a piece of paper, partially burned, into Wyatt's outstretched hand.

Hayes got a cold feeling in the pit of his stomach. "What is it?"

Eb smiled. "Part of a letter from the sheriff of Kansas City, telling a certain Reverend Perry that he's no longer welcome there. Evidently, after Savannah left, a lot of people came forward and complained about him to the sheriff and told him he would be out of a job if he let the reverend come back. They didn't like the way he treated Savannah."

Wyatt cursed. "Why the hell didn't they say something before?"

Eb sighed. "Savannah told them not to. My dad's been about the only one to talk, and the sheriff doesn't like him. It seems the sheriff's got a thing for Esmeralda and doesn't like that she's too crazy about Dad to see anyone else."

Phoenix came forward. "It looks like there were seven riders. We were just about to go look for any sign of them when we saw you coming."

Hayes looked toward the house. "Keep Savannah here. We'll go out and see if we can find them."

Eb nodded. "What the hell are they doing here anyway?"

"We had some trouble with them in town. Savannah knew that one of her uncle's friends was an outlaw. Turns out he's the one who took off with Savannah's mother. Paid the uncle to keep Savannah out of the way. With Savannah's mother gone, he gets no money and needs Savannah to keep his church solvent. Now that he's been run out of Kansas City, he's going to have to set up somewhere else. He needs Savannah."

Eb scrubbed a hand over his face. "What happened to the outlaw?"

Hayes waved a hand, anxious to get the matter of Savannah's uncle taken care of once and for all. "One of the others will tell you. We're getting fresh horses and heading out."

"How the hell did they beat you here?"

Wyatt shook his head. "Savannah was worn out and frantic, and so we let her sleep in. Then, we got married, remember? We stayed at the hotel. They must have thought we left and started out."

Hayes heard Blade start to explain what had happened, but didn't hear the rest. Intent on making sure Savannah's uncle was gone, he started out, with Phoenix leading the way. Hart and Gideon Sanderson joined them without a word, wearing their usual somber expressions.

Riding out, Hayes listened as Wyatt explained to Phoenix, Hart, and Gideon what had happened in town, speaking in the short, clipped tone Hayes knew so well.

His own anger boiled hot, but with a threat to Savannah, it became something much more. Possessiveness and the need to protect what meant the most to him added a layer of unease that he'd never before experienced when doing his job.

This time it was personal.

Savannah was his *wife*.

Hayes kept his gaze moving, scanning the outcroppings of rocks, looking for any sign of movement.

Riding in silence now, they listened for any sign of life, but heard nothing. After several more minutes of riding, Phoenix stopped and raised a hand, pointing to a clearing about fifty yards from where they'd stopped. The brush around it had been burned, and dirt had been scattered everywhere.

Leaning toward them, the Indian kept his voice low.

"That's where they had the fire. Luckily we got to it before it was too bad. Between the water we had in our canteens and the dirt we threw on it, we were able to get it out. A few more minutes, and who knows what would have happened?"

Hayes gritted his teeth.

"It appears this man's a menace in more ways than one. He's got sand, though, coming out here after what happened in Tulsa. He's got more riders with him, which means he recruited more in town. And he's desperate. He must need Savannah badly."

Wyatt slid from his horse, checking the ground.

"People like her, and she's the only reason he gets any donations to his church. Without her, he doesn't have a way to make a living. Yeah, he's desperate."

Hayes knelt and touched a finger to one of the tracks left behind. "And stupid, if he thinks he's going to be able to get through us to get to her."

Hart Sanderson, who knelt several yards away, dusted off his hands and came to his feet.

"Headed toward the ranch."

"Hell." Hayes and the others leapt onto their horses, not doubting the other man at all.

Hart hardly ever spoke, but when he did, he didn't waste words and people listened.

With his heart in his throat, Hayes raced with the others back the way they'd come.

"There aren't any tracks here. How the hell do you know they're going for the ranch?"

Gideon pointed toward the other side of the rocks. "They went that way. Probably stopped at the pond and then headed the long way around. They don't know these parts."

Hayes lifted a brow, sharing a look with Wyatt. "Gideon, I never heard you string so many words together at once." The fact that he did showed that they all shared the same alarm. He had to admit that he appreciated the sense of camaraderie, and that they all worked together to protect the women.

With a shrug, Gideon raced on. "Didn't have anything to say."

None of them spoke as they raced back to the ranch. The sense of urgency in the air increased as they got closer, until it became thick enough to cut with a knife.

Right before they cleared the trees, Hayes and the others stopped, the danger in the air unmistakable.

"Something's wrong."

Hart nodded. "Yeah."

Wyatt cursed from beside him.

"Son of a bitch! Look. Back of the house. Left corner."

Hayes couldn't breathe. "He's got Maggie and the baby."

Fear, unlike any he'd ever known, had him racing for the house. He pulled up abruptly, his heart in his throat when he saw that the men of Desire were in a standoff with Savannah's uncle and some of the roughnecks Jeremiah had pointed out to him in Tulsa.

Men for hire, they would do anything for money. The reverend had apparently decided his friends were useless and hired others to get what he wanted.

And Savannah stood right in the middle of it.

Seeing no way to sneak up on them, Hayes and the other men spread out, forcing the men with the guns to divide their attention. Since Savannah's uncle wasn't armed, that left the other six trying to keep an eyes on them while also watching Eb, Jeremiah, Duke, Hawke, and Blade.

Hayes kept his attention on the one holding the gun to Maggie's head.

"That's far enough. Get off those horses and drop those pistols real easylike."

Hayes spared a glance at Eb and Jeremiah, both men white as sheets as they watched the man who hid behind Maggie, keeping the gun to her head and jerking her in front of him. The baby in her arms cried incessantly as Maggie struggled not to drop him.

His gaze slid to Savannah. Dismounting, he kept her in his vision, surprised to see that she still wore her gun in the holster she'd worn since she left Kansas City.

Either the other men didn't see it or didn't consider her a threat.

"Now lose the pistols. No, reach out with your left hands only and drop the holsters or the little woman and screaming brat get bullets in their heads."

Hayes spared a glance at the reverend, unsurprised that the man seemed to have gathered some courage now that he had six other men with him that had guns.

Keeping his right hand in the air, he undid his holster and let it fall to the ground. His fear for Maggie and the baby had his heart racing.

He could only imagine what Eb and Jeremiah were feeling.

He couldn't understand why Savannah stood so far apart from the others, and wanted her close so he could shield her if necessary.

"Savannah, come over here to me."

"No." Savannah's uncle looked livid. "She stays right where she is. If we shoot Maggie and the baby, Savannah's next. I want her right in my sights, but not too close to Maggie."

For the first time since they'd arrived, Savannah turned her head slightly toward him.

He could see the fear in her eyes even from this distance, and it took every ounce of willpower he possessed not to run to her.

"What the hell happened?"

Duke spared a look at Eb and Jeremiah. "We had some trouble with the horses. Eb and Jeremiah came out to see what was going on, and these bastards broke in through the front door. Then all hell broke loose."

"Shut up."

With all eyes on Maggie, nobody moved.

Hayes went through a dozen scenarios in his head, but couldn't find one that wouldn't get Maggie killed. Inwardly cursing, he swore that he would never let Savannah out of his sight again.

Savannah stared at her uncle. "I told you I would come with you if you just let Maggie go."

"We can't go back, Savannah. Ace Tyler has the whole town against me. They have to pay!"

Savannah took a step closer. "Killing Maggie and the baby is only going to get you killed. You can't shoot me. You need me. That's why you told these men not to shoot me, isn't it? I won't go with you if you hurt Maggie or the baby. You know that. Let them go."

Hayes ground his teeth. If these men left here with Savannah, Hayes would be relentless in chasing them down and getting his woman back. Even the thought of her riding away with them filled him with terror.

The red-faced reverend looked a little confused.

"No. You're all coming with me. When we get away, we'll leave Maggie and the baby somewhere where they can find them."

Eb and Jeremiah stiffened even more. Shaking his head, Eb went whiter. "You can't leave a woman and a baby in the middle of nowhere."

Savannah took another step closer and kept speaking in that soft tone Hayes had often heard her use with her uncle.

"Leave the baby here. You don't want to hear all that crying, do you?"

The man holding the gun on Maggie shook his head. "We ain't takin' this crying brat with us. People would hear us from miles away."

Another of the men grinned. "There's a cliff not far from here. We'll throw it over that."

Shaking with rage, Hayes watched as Maggie took her eyes from her husbands and faced Savannah. Adjusting the baby lower in her arms, she and Savannah exchanged a look.

To his amazement, Maggie smiled through her tears, a smile of encouragement.

"You've done it a million times. I know you can do it. Do it, Savannah. It's a can. That's all. Just a can."

Hayes stiffened as everyone whipped their heads around to Savannah, his gut tied up in knots. He couldn't breathe. He could barely think. Something was about to happen, and he couldn't prevent it. He didn't even know what it was.

Savannah closed her eyes and slowly opened them, nodding once.

He'd never felt so helpless.

Savannah shifted her stance and took a deep breath, letting it out slowly.

It all happened so fast, he had a hard time believing what he was seeing.

Savannah whipped out the pistols at her side with a speed that left him dumbfounded, shooting the man holding Maggie right between the eyes.

Before he hit the ground, Savannah shot each of the others in the hands holding their guns, sending men and guns flying in the dirt.

Before the last shot rang out, Hayes and the others were already moving.

As Eb and Jeremiah dragged Maggie and the baby from the dead man's arms, and Duke and the others ran to kick guns out of reach of the other screaming men, Hayes and Wyatt ran straight to Savannah.

They reached her side before the smoke even cleared. Gathering her to him, he took one of the guns from her hands while Wyatt took the other.

"Savannah!" Christ, he couldn't believe what he just saw. He'd seen it with his own eyes and still couldn't believe it had happened. Gathering her shaking form against him reminded him once more of her frailty.

Her eyes glazed over, scaring him to death, her voice a raspy whisper.

"Told you I could shoot." Her body slumped as she fainted dead away.

Hayes blinked, panic-stricken, and scooped her up in his arms, vowing that as long as he lived, he'd never stop loving this woman.

Chapter Fourteen

Savannah shot up, her heart racing, and struggled to get to her feet, only to be tumbled back against Hayes's chest.

His arms felt warm and solid around her, the man himself a wall of strength she could lean on as he held her on his lap.

"Easy, honey. You're all right. God, I was never so scared, or so proud of you."

Four hands moved over her back and shoulders, while two sets of lips kissed her hair as Wyatt moved in at her back.

"You scared the hell out of us. Are you all right? Do you hurt anywhere?"

With the realization that they were on the back porch of the Tylers' house, Savannah closed her eyes against the looks of concern from several of the men standing in the yard only feet away.

"I killed a man. I killed him. He's dead because of me."

Hayes and Wyatt both stilled, but within seconds resumed their caresses. Hayes leaned back, tilting her face back.

"Yes, you did, and because you did, Maggie and the babe are alive and safe in their bed right now." His tone, softer than she'd ever heard from him, reached into her chest and wrapped around her heart.

Wyatt pushed her hair back and wrapped an arm around her from behind, his hand rubbing her thigh in firm, smooth strokes.

"He was one of those troublemakers from town. He and the others have been in trouble with the law ever since Eb and Jeremiah got here. Don't think for one minute that any of us wouldn't have killed him if we'd had the chance. You were brave enough to take the shot, and you were the only one who could have."

Savannah opened her eyes in the hopes of getting rid of the image of looking straight into the other man's eyes before taking the shot that killed him.

"Maggie and the babe aren't hurt?"

Wyatt stiffened. "Eb says her arm is covered in bruises from being jerked around and that her head is already bruised and sore as hell from where that bastard kept pushing the gun against it. All that ended when you were brave enough to take that shot, Savannah. You're a heroine around here."

Feeling very old and distant from everything going on around her, Savannah sat up, pushing out of their arms.

"Where is my uncle?"

Hayes kept a hand across her legs, rubbing her knee. "He and his other friends are the first official guests of the new jailhouse. We'll be taking them to Tulsa in a day or two."

Savannah nodded, looking out to the yard, but carefully avoiding meeting anyone's eyes.

"I want to see Maggie, and then I want to see him."

Coming to his feet with her in his arms, Hayes started toward the back door. "You can see Maggie and the babe, but I don't think seeing your uncle is a good idea."

Savannah didn't have the energy to argue with him, or to push out of his hold. She felt numb and disoriented. It was as if she could see and hear everything around her, but she was no longer a part of it.

She'd killed a man. She'd taken the life of another human being and didn't know if she could live with it.

* * * *

Wyatt left Hayes talking to Eb and Jeremiah in the kitchen and went out the back door, in need of air. As he approached the fenced area, Hawke turned.

"Hell of a woman. How's she doing?"

From beside him, Phoenix stepped forward. "She looked really shaken. Is she hurt?"

With a sigh, Wyatt hooked a foot over the bottom rail.

"She's not hurt, but she's shaken. She can't get over the fact that she killed a man. She did the same thing when she thought she'd killed the man in Tulsa. We should have expected it."

Hawke patted his shoulder, rare for a man who never touched anyone. "After this afternoon, I think we're all shaken. We've already spoken with Jeremiah. We're going to have to increase patrols around here, and strangers are going to be watched even more closely than ever."

Phoenix glanced toward the house.

"Doesn't she realize she saved Maggie and the babe's lives? I just can't believe she made that shot. I don't know if I would have had the courage to take it. Hell, even thinking about having to take that shot—"

Hawke turned back toward where Hart worked with an especially headstrong stallion.

"None of us would have relished taking that shot, but there isn't any one of us who wouldn't have taken it to save their lives. She's an expert shot. Everyone's talking about it. It looks like we're all going to have to practice more. Eb tells me that he and Jeremiah taught both women to shoot and that Maggie's as good as Savannah."

Wyatt blinked. "You're kidding."

Hawke's lips twitched, the closest he ever got to smiling. "I'm not. She was damned brave, lowering the baby and telling Savannah to take the shot, knowing Savannah could have been too nervous or that that bastard could have jerked her around again. She knew that once Savannah shot, it would be over, and at least the babe would have been saved. Brave women—both of them."

Duke spoke from somewhere behind them, the large man not making a sound as he crossed the yard.

"That courage is what's going to get Savannah through this. That, and a lot of patience. Do yourself a favor, though, and don't treat her like a child. She's in shock. She's probably numb. Get her mind off of it as much as you can and get her back to her old self again."

* * * *

With Maggie's words of thanks and praise still ringing in her ears, Savannah faced her uncle through iron bars.

"How could you do this? What kind of man are you?"

Savannah stared at him, shaken to realize her uncle was a stranger. Ignoring the lecherous comments from the other men jailed with him, she cleared the lump in her throat.

"I don't even know you. I killed someone because of you."

Her uncle glared at her. "Where'd you learn to shoot like that? I thought I told you to stay away from guns."

Savannah wanted to throw up. "Did you hear me? I had to kill someone because of you."

Her uncle's shrug shocked her. "He was nobody. Listen, we can pray about it. Why don't you go get the keys hanging there beside the door, and let us out of here? We'll head south. We'll set up somewhere new, and you can do your penance for killing him. We'll have a fresh start."

Shaking her head, Savannah wrapped her arms around herself and sank into the only chair. "I can't believe this. You want to use the fact that I killed another man to get me to be your slave again. Just like before. You blamed me for my mother leaving, saying that if I'd been a good little girl, she never would have left me. You never meant any of it. It took me years to figure out that being good wouldn't bring her back. You've used me all my life."

Anger at herself and her own stupidity made her stomach roll. "I'm not letting you out. I'm not leaving here. Ever. I'm happier here than I've ever been in my life. You can rot in hell for all I care." She stood and went to the door, glancing at him as she opened it.

"I hate you."

Her uncle wrapped his hands around the bars, his knuckles white. "You're going to pay for that! I'm not the one who's going to rot in hell. You're the one who took a life, not me."

Savannah closed the door behind her and ran, not wanting to hear any more.

She felt dead inside. Empty. Confused. Lost.

Everything she'd ever believed in meant nothing now.

Her uncle, a professed man of God, was even more evil than she'd ever suspected. He cared even less about her than she'd ever thought. The years wasted had saddened her before, but now made her sick.

Once on her horse, she paused to look again at the house Wyatt and Hayes had built for her. One day soon, it might be home, but right now it was empty.

Only one place in the world felt like home, and that was where she needed to be. Wiping away tears with her sleeves, she headed in the direction of the ranch, anxious to be in her husbands' arms.

She found them sooner than she'd anticipated.

Both looked frantic with worry as they approached only minutes later.

Wyatt pulled her from his horse and across his lap, holding her tightly.

"Where the hell have you been? Everyone's out of their mind with worry, looking for you. Why aren't you wearing a gun?"

Sobs broke free before Savannah even realized they were there. Shaking so hard she could hardly speak, she pressed her face against Wyatt's chest and held on, crying harder when his arms closed around her.

"Hold me. Just hold me."

Safe and warm, she cried for herself, the man she'd killed, and the unwanted child who'd only wanted to be loved.

She cried in fear that she would never be able to fit into the new life she'd chosen for herself, and that the numbness surrounding her would never go away.

She'd killed a man.

Wyatt held her close, rubbing her back.

"Anytime, sweetheart. I'll hold you anytime you want. I love you, Savannah. Never forget that."

The tenderness in his tone had her crying even harder.

"Don't let go of me."

"Never."

Savannah slumped, knowing he would keep his word. She needed something real to hold on to, and she trusted Wyatt and Hayes to keep the rest of the world away until she could handle it again.

Chapter Fifteen

Her scream scared the hell out of Wyatt.

She bolted upright, her face wet with tears, her words coming out in a rush.

"I killed him. He was looking right at me and I pulled the trigger. I pretended it was a can. Maggie and I practiced with cans. But, it wasn't a can. It was a man, and I killed him."

Hayes eased her back and rolled on top of her.

"You had to do it. He had to die so Maggie and the baby could live. He would have killed them, Savannah. I'd give anything to have been able to take that shot for you, but you did it. You're strong. Don't let that bastard take that away from you."

Savannah's whimper tore at him, and he couldn't deny the flare of jealousy that he wasn't the one on top of her when she lifted tear-filled eyes to Hayes.

"Take me. Make me feel."

While Hayes made love to Savannah, Wyatt stayed beside them, kissing her and caressing her hair, listening to the soft sounds of Savannah being eased into the ultimate pleasure and let down slowly.

Surprised to find Hayes capable of giving Savannah the soft, sweet kind of loving she needed, Wyatt promised himself that he would show her the same kind of tenderness and affection the first chance he got.

Minutes later, she slept, while he and Hayes lay awake on either side of her.

He was so mad he could spit nails. He didn't know what he could do to penetrate the fog that surrounded Savannah, and he wanted to hit something.

When Eb and Jeremiah offered to let them stay with them until their bed arrived, Wyatt readily agreed.

Savannah didn't need to sleep on a cold floor, and he definitely didn't want her anywhere near the jailhouse until they transferred her uncle and the others to Tulsa.

It had taken them hours to get her to sleep. Alarmed at her trembling, he and Hayes had kept the lantern low and gathered her close between them. She'd stared at the ceiling wide-eyed, apparently lost in another world—one in which he and Hayes couldn't reach her.

Every time her eyes had begun to flutter closed, she'd whimpered and opened them wide again, as though something had frightened her.

She wouldn't speak to them, but their low voices had seemed to comfort her. She'd breathed easier and her eyes had begun to close again.

When her eyes closed and remained that way, her breathing evening out, he and Hayes had looked at each other over her sleeping form, hardly daring to move for fear of waking her.

Only to have her wake up screaming.

When she turned on her side facing Hayes, Wyatt curled up behind her, tightening the hand at her belly to pull her close. Careful to keep his voice low, he breathed in the scent of her, trying not to think about her naked ass pressing against his cock.

"How the hell are we going to get her past this? She won't let either one of us out of her sight. She won't eat. She just sits there with that glazed look in her eyes. She won't even hold the baby, just cries when she sees him."

Hayes sighed and dropped the back of his hand over his forehead. "We give her time. We give her love. Maybe we should take her with us tomorrow when we go to Tulsa."

Wyatt sighed, the knot in his stomach growing larger.

"Or, taking her could be the worst thing for her. Christ, I don't want to hurt her any more. This husband stuff isn't as easy as it looks. I can't stand seeing her this way. She's breaking my heart, and I don't know what the hell to do to fix it."

Hayes shifted in the bed beside her.

"She's so damned fragile and insecure, and yet she shoots better than any man I've ever met. It took sand to draw those pistols. She knew it was the only thing to do when she did it. We just have to be patient and keep reminding her of that. Until she gets over it, we're going to have to walk on eggshells around her."

Wyatt sighed in the darkness, marveling at the woman beside him. Every time he closed his eyes, he remembered the way her eyes had gone flat and cold right before she took the shot that saved Maggie.

And then he remembered how she fainted right afterward, and how she'd clung to him today, her face wet with tears as she begged him to hold her.

Every time he thought he couldn't love her more than he did at that moment, she proved him wrong. His love for her grew every day, every minute, until he thought he would burst.

Keeping her safe and making her happy had become more important to him than anything else in the world.

If only he could get through to her.

* * * *

Wyatt came awake a few hours later, too restless to sleep any more. After motioning to Hayes, he dressed in the darkness and quietly made his way downstairs.

He couldn't stop thinking about Savannah and the pain she suffered for taking a life. He wondered if perhaps they should take her somewhere else, a city where she would be safer.

He went out the door and started down the steps, pausing as the hairs on the back of his neck stood on end.

In a move as instinctive as breathing, he reached for his gun, pausing when he heard a chuckle.

"Good instincts, but not up to your usual standards. I could have shot you in the back before you even noticed me."

Already in a bad mood, Wyatt didn't need to deal with Jeremiah this morning.

"Yeah, well, you didn't, now did you?" Turning, he started for the chow house, in desperate need of some of Duke's strong coffee.

Jeremiah fell into step beside him.

"Savannah all right? We heard her scream a couple of hours ago."

The fear that had made his heart burst nearly out of his chest when her screams of horror woke him came rushing back.

"Nightmare."

"Figured as much. Nearly fell off the bed when I heard it and was halfway to her before I remembered that you and Hayes were there."

Wyatt nodded and said nothing. Once inside the already bustling building, he went straight to the coffee.

Duke handed him a biscuit.

"Savannah all right? She hardly touched her dinner last night. I warned everyone not to say anything about her shooting, but the men are nearly bursting at the seams with pride. Damned fine shooting. Bravest little thing I ever saw."

Jeremiah poured his own coffee.

"She had a nightmare last night."

To Wyatt's surprise, most of the men gathered around, grim-faced. The concern in their eyes humbled him and reminded him just how much men here cared for *all* the women who lived here.

Under normal circumstances, he would have kept it to himself, but he couldn't deny the sense of relief he felt at being able to share his worry.

In more private areas, he shared concerns dealing with Savannah with Hayes alone, another benefit of the lifestyle they'd chosen, but since everyone knew what happened the day before, he figured it might help to get other opinions.

With a sigh, he dropped onto one of the benches. "She can't get over killing a man. She's not eating. She has a hard time going to sleep, just stares at the ceiling for hours. When we finally get her to sleep, she wakes up screaming. She doesn't want to talk but keeps us in sight at all times. Hayes stayed with her because we didn't want her to wake up alone."

The other men nodded, their expressions of concern making Wyatt feel a little better.

Blade frowned. "I saw that she wasn't wearing her guns at dinner. Maybe it wasn't such a good idea to take them from her right now."

Wyatt set his empty cup aside.

"Hell, we didn't take them from her. I feel better if she's armed, especially after seeing the way she can shoot. She took them off and won't even look at them."

It frustrated the hell out of him, wondering how long he could let her go around unarmed in a place like this.

Gideon spoke up from the next table.

"You'd better get them back on her soon or you won't get her to wear them again at all."

Wyatt nodded. He'd already figured that out, but had no idea how to do it, short of holding her down and strapping her holster on her.

Probably not a good way to treat an almost hysterical woman.

"We've got to take her uncle and the others back to Tulsa—including the dead man. We're not sure if Savannah's going to insist on coming with us or not. We hope not, but, like I said, she won't let us out of her sight, and I'm sure as hell not going to leave her behind if she wants to go."

Picturing her face as she'd clung to him he groaned inwardly. He'd never be able to leave her here if she wanted to come with them.

The look on her face alone would haunt him.

After pouring a cup of coffee for both Hayes and Savannah, Wyatt straightened.

"I'll let you know whatever she decides. If she stays, will you all help keep an eye on her?"

Jeremiah slapped his back, his expression somber. "That goes without saying. You're in Desire now, remember? Hell, we knew it was going to take all of us to protect the women, but I don't think we realized the extent of it until now. In Savannah's present state, she won't even be able to protect herself. We've got to do something. Until then, we're all going to watch her like hawks."

* * * *

Savannah came awake to the sound of her own scream, jolting upright only seconds before the door to the bedroom flew open and Eb raced to her side.

With a hand at the back of her head, he held her close, his other hand rubbing her back in long, smooth strokes.

"You're all right. There's nobody here. You're safe. It's all right, honey."

Slumping against him, she took a shuddering breath, wishing it was Wyatt or Hayes holding her.

"I'm sorry. It's stupid." Embarrassed that she'd woken him for the fourth night in a row, Savannah pulled the covers higher.

Eb eased back. "It's not stupid, and you don't have anything to be sorry about."

He stood and seconds later a match struck. Eb lit the lantern on the table close to the bed, raising the wick to provide plenty of light. Taking a seat in the chair next to the table, he ran a hand through his disheveled hair and sat back.

"You've had nightmares every night since the shooting."

She reached for the shawl lying on the end of the bed and wrapped it around her shoulders, her face burning.

"I know. I'm sorry I keep waking you up. Between me and the babe, you're not getting any sleep at all."

Eb came to his feet. "Stay put. I'll be right back."

He came back minutes later with two glasses and a bottle of whiskey.

Savannah grimaced. "I don't want a drink."

Eb poured them anyway and handed her one. "Too bad. I'm not drinking alone and I think a couple of sips will do you good. Drink it or I'll pour it down you."

Savannah took the glass and smelled it, watching as he went back to the chair.

"It smells awful."

Eb smiled. "It's an acquired taste." His smile fell, his eyes narrowing. "Just take a sip or two. You're still shaking." His tone, one of a man used to giving orders, made her smile.

"You're bossy. I don't know why Maggie puts up with you."

Raising a brow, he eyed her steadily.

"Yes, you do. It's the same reason you put up with Wyatt and Hayes. You love them and know that they love you just as much. Your men are just as arrogant as I am, and you wouldn't want them any other way. Now, drink your damned whiskey."

Holding her breath against the strong smell, she took a healthy sip, and immediately began choking. She tried to gulp in air, tears filling her eyes at the burning sensation that travelled all the way down her throat and to her belly. Coughing, she struggled for air and tried to shove Eb away when he rushed to her side and started patting her back.

Finally able to breathe, she met his look of concern over her shoulder, missing Hayes and Wyatt more by the minute.

Eb presence steadied her, but didn't give her the comfort Wyatt's or Hayes's would have.

Attempting to lighten the mood, Savannah smacked at his arm. "Are you trying to kill me?"

Eb smiled, a smile that didn't reach his eyes.

"Hardly. Are you ready to talk about it? I know I'm not Hayes or Wyatt, but you and I have known each other a long time, Savannah. You know you can trust me."

She didn't know if the whiskey loosened her tongue or if the frustration of waking in the middle of the night to her own screams had gotten to her, but she nodded in silent agreement.

Waiting until he took his seat again, she hesitantly took another sip of her drink. Surprised to find that it tasted a little better than it had the last time, and liking the way it warmed her insides, Savannah scooted back against the large headboard and cradled the glass in her hand, staring down into it.

"It's different now." She spit the words out in a rush before she lost her courage, surprised to find that just saying them made her feel better. Glancing up to gauge his reaction, she wrapped both hands around the glass.

Eb raised a brow and set his drink aside.

"Oh? How?"

Savannah took another sip, finding each sip easier to drink than the last. She found it also made the dream seem further away and easier to talk about.

"At first I kept seeing that man's face. I was staring at his eyes when I shot him. I was trying to pretend his face was a can. It was the only way I could do it. The only way I could shoot him was to pretend I was shooting a can like we did back in Kansas City."

Eb nodded. "I can understand that. I'll be honest with you, Savannah, my heart was in my throat when I heard what Maggie said to you and I realized what you were going to do. As long as I live, I'll never be able to repay you for taking that shot. You saved Maggie's and Ace's lives. That man wouldn't have stopped. He held a gun to a woman and a baby. Any man who would do that would do anything. You know that."

After tossing back the remains of his drink, he poured another, a muscle working in his jaw. "I have my own nightmares about that day."

Sitting back, he regarded her steadily. "So, how did the dream change?"

Savannah shrugged and took another small sip, surprised that her eyes seemed to be getting heavier.

"Sometimes I still see his eyes when I shoot him, but then I miss him and hit Maggie. I killed her over and over. I killed my best friend. Everyone hated me after that and my best friend was gone."

Eb set his glass aside, his eyes piercing and filled with his own horror.

"That didn't happen." He slammed his glass on the table and slid from the chair to kneel at her feet, gripping her empty hand.

"My nightmare is the same, but it didn't happen. Another nightmare is that you didn't take the shot at all and that bastard took her, or killed her himself, which he would have as soon as she was no longer useful. Don't think for one minute, though, that we would have hated you if you'd missed. We all know how much you love Maggie and Ace. Any one of us would have taken that shot rather than let him kill her."

Her vision blurred as her eyes filled with tears.

"Something like that could happen again. What if everyone counted on me and I failed? What if someone's life depended on me and I got them killed? What if I couldn't take the life of another human being again, even if it would save the life of someone here?"

She took another sip, surprised to see that her glass was empty. "I killed a man, Eb."

Eb stood and took her glass, setting it on the table as he took his seat again.

"Wyatt and Hayes should be home soon. I'm glad you stayed here instead of going with them. You've changed in the last couple of days. Settled some."

Savannah shrugged negligently, but tears continued to well in her eyes.

"I miss Wyatt and Hayes. I didn't think I could feel anymore, but I miss Wyatt and Hayes so much."

She took a deep breath, and met Eb's searching gaze.

"I love them. I hate what I had to do, but I would do it again. It took time to realize that. I'd hate it, but I'd do it. God help me, I'd do it again to save someone I love."

Struggling to keep her eyes open, she pulled the shawl tighter around her against the chill that went through her. "I didn't know how hard it would be here. How primitive. How dangerous."

She looked up as the door opened, expecting Maggie or Jeremiah.

Her heart leapt into her throat when Wyatt walked through, followed closely behind by Hayes. Both men looked dirty, tired, and worried—but to her, they'd never looked better.

All the love she felt for them broke like a dam inside her, and a sob broke free before she could prevent it.

They both rushed toward her, barely glancing at Eb, their eyes raking over her with a breathtaking mixture of hunger, concern, and love.

Her pulse tripped, her body already tingling with awareness and aching to feel their bodies against hers.

"But to have Wyatt and Hayes in my life, I'd face anything. I don't think I could live without them."

Wyatt stepped forward.

"Something you'll never have to do." Bending, he touched his lips to hers. "I need to get cleaned up before I hold you." He glanced over his shoulder at Eb. "Problem?"

Eb came to his feet.

"Another nightmare. I wouldn't be surprised if it was the last. I think she just needed the two of you to get home. What took you so long?"

Hayes was already stripping off his clothes, revealing a leanly muscular body that never failed to arouse her.

"Got all the furniture and dealt with the sheriff. We aren't planning to leave again anytime soon. We'll be moving into the house tomorrow. Good night, Eb."

Laughing softly, Eb stood and moved to the door. "I can take a hint."

Hayes eyed her in the mirror as he poured water into the bowl and reached for the soap.

"Good. I want my wife. Get out."

Chapter Sixteen

Savannah giggled in delight when Hayes grabbed the hem of her nightgown and whipped it over her head, reaching for him even before the material could hit the floor.

"I missed you, you know? I was starting to wonder if you were ever coming back. I'm all right now. I keep having dreams, though."

Snuggling into him as he got into the bed beside her, Savannah traced the line of his scar with the tip of her finger.

"This makes you look scary, but in a roguish way. Very handsome."

Hayes narrowed his eyes. "You're drunk. Eb give you whiskey?"

Savannah nodded, that warm feeling inside her growing as his hand moved down her body.

"A little. I had a bad dream, and he gave me a drink. I killed Maggie."

"What?" Hayes looked more than a little shaken, and even Wyatt stopped washing up to come to the end of the bed.

Shaking her head, Savannah grinned. "Not really. In my dream." Her smile fell as the horror of that dream came back to her. "I missed and killed Maggie. Eb says he has the same dream. It's scary. I don't like that I killed a man, but I think I would do it again if I had to. I hope I never have to."

Hayes rubbed her stomach, his eyes filled with affection.

"Instead of thinking that, you should be remembering how strong you were. You found out what you could do if you had to."

Wyatt finished washing up, tossing the towel aside as he climbed into the bed on her other side.

"We all saw what you could do. Word of your shooting is all over Tulsa. Unfortunately, I think you're going to be a legend around here." He kissed her shoulder.

"And you're all ours. We've missed you."

Writhing beneath their hands, Savannah smiled at each of them in turn. "That whiskey was making me tired, but suddenly, I'm wide awake. I missed both of you so much. It's been so cold at night. It's not fair that I get married and then have to sleep alone."

Now that they were back, she felt muscles relax that she hadn't even realized had been so tense. Her awareness of them sharpened as everything else faded in the background.

She loved the texture of their skin, the hard muscles beneath the surface bunching and shifting every time they moved. Their firm hands stroked her skin with a sureness and possessiveness that took her breath away.

She felt alive again, in a way she hadn't felt since the shooting.

Wyatt bent and kissed a nipple, smiling when she jolted.

"Not fair at all. I guess your husbands are going to have to make it up to you."

Safe and warm between them, Savannah giggled, the whiskey doing strange things to her insides.

"I like that word." Keeping her voice at a whisper, she giggled again. "My uncle didn't like that I married two men."

Sobering as the love for them welled up inside her, she blinked back tears. "Thank you for loving me."

Hayes slid his hand lower to cover her mound. "We couldn't have done anything else." He slid a finger through her folds, his eyes widening. "You're soaking wet. Aroused, are you?"

Trying to hold on to embarrassment proved futile. Lifting her hips, she began to rock against him, holding Wyatt's head to her breast.

"I missed you, and I think the whiskey is doing strange things to me."

Wyatt lifted his head.

"This might be a good time to take that ass, while you're all loose and warm. Christ, my cock's already throbbing." He brushed her hair back from her forehead, the heat and tenderness in his eyes creating an answering need inside her.

"We'll go nice and slow, honey."

Wrapping her arms around his neck, Savannah sighed. "It's hot in here. Take the blankets off. I want to be naked."

Hayes raised a brow, a slow smile spreading across his face. "Yes, ma'am."

When he tossed the covers aside and reached for her, a sense of vulnerability came rushing back, and Savannah grabbed him, wrapping her arms around his neck in desperation.

"It's going to be all right now, won't it?"

Cupping the back of her head, Hayes held her close, his hand moving in circles across her belly.

"It's already all right. It's all over now. Those other men won't ever be able to shoot again. Who knows how many lives you saved?"

Savannah stilled. "I never thought about that."

Remembering the evil on the other men's faces, Savannah felt as if a huge weight had been lifted from her shoulders.

Wyatt groaned, his cock jumping against her hip.

"You're a brave woman, Savannah. You always have been. You did what you had to do in order to survive your uncle, even knocking him out when he drank. Yes, we know all about his drinking and what he tried to do when he had too much. You left the only home you've ever known to make a fresh start. You're not afraid to do what needs to be done, even shooting a man to protect your best friend and her baby."

She didn't want to think about any of that now. Right now, she wanted nothing more than to get lost in the feel of her husbands.

Just being this close to them after so many days apart aroused her. The feel of them, the look of them, the sounds they made and the slide of their hands over her body had a familiarity now that soothed her, but at the same time excited her.

They knew her body now. They knew what she liked and touched her in ways that made her dizzy with pleasure.

With their hands and eyes moving over her body with increasing heat, and the potent whiskey running through her veins, Savannah smiled and dropped back onto the pillow.

Wanting to take away the worry she still saw in their eyes, she arched her back, delighted when their gazes both dropped to her breasts. Her nipples drew even tighter and ached with the need to have their hands on them.

She couldn't resist teasing them, loving the challenge that sparked in their eyes whenever she did.

"And I took on two lawmen as husbands. Do you think I'm tough enough to deal with you?"

Wyatt's eyes narrowed and gleamed as she'd hoped, his lips twitching. "Let's put it to the test."

Cupping his jaw, Savannah stared into his eyes, struggling to keep hers open.

"I don't want you to worry about me anymore. I'm all right now, I promise."

Hayes laid her flat, running his hands over her, sending ribbons of sizzling warmth from her breasts to her slit. "You're very all right, and in a few minutes, you'll be even better."

He took her hand in his and wrapped it around his cock. "I haven't taken you in days. I'm hungry for you." Bending, he touched his lips to hers. "Starving."

She folded her hand over his cock, once again amazed that something so hard and threatening could be so silky soft.

Curious and more than a little aroused, Savannah pushed at his chest. "Move. I want to see."

With a groan, Hayes rolled to his back, his reluctance obvious, as was his desire to please her. "I'm not gonna last."

Her movements clumsy, Savannah got up, sitting back on her heels, fascinated at the hard body laid out before her. Every time she remembered that they both now belonged to her, love rushed through her veins and warmed her from within.

With trembling hands, she ran her fingers over his cock, intrigued at the way it jumped beneath her touch, delighted at the deep sounds of pleasure emanating from him.

With another groan, Hayes closed his eyes, opening them again almost immediately at her cry. The feel of Wyatt's hands coming around her from behind and sliding over her abdomen had her crying out hoarsely and whimpering in frustration.

Wyatt's warm breath tickled her ear as he parted her folds, his cock pressing insistently against her back. His firm fingers slid back and forth through her slippery slit, gathering her juices before pressing a work-roughened finger against her clit.

With his muscular thighs against her legs, she couldn't straighten them, forced to remain in the position he held her in.

"Wyatt, it's too much. I'm gonna come."

Hayes sat up in a rush, coming to kneel in front of her. Using his knees to push hers wide, he covered her hand and guided it up and down the length of his cock, his voice like shattered glass as she took over and he released it.

"Yeah, just like that. Now you can't close your thighs at all, darlin'. Nice and wide open just the way we like them." Covering her breasts with his hands, he toyed with her nipples, sending white-hot heat to her clit and pussy.

Wyatt scraped his teeth across her shoulder and pulled her back against him, tilting her hips and sliding a hard finger into her pussy. "Hot and wet and helpless. Just the way you should always be. Take Hayes's cock into your mouth and suck it the way you did to me that night."

Giggling at the groan that rumbled from deep within Hayes's chest, Savannah bent forward and licked the drop of moisture from the tip, smiling when he groaned again.

Her smile fell when he tightened his fingers on her nipples, the slight pain making her pussy clench on Wyatt's finger, soaking it even more with her juices.

Holding on to Hayes's hips, she dropped back against Wyatt, rocking her hips in time to the strokes to her clit and his increasingly forceful thrusts into her pussy.

Her moans, muffled by the cock in her mouth, came out steadily now as their hands became even more devious and more insistent. She felt them everywhere, her pussy, clit, and nipples burning with sensation. Her bottom clenched, the promise of attention there almost too much to bear. The combination of pleasure and whiskey made her dizzy, forcing her to lean back heavily against Wyatt for support.

Her body gathered, each stroke to her clit making her stiffen, clenching on the finger inside her. When Hayes withdrew from her mouth, she reached for him again, only to have her hands taken in his. His mouth covered hers, swallowing her cries as the pleasure inside her exploded.

Unable to close against Wyatt's slow moving fingers, Savannah whimpered as the pleasure crested, pressing her thighs hard against Hayes's knees.

"Please. Oh, God. Too much. It's not stopping."

Alarmed that instead of starting to ease, the pleasure seemed never ending. It went on and on, and nothing she could do could stop it.

Her entire body tingled, from her neck to her toes, the wash of heat engulfing her in a wave of bliss.

Her clit became so sensitive that the lightest touch kept her orgasm rolling through her and making it nearly impossible to breathe.

Wyatt seemed to know it, his touch becoming lighter and slower, giving her just enough to keep the pleasure at its peak.

She couldn't breathe. She couldn't think, the dizziness growing stronger by the second.

All she knew was pleasure and the sensation of love and heat all around her.

"I can't stop. So good. Ah, God. I don't want it to end. Oh! No more. No more."

Even when Wyatt withdrew from her pussy and slid his finger from her clit, the pleasure lingered, warm waves of it that held her in its grip. Slumping against Wyatt, she whimpered and tried to open her eyes, desperate to see the men she loved, but it proved too much effort.

"I love you."

It came out as a whisper, and she wasn't sure they heard her, so she tried again. "I love…"

* * * *

Hayes ran a hand through her hair, watching as her eyes closed and didn't open again. Taking in her flushed cheeks and parted lips, he knew it was an image he wouldn't forget for a long time.

The huskiness in her voice sent another surge of lust to his cock, while the soft whimper in it brought all of his protective instincts to the surface.

A powerful combination.

"I love you, too, darlin'."

With a heartfelt sigh that their loving tonight had ended far sooner than he'd hoped, he smiled.

Wyatt chuckled and wrapped his arms around her from behind, kissing her neck and grinning when she murmured in her sleep.

"Our tough little wife."

Hayes threw back the covers as Wyatt lifted her and placed her on the bed. Sliding in beside her, he wrapped an arm around her and pulled her close, waiting until Wyatt settled in on the other side of her and blew out the lamp.

"Word got around Tulsa pretty fast about her shooting. I hope it keeps folks from bothering her."

Wyatt sighed. "My fear is that it'll go the other way. Some young gun is going to challenge her to prove he's faster."

"God forbid."

Exhausted from riding all night to get home to her, Hayes still couldn't settle. His cock still pounded, desperate for relief, and his mind remained restless. Just the thought of someone challenging Savannah would give *him* nightmares.

Chapter Seventeen

"Strip." Wyatt removed his hat and tossed it aside, his eyes narrowed on hers. Standing with his feet several inches apart and his hands on his hips, he looked every inch the furious lawman, while the hunger and impatience in his eyes reminded her of a disgruntled husband.

Hiding a smile, Savannah turned to face him fully and raised a brow. "Well now, that's real romantic."

"I'm not romantic. I'm aroused."

In fact, they'd been sweet and solicitous to her all day, treating her as if she just might break at any moment.

Apart from the fact that it had started to drive her crazy, she wanted her husbands to see that she was more than capable of handling whatever came at her—especially with the two of them by her side.

She didn't think she'd ever get over killing a man, but she'd thought about it for days and realized she'd had no other choice. She'd meant what she'd said.

She would do it again, if she had to. She wouldn't like it and would avoid it at all costs, but if her life or the life of a friend was in danger, she'd do it.

She just hoped that she would never have to point her gun at another human being for as long as she lived.

She didn't want to think about it, and their constant fussing had begun to get on her nerves. She'd spent most of the day doing what she could to prove to them that she hadn't fallen apart, and that she wanted her men again.

Teasing them mercilessly had been the only thing she could think of.

Evidently, she'd done a good job.

Wyatt had already begun stripping out of his clothes, his movements hurried and lacking his usual grace as he tossed each item he removed aside.

"I'm not in the mood for romance. I'm in the mood for hot, sweaty sex. I haven't had you for almost a week, and after falling asleep on us last night, you've spent the entire day teasing us and laughing at us. You're going to pay for that, *wife*."

Savannah struggled to hide a smile and started to undress, anxious to climb into the bathtub they'd filled and wash with some of the scented soap Maggie had sent with her to her new home.

"Honestly, Wyatt, I have no idea what you mean." Tossing her shirt aside, she bit her lip to keep from smiling as Wyatt's gaze lingered on her bare breasts.

"Yes, you do." Wearing only his pants, Wyatt strode across the room to her, yanking her clothing off with a haste that had her giggling. His hands roamed over her with an impatience she'd never seen in him before.

"We try to be gentle and understanding, and you start flirting and twitching your ass at us." His eyes lingered on her breasts, making them swell and ache. When he lifted his gaze to hers, the hunger in his narrowed eyes stole her breath.

Savannah held on to his shoulders as he knelt in front of her to remove her pants, digging her fingers into the hard muscle beneath her hands. Loving the texture and warmth of his bare skin, she let her hands roam, her breath catching as he tossed the last of her clothing aside. A moan escaped at the feel of his hands sliding up her legs, his thumbs brushing the tender skin of her inner thighs.

Throwing her head back, she threaded her fingers through his hair, her stomach muscles quivering beneath his lips.

"I'm all d–dirty and sweaty. Let me take a b–bath. It feels so good when you touch me. You've hardly touched me all day."

Hayes came through the door with yet another bucket of hot water, setting it down by the tub with enough force that water sloshed over the sides.

"Scared to. Probably would have attacked you. Take your bath. Move it."

Before she could move, Savannah found herself in Wyatt's arms and plopped into the bathtub full of warm water. With her body already humming with desire, she reached for the soap and a small cloth and watched as Wyatt and Hayes both finished undressing.

She ran the soapy cloth over herself as she admired every inch of skin that came into view. She hadn't become accustomed to bathing in front of her husbands, but found herself too busy watching them to mind much at all. Keeping her eyes on Hayes as he stripped off his shirt and yanked at the covers to pull them all to the foot of the bed, she lay back in the tub and lifted a leg to wash it.

"You're imagining things. I never flirt, and I've never *twitched* my bottom at anyone."

Wyatt paused with his hands at the fastening of his pants, drawing her attention once more to the large bulge just a few inches lower.

"Bullshit. You've been twitching that ass at us all day, bending over when you didn't need to and shaking your hips. Touching us every chance you got." The indulgence and mischief in his eyes took the sting out of his words.

She wet her hair and started to wash it, her breasts swelling under their combined stares. Pretending she didn't notice, she scrubbed furiously, knowing full well that her breasts swayed when she did. "You're my husbands. I'm not allowed to touch you?"

Wyatt's eyes narrowed. "You've been brushing your hands over our arms and chests every chance you get."

"I told you I was just brushing the dirt off of you."

"You rubbed up against me while we were standing in line for supper, giving me those damned looks."

Hiding how much he intimidated her, standing tall and half naked with his hands on his hips, Savannah blinked innocently. Her gaze drifted to Hayes, who shoved his pants down to his ankles and stepped out of them, his movements hurried.

She couldn't resist watching their strong bodies as they moved. Most of the time, she'd been naked and with their hands on her, and when that happened, she didn't get a chance to see much of anything.

Not knowing how long she'd have the chance to watch them in action, she wanted to take full advantage of the opportunity.

After rinsing her hair, she settled on one side with her hands at the rim of the tub and her chin resting on them. In this position, she could watch both of them, her stomach tightening as need overtook her. "What looks?"

Hayes lifted his head, narrowing his eyes in that way that always made her clit tingle. "*That* look. You've been giving me that look all day like you want to take a bite out of me. Then, you were brushing against me during supper, fidgeting in your seat and rubbing the side of your breast against my arm. I should have thrown you over my shoulder right then and there and brought you back here."

Not knowing how long she had before they took over, Savannah leaned back and lifted her legs out of the water to rest on the edge, delighted that both men stopped what they were doing to stare at them. She never would have imagined having this kind of power over two such commanding men, and found she enjoyed playing, something she had little experience with, very much.

Deciding to play a little more, Savannah shrugged and looked away. "I have no idea what you're talking about." Taking the soap, she worked it between her wet hands until they were slippery. Setting the soap aside, she began running her hands over her breasts, but her touch didn't give her the satisfaction she craved.

Lifting her gaze, she paused with her palms over her nipples, frozen at the looks of hunger on Wyatt's and Hayes's faces.

Wyatt's eyes narrowed dangerously. "That's it. I can't take anymore."

In three strides he reached her, using the cloth to rinse her and lifted her by her upper arms to stand in the tub.

"You're done." Running his hands over her, he held her at arm's length, his eyes taking in her nakedness and making her skin tingle everywhere.

"Damn, you look good naked and wet." He lifted her out of the tub and set her on her feet on a small piece of cloth on the wooden floor, and wrapped another around her.

"Let me get cleaned up. Dry off for me. Nice and slow so I can watch you."

She stood frozen, unable to look away from him as he got into the tub, her eyes drawn to his thick cock. Knowing that cock would soon be filling her sent a wave of longing through her that made it difficult to remain on her feet.

Wyatt sank into the tub and reached for the soap, lifting it to his nose and making a face before placing it back on the edge of the tub.

"Hayes, hand me the regular soap. This is Savannah's."

Hayes tossed him another soap and wrapped his arms around her from behind.

"It smells good on you." Cursing, he released her. "I'm too dirty. Hurry up, Wyatt. I want to get my hands on her. After what she's done to us today, I'm more than just hungry for her. As a matter of fact, I think I'm going to start now."

She'd started to lean back against him, only to have him set her upright and move around to stand in front of her.

"Stay back. I don't want you to get dirty." Hayes held her shoulders to steady her, his eyes hooded as they met hers.

"I like you wet. Everywhere."

He sighed, rubbing the cloth over her. "But I don't want you getting chilled. Let's get you dried off, and then you can spread those thighs for me so I can deal with something else that's wet."

She'd hoped that she would be able to get their interest by teasing them the way she had this afternoon, but she hadn't counted on their overwhelming responses.

She also hadn't anticipated the effect teasing them would have on *her*.

She found herself embracing her femininity in a way that was totally foreign.

And totally irresistible.

She couldn't wait to explore this feeling further, but for now, she wanted nothing more than to get lost in delicious pleasure.

Her breasts, already sensitive, seemed to swell under the firm hands guiding the rough cloth over them. Her nipples, already beaded and needy, tightened even more under his ministrations, each touch to them sending waves of delight to her slit.

The friction of his slow, circular strokes continued downward, passing over her belly and to her mound and then to her inner thighs, each brush of the cloth heightening her body's sensitivity until she shook with need.

"You're trembling. Wait until I get my mouth on you. I've been thinking about eating and fucking this pussy all day."

Shaking harder now, she had to hold on to him, locking her knees against the weakness that settled in her limbs. Her hands slipped from his shoulders as she turned to watch Wyatt, and she grabbed for him again, delighting at the play of muscle under her fingers.

She got her wish to see more of Wyatt when he stood, her mouth watering at the sight of his thick cock jutting out from his body. With Hayes rubbing her dry and Wyatt standing only feet away, naked and soaking wet, Savannah's lust soared, her juices dampening her thighs as her body prepared for them.

Wyatt stepped out and ran a cloth over his body as if he didn't care if he dried or not, and started toward her, his thick cock bobbing with every step.

"I'll finish drying her and getting that ass slick while you wash off."

Their fascination with her appeared to be just as strong as her own fascination with them. Neither one of them seemed to be able to look away from her for long, their eyes narrowing as they travelled repeatedly up and down her body. They licked their lips, the hard lines of their own bodies seeming more and more tense every minute, and they touched her each time they got close.

Taking the cloth from Hayes as he approached, Wyatt circled her and wrapped it and his arms around her from behind. Bending to touch his lips to her shoulder, he inhaled sharply.

"Are you sure you're all right?"

In contrast to the hard cock pressing into her back and the huskiness of hunger in his voice, Wyatt held her with such tenderness it brought tears to her eyes.

Letting her love for him shine in them she turned to smile up at him over her shoulder, aware of Hayes's stillness across the room.

"As long as you and Hayes love me, I'm wonderful." She started to turn in his arms, but he held firm.

Different, but no less arousing than Hayes's slow caresses, Wyatt's firm, demanding ones changed the mood in just seconds.

"In that case, you're going to be wonderful for the rest of your life."

The loving tenderness beneath the hard edge of need proved to be an irresistible combination, the affection making the need even stronger.

After Wyatt dried her back, he turned her slightly toward the bed and knelt behind her, pushing her feet apart.

"Bend over and put your hands flat on the bed."

Shivering at his tone and at the slide of his hands up and down the backs of her thighs, Savannah did as he wanted, shocked at how exposed she felt in this position.

The sensation became even stronger when Wyatt slid his hands to her bottom and parted her cheeks, exposing her bottom hole until she could feel the air move on her there.

Sucking in a breath at the slight sting, she turned her head when the sound of water splashing got her attention.

The water ran in rivulets down Hayes's hard frame as he stepped from the tub, making her fingers itch to follow them with her hands.

Biting her lip as Wyatt's tongue traced a pattern over her bottom, she couldn't take her eyes from Hayes as he raised his arms to push his wet hair back from his face, the muscles in his arms and chest more pronounced at the movement.

Another rush of moisture escaped, her bottom and pussy clenching as Hayes stepped from the tub, her bottom hole tingling at the attention from Wyatt.

The sensation of being so exposed made it harder to concentrate on watching Hayes, especially when Wyatt touched his tongue to her puckered opening, tightening his hands until it stung even more.

She jolted with a squeal, falling to her face on the bed as her arms gave out, the sensation so incredibly alarming and decadent that it completely disarmed her.

Wyatt ran a hand over her bottom, using his thumbs to trace circles over her tight opening.

"Even better. Stay that way. I've been thinking about fucking this ass all day. Hayes, she's real responsive here. She keeps pushing back against me. She's almost ready. Once I get some salve worked into her and play with her a little, she'll be begging to have her ass fucked."

Savannah gasped as his finger slid over the sensitive skin, her hands tightening into fists when he started to put pressure against the ring of muscle.

"Just take me, damn it." She couldn't take any more games. "I need you. I don't want to play anymore."

Hayes knelt on the bed in front her, reaching under her to cup her breasts.

"After what you did to us today? You've got me so wound up, my cock's ready to explode."

Taking her nipples between his thumbs and forefingers, he pinched slightly and rolled them, moving closer to kiss the center of her back.

"But I'm going to tease you, lady, as long as I can, to make *you* suffer some of what you put us through all day." The tension in his voice made it clear the play couldn't last for long, and she was determined to make him lose that last bit of control as soon as possible.

Feeling his cock brush against her shoulder, Savannah turned her face toward it and licked it, sucking in another breath when Wyatt nipped the tender flesh between her thigh and buttock. Pleased when Hayes stilled, she licked his cock again.

"I thought you liked it." Her breath came out in raspy pants, the effort to remain still against Wyatt's teasing costing her dearly.

Hayes groaned, his hands covering her breasts and massaging them, the muscles in his thighs tightening when she swiped his cock with her tongue.

"I did. You will, too. Wyatt, move her back a little to give me some room. You can work on her ass while I have some fun. I'm going to tease her clit until she's screaming for mercy."

Wyatt chuckled. "She's already soaked. Don't make her come. I don't want her to come until I'm in her ass."

Savannah couldn't believe how much their talk excited her. She should have already realized from teasing them today that the anticipation excited her almost as much as having them touch her, but she hadn't known how much it would arouse her to hear them talk to each other about what they planned to do to her.

They handled her with an ease that made her heart race even faster, standing her up briefly to make room for Hayes to sit on the floor and then forcing her to bend over him.

Hayes leaned back against the high bed, holding on to her hips as Wyatt spread her legs again. This position left her pussy and clit brushing Hayes's mouth and her ass spread wide and exposed to whatever devious plans Wyatt had for it.

Shaking uncontrollably, she fisted her hands in the covers in an effort to brace herself, but Hayes and Wyatt seemed to have no problem supporting her.

Hayes drove her crazy, the quick flicks of his tongue over her clit sending her higher and higher, but not giving her the relief she needed.

His hands held firm, keeping her clit pressed against his mouth no matter how much she squirmed, something she did more and more as Wyatt continued to play with her forbidden opening.

Using one hand to lift and part her buttocks, Wyatt teased her bottom opening with his finger.

"In just a couple of minutes, I'm going to be balls deep inside this tight little ass. Let's see how much you're teasing us then."

Savannah tried to rub her clit against Hayes's mouth, shaking even harder as the tingling heat started to spread.

"You gonna talk, Sheriff, or are you going to—ah, oh God, more—take me?" She didn't want to admit her fear of being taken there, especially when Wyatt's attention awakened her ass and made her crave the need to be filled in her most vulnerable opening.

Hayes chuckled against her clit, sinking his finger all the way into her pussy.

"Like that, do you? Wyatt, hurry up."

Wyatt groaned, his hands disappearing and leaving her feeling bereft. Just seconds later, she heard the unmistakable sounds of the tin of salve being opened, and a second later, it hit the floor.

"Hold her."

Savannah bucked as a slick finger pressed hard against her bottom hole and forced the tight ring of muscle to give way as he entered her. Her entire slit burned, from her clit to her ass, each stroke of their fingers and swipe of Hayes's tongue driving her need even higher.

Moans poured out of her, each one more pitiful and needy than the last as the pleasure mounted. Her clit throbbed so badly it almost hurt, her bottom clenching on the finger Wyatt had speared into her, and the one Hayes moved way too slowly in and out of her pussy.

By keeping her in this position, they controlled just how they could touch her, and she couldn't do a thing about it.

She loved it.

She reveled in being under their control, especially when she knew that they would never do anything to harm her, and that the slightest word from her would halt everything.

It allowed her to give in to them as she would never have dreamed of giving in, letting her give up some of the control she'd kept such a tight rein on her entire life.

With a hard arm around her belly, Wyatt held her steady, groaning when her knees gave out.

"Now I'm going to use two fingers. I want to stretch you out a little more."

"Oh, God."

Anticipation heightened her senses, making every touch more potent and causing her to shake even harder.

As Wyatt's finger slid out of her, she held her breath, sucking it in again when two fingers pressed at her opening. Chills raced up and down her spine as he began to push them into her, the sting of being stretched almost more than she could bear.

"Oh, God. Oh, God. It stings. It burns. I need to come. I need to come *now*."

Hayes withdrew from her pussy with a speed that left her clenching, each of his infrequent and light licks to her clit making her jolt.

The fingers in her bottom, though, held most of her attention, the slow, relentless invasion making her even more aware of her vulnerability. The friction of his callused fingers against her inner walls proved to be so disarming, she slumped weakly, her body a mass of trembling nerves.

"I can't. Oh, God. I need to come. It's…it's too much. I can't think. No!"

Wyatt slipped his fingers free at the same time Hayes lifted her from his mouth.

"You're not fucking coming until I get my cock up this tight ass."

She might have taken offense at his words if they hadn't come out in such a tortured groan.

"What if it doesn't fit? You're not going to leave me like this, are you?"

As Wyatt released her, Hayes gathered her close and sat on the edge of the bed with her on his lap. Brushing her still-damp hair back from her forehead, Hayes kissed her hard. When he lifted his head, the blazing heat in his eyes threatened to scorch her as his hands went to her waist.

"It'll fit. It'll work. We're not done until we're all done. Come here."

Wrapping her arms around his neck, she cried out at the flick of his tongue over her nipple as he raised her and then lowered her onto his cock, impaling her with his thick heat.

Her juices made it easy for her to take him, but the sensation of being so full kept her from moving.

"Hayes. It's so deep. It's so big. Oh, God. I can't stop. I'm gonna come."

With his brilliant green eyes steady on hers, Hayes squeezed her bottom cheeks, making her puckered opening sting.

"Darlin', you know how to make a man feel ten feet tall. In just a minute, this ass is going to be just as filled with cock as your pussy."

Savannah couldn't stop clenching, the awareness in her bottom demanding that she be taken there. Now that Wyatt had brought the nerve endings in her bottom to life, she needed attention there, but she didn't know if she could handle what they had in store for her.

Kicking her feet, she dug her fingers into his shoulders. "I burn everywhere. Do something."

Hayes chuckled again, his laugh stopping abruptly when she clenched on him again. Wrapping his arms around her, he dropped to his back, taking her with him.

"Be still. I can't move until Wyatt's inside you. Then we're going to both move, so you'll be fucked in both openings at the same time. Stay still, Savannah."

A sharp slap on her ass made her squeal a second before Wyatt grabbed a buttock in each hand and spread her wide.

"Slow, Savannah." His voice, barely recognizable, held a determination she'd never heard in it before. "Don't you fucking move."

Hayes held a firm hand at her lower back and one in her hair. "I've got her. She's not going anywhere."

Savannah cried out when the huge head of Wyatt's cock pressed at her opening, feeling much more threatening and dangerous than his fingers had. It burned as it entered her, her breath coming out in sharp pants as she tried to adjust to such a heart-stopping invasion. She couldn't move so much as an inch in any direction as Wyatt and Hayes forced her to remain immobile while Wyatt pushed his cock relentlessly into her ass.

"Oh, God. Hayes. Wyatt's inside me. He's putting it in me." She groaned as Wyatt's cock went a little deeper, each inch taking as much of her heart and soul as it did her body.

She'd never imagined she could ever feel so taken, but in that moment, they took everything. Nothing existed except them. Nothing else mattered.

Hayes groaned, his hands firming and keeping her against his chest.

"How does it feel? Tell me."

Shaking her head from side to side, Savannah buried her face against his throat and whimpered.

"I'm so full. It's not possible to feel this full. It's so hot. So hard. So deep." A shiver went through her as the tingling feeling increased, spreading everywhere. "It's like I'm coming, but I'm not. Maybe I am. Oh, God. I don't know. Oh! It's so deep. It's stretching me, and it burns."

With the heat of their bodies surrounding her and fuller than she even thought possible, Savannah struggled to adapt, her body clenching on the thick cocks filling her and making her feel even fuller. Taken as never before, she didn't even recognize the sensations running through her, the feeling so foreign and naughty she struggled to fight it.

Every inch of her skin shivered and tingled, the hot and cold mingling into something that sent her pulse soaring.

Wyatt's hands tightened. "She can't take any more. She's so fucking tight. Jesus, I've never felt anything so good. I could spend the rest of my life right here."

Running his hands up and down her back, Hayes kissed her hair. "You all right, honey?"

Everything trembled, shivers and sizzling heat racing over her in waves. "I don't know. Oh, God. I never felt like this."

Suddenly, the need to sit up became overwhelming. Pushing against Hayes's chest, she gingerly rose, surprised that he let her, her breath catching at the shifting of the cocks inside her.

Her breasts felt so swollen and heavy, her nipples tingling with the need for attention. Her clit ached unbearably and she knew that the slightest caress there would send her hurtling off the edge.

Sensation seemed to pound at her from all sides, so intense that she didn't stand a chance at holding back.

Her cries and moans filled the small room, mingling with the groans of her husbands as they began to move.

Nothing could have prepared her for the feel of being taken in both openings at the same time. The friction of their cocks against the inner walls of both her pussy and ass as they moved together overwhelmed her and she found she couldn't focus on either.

Both men seemed more caught up in it than ever before, adding to the intensity.

Hayes groaned hoarsely, holding her slightly above his chest, his hips moving continuously as he fucked her pussy, drawing his length about halfway out before thrusting deep again. In the low lamplight, the look on his face appeared anguished, the scar on his cheek more pronounced than ever.

He looked dark and dangerous lying beneath her, holding her to him as if he would never let her go. His slow, deep thrusts never faltered, the rhythm of them matching that of Wyatt's.

He withdrew several inches as Wyatt's smooth stroke filled her ass, and thrust deep again as Wyatt withdrew almost completely.

She'd never felt so primitive before, so wild and hungry for physical satisfaction. Her body no longer felt like her own, locked in the grip of something so powerful she had no control.

Shaking with pleasure, lost in sensation, Savannah held on to Hayes, the only solid thing in her world. The tingling heat that encompassed every part of her body grew stronger with each stroke, making her nipples sizzle and bead even tighter. She tried to move faster as the heat at her slit grew, those incredible tingles growing too sharp and focused for her to be still, but her men held firm.

Through it all, Hayes stared up at her, his eyes watchful and hungry. His hands held her steadily as he surged into her.

"Easy, darlin'. Slow. And. Easy. Too fucking good."

"No." It came out in a whimper as Wyatt filled her ass again. "I c– can't. It's…I…oh, God!"

It slammed into her, the shock of its strength stealing what little breath she had. It rolled through her, the heat and pinpricks of sensation starting at her slit and spreading outward, taking control of her body as it went through her.

She felt it everywhere, the sublime pleasure making her body tighten and her muscles quiver. Her clit felt huge. The cocks in her ass and pussy jumped inside her, making her feel fuller than ever, the hard thickness in both places suddenly more threatening than ever.

She'd never felt so full, never felt so taken, never felt so completely lost in sensation. She belonged to them as never before, giving herself over to pleasure that went way beyond just physical.

Stiffening, Savannah cried out, her voice raw and hoarse as the wave of pleasure crested. It held her in its grip, her pussy clenching in hard spasms.

Hayes groaned, his hands tightening on her hips as he surged deep.

"Jesus!"

Wyatt's hands slid from her waist to her shoulders, his harsh groan sounding tortured and filled with pleasure.

"It's killing me."

Savannah whimpered as her orgasm released her from its hold, the shimmering waves lessening in slow increments, leaving her weak and trembling. The sounds of harsh breathing and low moans mingled together until she didn't know which belonged to her and which belonged to her husbands.

She didn't care.

Too weak to hold herself upright, she allowed Hayes to lower her to his chest, grateful for the strong arms that came around her and for the solid heat beneath her.

She couldn't stop shaking. Each small movement by any one of them, even drawing a deep breath, moved both cocks inside her, making her pussy and ass clench. As another wave of tingles went through her, she moaned and buried her face against Hayes's chest.

"What just happened?"

Wyatt's chuckle broke off and became a moan.

"I don't know. We loved you. Give me an hour or so for my heart to settle down and the blood to flow back into my brain and we'll talk." With another groan he slid free of her ass and straightened, running his hands over her bottom and thighs.

"You all right, darlin'?"

Savannah jumped when the damp cloth touched her bottom, wiggling on Hayes's cock when Wyatt started to wipe her clean.

Wrapping his arms more firmly around her and tangling his hands in her hair, Hayes touched his lips to her forehead.

"She's good. I was watching her the entire time. I loved watching her fall apart like that."

Savannah started to lift her head, but decided it would be way too much effort. Smiling, she breathed in the clean scent of soap on Hayes's skin.

"I'm right here, you know."

Running his hands up and down her back, Hayes lifted his hips, moving his cock inside her.

"I know exactly where you are. Say it."

Knowing exactly what he meant, Savannah lifted her head, propping her chin on the hand she laid flat on his chest. Breathing a sigh of relief when Wyatt dropped the cloth and moved to lie beside her, she smiled at Hayes, recognizing the underlying intensity in his deceptively mild tone.

"I love you. Now, you say it back to me."

Wyatt chuckled, never opening his eyes. "She's gonna be trouble."

Hayes smiled, a mere twitch of his lips, but the muscles beneath her relaxed, the tension leaving his body in a sigh.

"Love you, too. Hell, you're going to make me say it all the time, aren't you?"

Despite his gruff tone, she could tell that the idea didn't bother him at all.

Hayes rolled her to her back in a quick move that made her giggle as Wyatt cursed and moved out of the way.

Brushing her hair back from her face, Hayes withdrew from her and dropped to her side so that he and Wyatt lay on either side of her. He bent to brush her lips with his before lifting his head and staring down at her, running a finger over her breast and lightly circling her nipple.

"It's getting easier. I might just get used to it."

Rubbing her thighs together, Savannah groaned, lifting into his caress, surprised at the shiver of pleasure.

"You'd better get used to that. God, that feels good. I'm so worn out I can barely keep my eyes open, and it still arouses me when you touch me."

Wyatt lifted her thigh over his and teased the sensitive spot behind her knee before running his fingertips up her inner thigh, smiling at her moan.

"Obviously not worn out enough. Tell me you love me, too, and I'll make you come again."

Cupping his cheek, Savannah let out a cry as he parted her folds and began to caress her clit. Lifting her hips, she held on to him, another cry escaping when Hayes propped his head on his hand, his eyes indulgent as he toyed with her nipples.

Thrusting her fingers into Wyatt's still-damp hair, she pulled him closer, brushing her lips over his chin. Despite her drowsiness and need, she couldn't resist the urge to tease him. She felt closer to him and to Hayes now than she ever had before, her pussy and bottom still tingling with awareness.

"How will you know if I'm telling the truth, Sheriff?"

Wyatt smiled and touched his lips to hers, increasing the strokes to her clit. "I'll know. Say it."

Her clit had become so sensitive that even the slightest touch of Wyatt's finger sent her senses soaring. With the attention to her nipples and the still-sharp awareness in her pussy and clit, she started to tremble almost immediately. Her weakened condition and the confident touch of a man who knew her body intimately made it impossible to hold back anything. Much faster than she'd thought possible, he sent her over the edge again.

It happened so fast she couldn't breathe, the last of her strength gone. Completely spent, she whimpered as he slowed his soft caress, leaning into him.

"I love you."

Wyatt pulled her close and settled her against him. "I know, honey. I know."

* * * *

She woke hours later, still settled against Wyatt. Blinking at the low light, she watched curiously as Hayes unfolded a piece of paper he'd just retrieved from the pocket of the shirt that he'd picked up from the floor.

"What's that?"

Hayes didn't seem the least bit self-conscious about his nudity as he crossed the room to the small table by the door and used a key to open the small chest that sat on top of it.

"The written laws of Desire. It's a paper we drew up and that every man who lives here must agree to. They decided the sheriffs should hold on to it for safekeeping."

Sitting up, Savannah smiled at Wyatt's low grumble and tucked the sheet around herself.

"Can I see it?"

"No."

Savannah blinked at his abrupt answer. "Why not?"

Hayes locked the chest and set the key aside.

"Because it doesn't concern you." He blew out the lamp and got into bed next to her, pulling her to him until her head was pillowed on his chest.

"Don't make that face at me. It's just the laws that protect the town and the women and make it possible for us to live the way we want to live."

Savannah stilled, an uneasy feeling settling in the pit of her stomach.

"Will we be all right? Will this thing work between us? One wife. Two husbands. Promise me it'll be all right, Hayes. I never thought it would be possible to love two men, but I couldn't stand it if I lost either one of you."

Hayes pulled her closer, lifting her chin and pressing his lips unerringly to hers, somehow finding her mouth even in the darkness.

"There's no way you're going to lose either one of us. I'll love you until the day I die."

Wyatt reached for her hand and laced his fingers with hers. "And beyond. If it doesn't work here, we'll find somewhere else." Chuckling softly, he kissed her shoulder. "With the determination of the men here, I have no doubt that it'll be fine here, and others are going to be coming here in droves. Now stop worrying and go to sleep."

Savannah smiled in the darkness as Hayes pulled her more firmly against him, while Wyatt curled up at her back.

She'd found more love than she'd ever thought possible, and looked forward to the rest of her life with a giddiness that made her dizzy.

Desire.

She'd found it, in more ways than she'd ever anticipated.

Epilogue

Savannah grinned as her husbands approached, admiring the fine figures they made as they rode toward her. All hard lines and muscle, they looked damned intimidating, but their eyes held nothing but gentle concern and hunger as they met hers.

She'd been married for two months now, and her heart still skipped a beat each time she saw them. Even covered with dirt and sweaty, they were the most beautiful men she ever saw.

"Hello, Sheriffs. You look like you've had a busy morning."

Removing his hat, Wyatt let his gaze roam over her as he used his sleeve to wipe his forehead.

"Couple of the Tylers' purebreds got caught up in some brush. Could have cut them loose, but the stupid things wouldn't cooperate." Lowering his voice, he leaned forward. "You, wife, look good enough to eat."

Even though she'd been on the receiving end of their flirtatious and sometimes even lewd comments, Savannah couldn't keep her face from burning as need shot through her. The remembered feel of his mouth on her pussy, his soft hair brushing against her inner thighs came rushing back.

Hayes moved closer, his eyes hooded beneath the brim of his hat.

"Where are you headed in such a hurry?"

Taking his outstretched hand, Savannah allowed him to pull her up onto his lap, relaxing against him.

"Supply building." Closing her eyes, she slumped, placing her hand on his forearm, smiling when his lips touched her hair. Just being in his arms warmed her, and, as always, made her feel like she was right where she belonged.

His hot hand covered her thigh, warming other parts of her, and she sighed, knowing it would be hours yet until they could be alone.

Hayes cursed and straightened. "Don't lean on me, darlin'. I'm filthy."

Lifting her head, she met his gaze, smiling at the flash of heat in his eyes when she rubbed her breast against his chest.

"I've got to admit, Sheriff, I like that about you." Thrilled that she'd been able to surprise him, she lifted her face for his kiss.

"Why did you pick me up and put me on your lap if you didn't want me to get dirty?"

His lips twitched, indulgence and love shining in his eyes as he tugged her braid.

"Habit. I can't seem to stop reaching for you anytime I'm anywhere near you. What do you need from the supply building?" He ran his hand up and down her back, his eyes constantly scanning their surroundings. Even when he didn't look at her, she knew that nothing she said or did would escape his notice.

"Some fabric to make curtains. With so many men building their own homes around us while they're waiting for the mail-order brides to arrive, and building the house for the women to live in across the way, we never know who's going to ride by our windows."

Hayes glanced down at her, his eyes lingering on her breasts. "Good idea. I'd hate to have to kill one of these men for seeing you naked."

Wyatt urged his horse closer and reached for her, the gleam of remembered pleasure in his eyes as well as the promise for more.

"Come here, honey."

Savannah smiled, something she did quite often now, and went willingly into his arms.

Bending his head until the brim of his hat hid her from view of the other men, he kissed her, one of those hot, hungry kisses that made her heart race.

She moaned into his mouth as the awareness increased, and rubbed her thighs together at the surge of heat that settled there. Wishing they could be alone, she lifted her hand to his neck, moaning in protest when he lifted his head.

He studied her with narrowed eyes, a slow smile of satisfaction spreading across his face.

"I love when you get that look on your face. Makes me want to strip you naked right here, wrap your legs around my hips, and sink my cock into you."

Savannah groaned, her pussy clenching with anticipation.

"I hate when you say things like that when I know I have to wait hours before you can take me. I think I'm mad at you."

Wyatt chuckled. "Yeah, but you love me."

With a sigh, she leaned against him, eyeing Hayes.

"I do. I love both of you, which is another reason for me to make those curtains. When those mail-order brides come, they're going to see you two and decide they want a closer look. If they see my husbands naked, I'm going to get jealous and might have to hurt someone."

Both men smiled, their eyes dancing with amusement.

Wyatt tightened his arm around her and turned his horse, riding the short distance to the supply building. Running a hand over her thigh before helping her down, he grinned.

"Get your fabric. We wouldn't want to have to arrest you for hurting someone." He tapped the brim of her hat, pushing it down to cover her eyes.

Pushing it back, she grinned up at him. "I have two husbands who wouldn't let that happen. Believe me when I tell you that you don't want to mess with either one of them!"

Turning her back when Wyatt roared with laughter, Savannah hurried into the supply building, laughing with pure joy at their banter.

Still smiling, she worked the bolt of fabric she'd picked out earlier loose. Holding it in front of her, she made her way back outside, anxious to see her husbands again.

Surprised to find them both gone, she closed the door behind her, her smile falling.

She knew it was ridiculous to be so disappointed. Her husbands had been busy every day since they'd moved here, riding the perimeter of their new town and getting to know each and every person who lived here. They spoke to Eb and Jeremiah every day to keep track of everything going on, and even took time to see little Ace, completely fascinated by the baby.

Even so busy, somehow, they always made time for her, one or the other stopping to see her every chance they got throughout the day.

It seemed strange that they hadn't waited for her today.

Mentally shrugging, she started across the yard, smiling and waving to acknowledge greetings from the other men, far less than had been there just moments ago. After stashing the fabric in her saddlebag and getting on her horse, she took a last look around, hoping to get a glimpse of her husbands.

"They're checking something out."

Turning, she saw Duke coming out of the chow building, wiping his hands.

Something about his tone sent off warning bells in her head. "Oh? Is something wrong?"

Duke's expression appeared harder than usual, the muscle in his jaw working and making his large scar, so much like Hayes's, seem larger than normal.

"Don't know. They say the backs of their necks are itching. Out here, we all respect that, and the men are out checking things out. You riding out?"

Savannah nodded, looking around. "Yes. I'm going home. I want to get started on these curtains while there's still a little daylight left."

"I think you should stay here until your men get back."

Savannah shook her head. "No. They know I'm going home. They know where to find me. If you see them, please tell them that I'll wait for them to bring me back here for supper."

"I think you should stay here."

Savannah smiled at the authority in his voice. "I just saw them two minutes ago, and they didn't say a thing to me about staying here. I'll see them at the house, and I'll see you later for supper. Thanks, Duke."

She rode away before he could say anything else, anxious to get back home. Hopefully, she would have the chance to get some water hot and ready for Hayes and Wyatt to take a bath before they came back for supper. While the water heated, she could start measuring and cutting the curtains.

Thinking about her evening plans, Savannah rode toward the house, slowing to check the progress of the house the men seemed intent on finishing first, the house the women who came here would live in until they were claimed.

The men figured that building the house close to the sheriffs' home and the jail would be the safest, and many of the other men who eagerly anticipated being married had begun to build their houses close by.

The beginning of a town.

"Savannah Hawkins?"

Startled, Savannah whipped her head around, alarmed to find a stranger sitting on his horse only about twenty yards away.

Her hand went to her gun, some instinct warning her that this man wasn't from the ranch.

"Who are you?"

"Name's Slick. They call me that 'cause I'm so fast with the pistols. Heard you was, too. I got a reputation for being the fastest gun out here, but lately I ain't heard nothin' but talk about you. Say you're fast and could shoot the wings off a fly at twenty paces. They tell me I wouldn't be nothin' against you. Can't have that now, can I? You're ruinin' my reputation."

Savannah had seen that not quite sane look in her uncle's eyes often enough to respect it.

"I think you're mistaken." *Damn it.* She should have stayed at the ranch. Just the thought of having to shoot another man made her sick to her stomach.

To her dismay, four other men on horseback came out of the woods behind Slick, two stopping on either side of him.

"This her, Slick?"

Slick nodded, straightening in his saddle. "Yep. You all can watch me kill her and then tell everyone in Tulsa that you seen me outdraw her with your own eyes."

"That's going to be a little hard to do when you're all dead."

Wyatt's deep voice came from somewhere behind her, razor sharp and cold as ice.

She'd never heard anything so wonderful in her life.

To her further amazement, several of the other men from the ranch came from everywhere, surrounding Slick and his friends.

Hayes spared a glance at her before turning his attention to Slick. "That's my wife, and I don't appreciate it when men want to draw on her."

Hawke, Blade, Phoenix, Hart, Gideon, Eb, and Jeremiah surrounded the men, each with a gun pointed at them.

Wyatt rode up beside her. "Don't draw those guns, Savannah." He continued ahead, placing himself between her and the other men.

"If you apologize to my wife, and turn around, we'll let you go, but only because we want you to tell anyone you come across that women are treated with respect in Desire. We take any slight to them real personally."

Slick frowned and pointed at Hayes. "I thought she was *his* wife."

Hayes smiled coldly. "She is."

Wyatt nodded. "She's married to both of us. The women here are protected. Any man who harms a woman here will have no mercy shown to him. The only reason we're letting you go is so you can pass the word. Uh-uh. Get those hands away from those pistols."

Savannah couldn't breathe, the atmosphere so highly charged, she started to shake. With her heart thumping nearly out of her chest, she stayed as still as she could, scared to death one of those men would draw and—

In the blink of an eye, all hell broke loose around her. Before she even knew what was happening, two shots rang out, almost simultaneously.

Smoke still rose from the end of Hayes's gun, while Slick screamed and held his gun hand.

The other men sat frozen, slowly lifting their hands away from their own guns, while eyeing the men of Desire, who still held guns on them.

Jeremiah grinned. "None of you gonna go for it?"

Wyatt backed his horse up until he sat next to her, glancing at her while still keeping his gun trained at Slick's friends. "Savannah?"

Savannah nodded, drawing her first deep breath.

"What just happened?"

"Slick there decided to draw on Hayes. Hayes shot the gun out of his hand."

"Anybody hurt? I thought I heard two shots." She looked at each of the men from the ranch, searching for blood, but the only blood she saw was on Slick's hand.

Hart picked up his hat from the ground, poking his finger through a hole in it.

"I just got it broke in."

Wyatt chuckled, his eyes still hard as they raked over her. "Hart goes through hats like you go through peppermint sticks. Every time he gets a new one, something happens to it."

It didn't escape her notice that he searched her eyes while talking to her, or that even though he tried to sound playful, his voice still carried an edge.

Holding a gun on the men now sitting on the ground while Hawke and Gideon tied Slick and his friends' hands behind their backs, Eb smiled, a smile that didn't even come close to reaching his eyes.

"Hart hates new hats. He'll be complaining until he gets it broke in. You all right, honey? You look pale."

"I thought I was going to have to shoot him." The words slipped out before she even knew she wanted to say them.

She met Hayes's eyes and then Wyatt's. "I knew I could do it. I wasn't looking forward to it, but I knew I could do it. It was a relief that I didn't have to." Aware of the tension coming from both of them, she searched their eyes, but their icy ones revealed nothing.

Wyatt pulled her close, running his hands up and down her back. "You're going to have to be watched closely. I don't know what I'd do if anything happened to you."

"Nothing's going to happen to her." Hayes came close and dragged her from her horse to his. "We're going to take these men to Tulsa and let everyone see what happens to men who come to Desire to cause trouble."

Hayes gathered her close, burying his face in her hair. "I love you so damned much. When I heard what that man said to you—"

Grateful for something solid to hold on to, Savannah smiled, staring at Wyatt, who'd moved closer.

"If that man got a shot off, that means that he outdrew Hayes, doesn't it?"

Wyatt blinked. "Slick's gun went off just as Hayes shot it out of his hand. Messed up his aim enough that he couldn't shoot him."

Savannah smiled. "Uh-huh."

Hayes stiffened. "He didn't outdraw me. We drew at the same time. I hit my target. He didn't."

"If you say so." She couldn't resist teasing him, wanting to erase the horror still lingering in his eyes. She needed to prove that she was tough enough to survive life out here, and that even though she'd fallen apart before, she wouldn't let it happen again.

Leaning back, he glared at her. "He did *not* outdraw me."

Savannah leaned back against him. "Of course not."

The other men did their best to hide their smiles, Eb shaking his head, not even bothering to hide his.

"I always knew you were trouble, Savannah. Hayes and Wyatt are both hell with guns and with their aim. I've seen Slick here in action. He's fast, but against your husbands, he didn't stand a chance."

Savannah shrugged, winking at Eb, keeping her tone thoughtful. "Hmm, I'm sure you're right. I wonder if I could outdraw them."

Wyatt placed a hand on her thigh and leaned over her threateningly. "Savannah Hawkins, you're treading on thin ice here."

"Everything all right here? I heard shots."

All eyes whipped around to see Duke ride up, his eyes scanning the clearing.

Wyatt nodded. "Everything's fine. The one bleeding over there wanted to draw on Savannah. The others are his friends."

Duke's eyes met hers and then lifted to Hayes's. "Told her to stay back at the ranch and wait for you. She wouldn't."

Hayes leaned back, lifting her chin to stare down at her, his eyes hooded and swirling with anger as he turned his horse, putting himself between her and the other men, and her between him and Wyatt.

"Is that a fact?"

His deceptively low tone didn't fool her one bit.

Chills went up Savannah's spine. "Well, I—"

Wyatt squeezed her knee, and she heard several *uh-oh's* from behind her.

"We're going to have a talk about that later, Savannah."

Memories of the time he'd spanked her came rushing back, making her clit swell.

She actually looked forward to it, but didn't want her husbands to know that.

Over the last two months she'd learned a great deal about her husbands and used that knowledge now.

Out of sight of the others, Savannah stared up at Hayes and lifted his hand to her breast.

"Thank you so much for coming to my rescue. I love you so much."

His eyes softened, the flash of heat in them unmistakable. His fingers moved on her breast as though he couldn't help himself. His touch intensified her need, making her pussy clench and her clit begin to throb.

"I love you, too, but don't ever do that again. You need a damned spanking for the things you put us through."

Savannah smiled coyly, placing her hand on his chest, no longer able to sit still. "I'm looking forward to whatever punishment you think I deserve, Sheriff."

Hayes unerringly found her nipple and squeezed lightly, his eyes flashing again at her soft cry.

"We'll just see about that tonight, now won't we?"

Wyatt groaned.

"Now I'm going to spend the rest of the day hard. Give her to me."

Hayes pinched her nipple before releasing her. "Until tonight. Then you're mine."

Savannah touched her lips to his chin, tracing a finger down his scar. "I'm always yours."

After Hayes passed her to Wyatt, he rode away, leaving her staring after him. Watching the men put Slick and his friends facedown over their horses' backs, with their arms tied behind them, Savannah leaned back against Wyatt.

Concerned at his stillness, she turned her face to look up at him, surprised to find him staring down at her. Concerned that he might be jealous, she stiffened. "What's wrong, Wyatt?"

He took a deep breath and let it out slowly. "I would die for you, Savannah. I don't know how I could ever live without you now."

Incredibly touched, she blinked back tears. "You won't have to."

Wyatt nodded. "You won't be able to get away with what you did today. Your safety is the most important thing in the world to us. You're going to get a hell of a spanking tonight."

He gathered her close, turning her in his arms and burying his face in her hair. "Then I'm going to love you like there's no tomorrow."

"That's all I need."

She looked forward to a lifetime of tomorrows with two men she now couldn't live without.

She'd found more love than she'd ever known existed, and lived in a wonderful place unlike any other.

She had it all.

She had love—and Desire.

THE END

WWW.LEAHBROOKE.NET

ABOUT THE AUTHOR

When Lana Dare's not writing, she's spending time with family, friends and her puppies.

For all titles by Lana Dare, please visit
www.bookstrand.com/lana-dare

*For titles by Lana Dare writing as
Leah Brooke, please visit*
www.bookstrand.com/leah-brooke

Siren Publishing, Inc.
www.SirenPublishing.com

Lightning Source UK Ltd.
Milton Keynes UK
UKOW031713270912

199760UK00011B/106/P